Dear [...]

They s[...]
it's a small village on the sea, a mining town nestled in the mountains, or a whistle-stop along the Western plains, we all share the same hopes and dreams. We work, we play, we laugh, we cry—and, of course, we fall in love . . .

It is this universal experience that we at Jove Books have tried to capture in a heartwarming series of novels. We've asked our most gifted authors to write their own story of American romance, set in a town as distinct and vivid as the people who live there. Each writer chose a special time and place close to their hearts. They filled the towns with charming, unforgettable characters—then added that spark of romance. We think you'll find the combination absolutely delightful.

You might even recognize *your* town. Because true love lives in *every* town . . .

Welcome to *Our Town*.

Sincerely,

Leslie Gelbman
Editor-in-Chief

Titles in the Our Town series

OUR · TOWN

BLUE RIBBON

JESSIE GRAY

JOVE BOOKS, NEW YORK

BLUE RIBBON

A Jove Book / published by arrangement with
the author

PRINTING HISTORY
Jove edition / January 1997

The Putnam Berkley World Wide Web site address is
http://www.berkley.com/berkley

ISBN: 0-515-12003-0

A JOVE BOOK®
Jove Books are published by The Berkley Publishing Group,
200 Madison Avenue, New York, New York 10016.
JOVE and the "J" design are trademarks
belonging to Jove Publications, Inc.

PRINTED IN THE UNITED STATES OF AMERICA

10 9 8 7 6 5 4 3 2 1

This one could be for no one but you, Tony.

Acknowledgments

My sincere thanks and appreciation to the following people and organizations:

Ron Bryant with the Kentucky Historical Society,
Candace Perry and the Kentucky Derby Museum,
Samuel Wilson Thomas, Ph.D.—one of Louisville's local historians,
To Tammy, my little sister and my ever-faithful reader. What would I do without you?
Evan M. Fogelman—for keeping the faith . . .

And as always—to all of you out there . . . my readers, my family, and my friends—old and new alike. This book, in particular, could not have been written without your encouragement and love.

Jo Anne Cassity
A.K.A.
Jessie Gray
February 7, 1996
P.O. Box 732
Canfield, Ohio 44406

BLUE RIBBON

PROLOGUE

Louisville, Kentucky
May 14, 1885

THE FLAG DROPPED, and the horses bolted from their starting positions.

An explosion of cheering erupted as the crowd rose from their seats in the grandstands to watch the Thoroughbreds thunder down the front side of the one-mile oval track at Churchill Downs. Dust billowed up from their hooves, and the jockeys bowed low over their mounts' necks.

A quick starter, Favor, shot forward and took the lead. Behind him came Keokuk, with the other eight horses following. Then from out of the pack came a big black stallion. He was a magnificent creature, a magical, mystical being that seemed to have ridden right out of the pages of an Arthurian legend. He was tall and muscular and black as night, marked only by a blaze of white that began high on his forehead and ran down the center of his face.

Astounded, the crowd quieted, and the air became charged with excitement. The great horse seemed to glide on the wind, his stride pure and powerful. The jockey who rode him hung low over his body, the sunlight glinting off the fringe of blond hair that shone beneath his helmet.

In seconds the stallion was challenging the lead, and the crowd roared and took up the chant, "Knightwind! Knightwind! Knightwind!"

Darby Lynn Greene felt a shiver of excitement travel down her spine. She gripped her father's hand and stood up on tiptoe, trying to look over the sea of bodies in front of her. She glanced over at her father. "Isn't he beautiful, Papa?"

Henry Greene smiled and looked up at his daughter, who topped him by two full inches. He was a short, stocky man with a thatch of graying hair and a heavily lined face that often looked stern through no effort of his own. But to his four daughters, especially Darby, his youngest, he was ten feet tall. "Yes, he is," Henry agreed.

"I wish he were mine," she said wistfully, returning her attention to the race.

"I imagine you do," Henry said, and squeezed her hand.

"Thank you for bringing me, Papa," Darby said, her gaze riveted to the track.

"You're welcome, sweetheart." Today was her fifteenth birthday, and the only thing she'd asked of him was to attend the Kentucky Derby. The Derby was considered a social event for many of Louisville's residents, but that was not why Darby had wished to come. Darby was different from most girls her age. Her sisters would have asked for a length of material for a new dress or a pretty new bonnet from one of Louisville's finest hat shops, but Darby had no interest in such things. She loved horses and spent most of her time reading about them, dreaming of the day she would raise fine horses of her own.

Knightwind pushed his nose out into the lead, and the crowd screamed encouragement. Darby's heart froze in anticipation.

But suddenly the great horse faltered and fell behind, and the cheering died as Knightwind lost ground by one length, then two. Although he valiantly kept on running, it was obvious something was terribly wrong.

The crowd moaned its disappointment, and the other horses

pounded down the last stretch of track, one by one overtaking the black stallion, until finally a horse named Joe Cotton edged forward and crossed the finish line, winning the Kentucky Derby by a neck over a horse named Bersan.

Darby sighed and dropped her chin to her chest. Her young face mirrored her concern and disappointment.

Henry Greene pulled his daughter close and gave her a hug. "It happens that way sometimes, honey."

"But he was the best, Papa," she said quietly. "I know he was. . . ."

Three weeks later, the hot June sun blazed high in the Kentucky sky as Darby bent low over her mount's neck and raced for the hill in the distance. In her fantasy she was astride Knightwind, picking off the contenders one by one.

She allowed herself the dream, even though she knew the stallion would run no more. The newspapers reported that he'd fractured the cannon bone of his right hind leg, and at his trainer's urging, after just two short, undefeated seasons at the track, he'd been retired. Some owners and trainers would have allowed the horse's injury to heal, then tried to run him again, but not his owner, Benjamin Rhinehart and his trainer, Luke Richards. The horse would be moved from Rhinehart Stables, the Thoroughbred training farm located a mile east of Louisville in Jefferson County, to Rhinehart's breeding farm in Fayette County, where he would be standing stud.

Despite grumblings from other trainers and owners, who believed Knightwind had been retired too early, Rhinehart and Richards felt the stallion had earned his rest.

Darby's daydream came to an abrupt halt when her horse veered sharply to the right and charged toward a large, low-limbed oak tree down in a meadow. "Nooooo, Francine!" she cried out, pulling back on the reins. But the old mare stubbornly fought the bit in her mouth and kept on running.

The tree limb caught Darby across the middle and sent her sailing. She hit the ground with a thud that knocked the wind from her lungs and made her teeth ache. For an endless moment she lay sprawled on her back, straining for air, staring at dappled spears of sunlight stabbing down at her through the leaves above.

Then, quite suddenly, relief came; her lungs expanded and filled with air. She took several deep breaths while her vision cleared.

Wincing, she sat up and shook the cobwebs from her brain. She blinked back a hot rush of tears, then turned and glared at the old mare grazing peacefully a few feet beyond. "Now you've really done it, Francine!" Darby's left arm throbbed painfully. She tried to move it, but the effort cost her. An arc of pain shot up into her shoulder, causing fresh tears to burn. She swallowed and cradled the injured arm close to her body. "I shoulda let Pa sell you a long time ago!"

The horse snorted a response and swung her head from side to side.

"Don't you sass me—" Darby began, ready to deliver a sound scolding, but her words died beneath the sudden thunder of hooves.

Still dazed, she turned to watch the rider approach. When he reached her, he reined in and eyed her with mild curiosity from beneath the low brim of his dusty brown Stetson. "You're trespassing," he finally said, and pushed back his hat, squinting against the harsh glare of the sun.

Struggling to hold her dignity intact, Darby returned his long stare. "Who says so?"

"I do." His expression remained fixed, though her tenacity amused him. She was young—fourteen, maybe fifteen at the most. Her hair was cropped unfashionably short into chestnut curls that defied all sense of order. Her wide eyes were surrounded by short, dark, spiky lashes.

"Yeah, so . . . who are you?" she challenged, refusing to back down.

"Luke Richards," he said, unable to keep the smile out of his voice. "Trainer here at Rhinehart Stables."

That revelation shook her composure a bit, but she hid it

well behind a cloak of silence. She eased herself up off the ground and brushed off the rear of her worn blue britches, then pushed her short curls back from her forehead. She held her injured arm pressed to her side, walked over to the mare, and took the reins with her other hand.

Luke watched her in silence. She was tall and slim, leggy as a colt, but her cheeks were round and plump, emphasizing her youth.

"You hurt?" he asked, noting a suspicious glint in her eye.

"I'm fine," Darby answered shortly.

"You sure?"

"Said I was, didn't I?" she snapped, lifting her chin and meeting his gaze head-on. He sat his horse with an easy confidence that annoyed her. He was a young man, but lines were already etched into the tanned skin at the outer corners of his eyes, eyes that were quite remarkable really, clear and blue and timeless. His face was lean, his jaw square, his chin dented with a deep cleft. His hair, falling onto his forehead, was thick and black. He wore a light blue shirt that stretched across his broad shoulders and was open at the throat, with the sleeves rolled up over his tanned forearms. Dark brown trousers were tucked into scuffed black boots. A scabbard holding a rifle hung alongside his saddle. Attached to the saddle was a leather loop on which hung a pair of binoculars.

"Mr. Rhinehart doesn't take kindly to strangers," he stated quietly, the amusement gone from his voice.

"I'm not a stranger," Darby said, her gaze unwavering. "My father's land connects with Rhinehart land." She pointed down Brownsboro Road, in the direction of her father's farm.

"Doesn't matter," the young man said, his expression fixed. "You're still a stranger to Mr. Rhinehart."

Pride held her silent. His words stung, but they were true. Henry Greene's small tobacco and soybean farm might connect with Rhinehart land, but the two men lived in very different worlds.

She was saved from responding when a horse rode over

the hill and drew their attention away from each other. The rider reined in a good distance away. He waved at them, his blond hair shimmering in the sunlight. With a start, Darby recognized him as the young jockey who had ridden Knight-wind in the Derby.

As she stared at him, something as old as time stirred within her young breast. Abashed, her face flamed, and her heart broke into a weird canter. She looked away, feeling transparent and foolish and sure that Luke Richards could see the effect the young jockey had on her.

"Everything all right, Luke?" the young man hollered.

"Yeah! Fine!" Luke returned.

"Is she all right?" Bo Denton asked with a nod at Darby.

"Seems to be!"

"Did you get his time?"

Luke nodded. He'd been clocking Bo's time on one of Rhinehart's two-year-olds when he spotted Darby.

"How was it?"

"It'll do," Luke answered, always the conservative, though he was pleased with the horse's run. The horse's time had been damn good, but it was still too early to tell if this colt or any other could ever be as consistent as Knightwind had been. "Take him on in and cool him down!"

"See you at the stables!" Denton turned the horse around.

Watching him go, Luke added, "And take it easy on him! No need to wear him out!"

The young man flashed a white, nearly perfect smile over his shoulder, then gave the horse a nudge that set him trotting off at a modest pace.

Luke turned back to the girl. She was already walking away. "You sure you're not hurt?"

"I'm fine." Darby squared her shoulders. She was far too proud to let him know how badly her arm was hurting. "Come on, Francine." She gave the mare's reins a gentle tug.

"I could see you home," he said on impulse. He'd be

willing to bet a month's pay that she'd hurt that arm she held tucked against her body.

She threw him a look of disgust and kept on walking. "I can see myself home just fine, mister."

The fiery flash in her eyes told him it would do no good to argue with her. He'd have to hog-tie her to her saddle to escort her anywhere. "All right, then." He turned his horse toward Rhinehart Stables and gave him a slight nudge with his boots. He left without a backward glance, and within seconds disappeared over the blue-tinged hillside.

Darby sighed heavily. Her arm was throbbing painfully. "Friendly sort, isn't he?" she mumbled to herself. But her thoughts quickly abandoned Luke Richards in favor of the other young man—the handsome young jockey with the halo of sunshine hair. Once again that primitive, timeless feeling caught at her, and she realized with a start that she was every bit as female as her sisters, whom she'd berated countless times for entertaining thoughts of handsome beaus who would turn into fawning husbands.

Wait till she told Millie!

Millie Johnson was her best friend. They'd known each other forever. Millie's father, David Johnson, was the pastor of their church, the Walnut Street Methodist Church in Louisville.

Years ago Darby and Millie had vowed that they would never grow up mooning over men like the older girls of their assemblage did.

Remembering that vow, Darby wondered if she should mention anything about her feelings for the jockey to Millie after all. Maybe she wouldn't understand.

With her mind mulling over that thought, it wasn't long before she came to the line that separated Rhinehart's property from her father's. Trudging along, she kicked at a stone and rehearsed aloud the story she was going to tell her father about how she'd hurt her arm, even though she knew he probably wouldn't believe her. It wasn't the first time she'd abandoned her chores to ride Francine.

Suddenly she heard a shrill whinny and stopped in her tracks, her head snapping up. Several yards in front of her, near the fence, stood a horse. He whinnied another greeting, then lifted his head nervously into the air and snorted. After a few seconds he lowered his head and pawed the ground with one hoof. His saddle and bridle were intact. His reins hung limply to the ground.

And then she saw the man. He lay on the ground on the other side of the horse, unmoving.

Stunned, Darby stood stiff and silent for a moment, then she gave Francine's reins a tug, and despite the ache in her arm, she broke into a run. She knew who the man was. Benjamin Rhinehart was an imposing figure, a big man with silver hair.

Reaching him, Darby released Francine's reins and dropped to her knees. Her immediate thought was that he, too, had been unseated from his horse somehow. She poked at his shoulder. "Mr. Rhinehart?" she said softly.

There was no answer, and he didn't move.

"Sir?" She poked him again, harder this time. "Mr. Rhinehart!" Still there was no response. She waited a few seconds, then forced her hand under him and tried to roll him over, but he was too heavy, and her efforts were wasted. She withdrew her hand from beneath him and felt her stomach take a dive. Her hand was covered with blood.

Slowly she got to her feet and looked over at Francine, then over at the huge, sleek gelding who waited so patiently for his master to rise. She bit her lip, pondering her decision, then walked over to Francine and tethered her reins to the top rung of the fence. "You wait for me, Francine."

She approached the gelding cautiously. "You and me are 'bout to get acquainted, fella. That old girl over there can't get me where I need to go near as fast as you can." She took hold of his reins and stroked his nose gently. The horse snorted and reared back slightly, but she continued to speak to him in soft, soothing sounds until he quieted. She took a firm hold on the reins and saddle horn, ignored the pain in her arm, and lifted herself up into the saddle. The horse's ears flattened instantly, and he danced sideways. Darby felt a hump rise up in his back and, for a moment, she thought he would unseat her. "Easy, fella," she crooned quietly. "Come on, now." A few tense seconds passed, then the hump melted beneath her. "That's better," she said, praising him, and stroked his neck. "That's a good horse."

With one last look at the man on the ground, she turned the horse toward Rhinehart Stables, dug her heels into his side, and rode harder than she'd ever ridden in her life.

❖ *1* ❖

IT WAS EARLY morning when Luke Richards left Rhinehart Stables. He rode for some time, then, as he crossed over onto Henry Greene's land, dawn finally broke in a pearly swirl of incandescent color.

Luke held the colt's reins loosely, allowing him to trail behind his own horse, Toby.

His heart was heavy. His job at Rhinehart Stables was finished once he carried out this last request. It was a difficult task for him, but he'd promised Benjamin Rhinehart he'd follow through with the request, and he was honor bound to do so.

He did not know what he would do afterward. He could always go back to New York. The state had its share of Thoroughbred farms, and a good trainer could always find work.

But Kentucky was horse country to him. It was also home to him. He'd left New York and the orphanage at sixteen and headed straight for Kentucky. He was hired on immediately as a stable boy by one of the best trainers in the state. He'd never worked with horses before, but it was soon apparent that he had a special knack with them.

As a child, he'd been a loner and had spent most of his time reading and daydreaming about horses, the finest horses, Thoroughbred racing horses. As he grew into adolescence, he realized that he would be too tall to race them as he had hoped, so he decided to satisfy the desire in his heart another way: He would train them.

After six years of working as a groom and apprentice trainer at Thoroughbred farms all over the state of Kentucky, he heard Benjamin Rhinehart was looking for a head trainer. He wasted no time in applying for the job. Young as he was, he managed to convince Benjamin Rhinehart to take him on. He was hired on as a full-fledged trainer at Rhinehart Stables, where he'd remained over the past six years, gaining himself quite a reputation in racing circles. Now, at twenty-eight, he'd not only made a name for himself, but he'd also made a respectable sum of money, enough that he wanted for nothing.

But things had changed. Benjamin Rhinehart was dead.

If Luke had his choice, he'd stay in Kentucky, where he could keep an eye on his horses. But it would not matter. Bradley, Benjamin's only son and heir, would do what he wished with them.

Luke would miss the stables and the horses. He would miss Benjamin. The old man had not only been his employer; he'd been a good friend.

Which was why he was determined to see his last wish carried out. Benjamin had wanted the colt gone before his son came home from the eastern farm in Fayette County for the funeral. Although Luke was reluctant to turn the colt over to a girl who knew nothing about the prize she was getting, he knew it was in the yearling's best interest. The colt, though he would never know the world he had been bred for, would be better off with the girl than with Bradley, who would have run him into an early grave on racetracks all over the country.

As Luke rode up to Henry Greene's house, a big hound dog rose dispassionately from his spot on the porch and announced Luke's presence with one long, loud bawl of welcome. Luke reined his horse up in front of the house.

The big house was an unadorned, whitewashed two-story structure surrounded by a sprinkling of maple and oak trees. Over to the right of the house was a grouping of outbuildings:

a huge weather-beaten barn stood between a chicken-coop and a windmill, and a short distance beyond was a small bunkhouse.

The big house lacked any ornamentation to relieve its simplicity. It had seen better days, but Luke figured that Henry Greene, like most farmers, had little time to spare for repairs or money to spend on frivolities. Most of the area's farmers worked right along with their hired help, their workdays beginning at dawn and ending at dusk.

The yearling whinnied, and Luke's thoughts returned to the duty at hand. The colt nipped playfully at Toby's rump, but the older horse was used to the youngster's antics and ignored him.

"You're gonna miss that young fella, aren't you, boy?" Luke said quietly. The horse snorted, and Luke sighed and swung down to the ground. "Yeah, well . . . so am I."

Darby was asleep when her father knocked at her door. "Darby," he called out.

She pulled the covers over her head and groaned.

"Darby!" her father repeated, louder.

"Yes, Pa," she moaned sleepily.

"Get up, honey. You're wanted downstairs."

She groaned again, and her oldest sister, Emma, elbowed her in the ribs. "Get up!"

"Ouch!" Darby sat up. "That hurt!"

"Hush!" Emma said, and turned over in the bed. "I'm trying to sleep."

"So am I," Darby snapped, wanting to pop her sister a good one, despite her supposedly mature age of twenty years. She swung her long legs over the bed and stood up. Splinters of sunlight poked through the windows, chasing the night shadows into the far corners of the large, simply furnished room.

"Darby?" Henry Greene called again.

"Coming, Pa," Darby said, and pulled her nightdress up over her head and tossed it onto the bed. Emma would complain when she found the nightdress cast aside so carelessly. Darby grinned at the thought. She was glad Emma was getting married in another year. Emma was the last sister she had to marry off. The other two, Ardis, at twenty-two, and Linette, at twenty-three, had gone on to husbands and homes of their own a couple of years before.

Once Emma was married to Noah Sanders, life would be simpler with only herself, Pa, Aunt Birdie, Yancey, and Eugene around.

She went to the washstand and splashed cold water on her face, then took a towel and rubbed her face dry. She tugged on a blue-checked cambric shirt, buttoned it and tucked it into her britches, grabbed her boots, and left the room, slamming the door hard behind her.

Satisfied with Emma's muffled complaint, Darby grinned, sat down on the top step, and tugged on her boots. Then she tromped down the stairs to find her father and Aunt Birdie waiting for her in the spacious, cozy kitchen.

"Darby," Henry Greene said, "Mr. Rhinehart has sent Mr. Richards to see you about something."

Surprised, Darby stared over at Luke Richards in silence. Although five years had passed since she'd last seen him, he'd changed very little. The lines around his eyes had deepened somewhat. She walked over to where he stood beside her father.

She'd read about him many times in the *Louisville Commercial,* the *Louisville Courier-Journal,* and the *Times.* The newspapers compared him to Henry Brown and Dudley Allen—two great Thoroughbred trainers—claiming Richards was one of the finest young trainers in all of Kentucky, maybe the finest in all the country, having led many of Rhinehart's horses to victory.

Pondering those things, her brow puckered while she waited for him to speak. She gave no thought to the antagonism she'd felt toward him that long-ago day. He'd been most sincere in his thanks to her for what she'd done for Mr. Rhinehart.

"How 'bout a cup of nice hot coffee, Mr. Richards?" Aunt Birdie asked, taking a pot from the cookstove and filling two thick mugs to the brim.

"Thank you, ma'am," Luke said, accepting her offer.

Aunt Birdie smiled at him and nodded her approval at both his acceptance and good manners.

Bertha Greene was a small, unassuming woman with big, round brown eyes, and a dull, almost wrenlike appearance, which had earned her the nickname of Birdie at birth. She'd come to Kentucky from Missouri to join her brother, Henry, six years ago when his wife, Laura, had passed away. At forty-two, she'd long ago given up hope of marrying and having children of her own. But she was not bereft. Henry and Laura's daughters had become her own, and she'd taken it upon herself to see that all of her girls were married off to good men. The three oldest girls had been easy, but she knew getting Darby hitched would be a tribulation. Darby Lynn was different. Darby would rather raise horses than children any day, and Birdie had no misconceptions about that fact.

Luke took a sip of hot coffee. "That's fine coffee, ma'am." He tucked his hat beneath his right arm, then looked over at Darby. Her eyes, which he had first thought to be light brown, were really more of an amber color, flecked with bits of green. Dark curls sprang out from her head in riotous disorder. Though her cheeks were still plump, it was clearly evident that she was no longer a child. Nature had ripened her tall, slender figure with small but noticeable breasts and by adding a gentle curve to her hips.

Luke forced that observation to the back of his mind and got right to the reason for his visit. "Mr. Rhinehart passed on this morning."

Darby was silent for a moment. "I'm sorry," she said, her confusion growing.

"He was ill for a little over a year," he went on, then paused, searching for the right words. "Before he died he made it clear that I was to bring you something."

Darby's frown deepened. "I don't understand."

"He wanted to repay your kindness."

"I told him there was no need." She knew Benjamin Rhinehart believed differently, however. She had saved his life by riding his horse to his stables for help. Luke had sent one of the stable hands into town for the doctor, while he and Darby had ridden back to Benjamin Rhinehart. As it turned out, Rhinehart had been shot.

Funny thing was, the law never did find out who had shot Mr. Rhinehart, and now it seemed they never would.

"He felt it was necessary," Luke said, bringing her back to the present. He set his coffee cup down on the sturdy oak table in the center of the kitchen. "Thank you for the coffee, ma'am," he said again to Birdie, then placed his Stetson back on his head.

Birdie smiled. "You come back, now, Mr. Richards. It's always nice to get a visit from a nice young man with manners."

Luke turned to Darby and Henry. "If you'll follow me . . ." He walked to the kitchen door and out onto the back porch. The hound dog, his eyes bloodshot and droopy, lifted his head and stared at them, his expression one of dazed disinterest.

"Mornin', Remus," Darby said, and the dog plopped his head back down on the porch with a heavy thud.

As they made their way around to the front of the house, their boots made wet impressions in the dewy grass. Around them the morning awoke. The sun glistened down on them, and a spotted sandpiper ran across their path and took to flight. A half dozen chickens pecked halfheartedly at yesterday's scattering of feed and, out in the pastures, flies buzzed and butterflies dipped.

Yancey Latimer, one of Henry Greene's hired hands, stood near the open doors of the big barn. Yancey was a tall, lanky man with an easy smile and a tuft of thinning brown hair he kept hidden beneath a floppy old hat that had seen better days. "Mornin' folks!" he greeted them, and waved.

"Mornin', Yancey," Henry returned. "Eugene up yet?"

Yancey half snorted, half laughed. "What do you think?"

Eugene Kellar was Henry's other hired hand. Eugene was prone to sleeping late, but once he was up and about, he was a hard worker who labored well beyond dusk, which was why Henry tolerated his morning slackness.

A high-pitched whinny cut through the air, drawing Darby's and Henry's attention away from Yancey.

Darby's gaze found the culprit immediately. He stood to the left, beneath a maple tree, tethered to a low-hanging limb. Beside him was Toby, Luke's horse.

Darby's gaze found Luke. Her round hazel eyes were full of questions.

"He's yours," Luke said quietly, without preamble. "Mr. Rhinehart wanted you to have him."

Stunned, Darby looked over at the colt again, her jaw going soft with surprise.

He was beautiful—the most beautiful colt she had ever seen.

His coat was so black, it flashed spears of blue light in the early morning sunlight. A white, irregularly shaped star marked the very center of his forehead. "Oh, my," she said, her mind spinning with the realization that her dream of owning a fine horse, one that she could breed, was suddenly a very real possibility. She took a few steps toward him, then halted and said again, "Oh, my . . ." She stole a glance over at Luke, then over at her father.

Henry Greene shrugged and gave her a small smile. Darby understood: This was her business, and she should handle it as she saw fit. Her father had raised all his daughters to be independent, to think and reason for themselves.

Henry was as surprised as his daughter at the gift, however. Rhinehart had been profuse in his thanks to Darby, offering her a generous sum of money for her kindness. But she had refused. Now it seemed Rhinehart was making another effort to repay her with a gift she would find much harder to refuse.

"I can't accept him," Darby finally said, her voice tinged with regret. She lifted her gaze to Luke's. "I wish I could, but it doesn't seem right. What I did for Mr. Rhinehart is what I would have done for anybody. I can't accept payment for doin' what should be done anyway.''

Luke shrugged, as though her decision made no difference to him. ''That's your decision, but Mr. Rhinehart would have been disappointed. He wanted you to have him.''

Her emotions warring, Darby cocked her head. ''How old is he?'' she asked, curious.

''He's a yearling . . . born a year ago this past April.''

''My,'' Darby said, ''he's big.''

Luke nodded. ''A full hand taller than any yearling I've ever seen, and I've seen a lot of them.''

Darby smiled, and a matching pair of beguiling dimples appeared in her ripe cheeks, causing her entire face to come alive. Luke found himself returning her smile.

''He's fat, though,'' she said, and she was right. The colt's legs were long and lean, but his body was round and full, like a big, fat spider's.

''He's a baby. He'll lose that fat in time.''

Darby took a tentative step toward the colt, and he cocked his ears and stared at her with huge, heavily lashed brown eyes that gleamed with intelligence. Quite suddenly he bobbed his head up and down and whinnied furiously.

''He likes a lot of attention,'' Luke said. ''But he's good-natured like his mother.''

''His mother?''

Luke looked down at his boots and shifted his weight from one foot to the other. ''His mother is Merry Molly.''

Darby sucked in her breath sharply. ''Oh, my . . .'' she whispered, feeling even more certain that she could not accept the colt. Merry Molly was one of the finest Thoroughbred broodmares in the state. Though not incredibly fast, she had been known for her strength and endurance on the racetrack. An overwhelming desire to touch the colt prompted Darby to hold out her hand. The colt hesitated a moment, then pressed his velvety nose into her hand to see if she had a treat. When he realized she didn't, he lifted his head and snorted his disappointment. She laughed, then said, "He's so pretty."

Although she had loved Francine right up to the day she had died, this colt was the magical, spirited horse of her dreams, the one she'd always longed for. "His father?" she asked, her curiosity rife, looking back up at Luke.

Luke was silent a moment. "His father is Knightwind."

Flabbergasted, Darby's mouth dropped open. She looked back at the colt, then shook her head in disbelief. "Are you sure about this—about Mr. Rhinehart wanting me to have him?" She glanced over at her father, then back at Luke. "Why would he give me such a valuable horse?"

"Because he wanted to," Luke said simply. He drew the papers from his pocket. "These are yours." He held them out to her. "If you want him, you'll need them. They verify his bloodline."

Her mind churning, Darby took the papers from his hand.

Studying the younger man's face, Henry broke his silence. "This is a very hard thing for you to do, isn't it, young man?"

"Yes sir," Luke answered easily.

A smile threatened the leathery surface of Henry's face. "What would you have done with the horse if you'd had the choice?"

"I would have trained him to race, sir. He was bred to run."

Henry's gaze was sharp and discerning. He liked the young trainer. He was honest and forthright. "Then why didn't you leave him at Rhinehart Stables? Young Rhinehart would have raced him."

"I suppose he would have, but he wouldn't have raced him the way a horse should be raced. He would have used him up early on. Besides, Mr. Rhinehart made sure his orders were to be carried out through his lawyer, his brother Nathaniel. He had Nathaniel write Darby into his will to make sure the horse was delivered to her. If I hadn't brought the horse out to her, Nathaniel would have seen to it that someone else would have."

"Does the colt have a name?" Darby asked, breaking into their conversation.

"Mr. Rhinehart left that up to you. We've always just called him 'the baby' at the stables."

Seconds ticked by while indecision weighed heavily on Darby's heart. She wanted the colt desperately. Was it wrong to accept him—especially when Richards said that Rhinehart's son would not treat the colt kindly?

With that thought in mind, her heart made the decision for her. She would keep him, and she would love him, and someday she might even be able to breed him.

But what would she name him?

And then it came to her—a simple name really, but one that seemed most appropriate. She looked over at Luke, her eyes bright with excitement. "I'll name him Kentucky Blue," she said softly. "Because his coat is so black it flashes blue in the sunlight, and because he's Kentucky born and bred."

Luke nodded and steeled himself against the expected wave of sadness. His worst weakness as a trainer was that he became attached to his horses. Though he vowed to gain victory over that fault, he'd yet to do so. "That's a fine name," he said quietly, realizing his mission was complete. She would keep the colt. "Well . . ." He hesitated a moment and cast a quick glance over at his baby. He looked away and nodded. "I'd best be going, then." He turned and walked over to his horse. He swung himself up into his saddle and turned Toby toward Rhinehart Stables. Then he looked over his shoulder at Darby and said, "Take good care of him, miss."

"I will," Darby said, staring up at him. She read the sadness in his eyes and felt the need to reassure him. "I promise I will," she called out.

The colt whinnied and bobbed his head, trying to get Luke's attention, but Luke ignored him. He could not say good-bye. His work with Kentucky Blue was done, finished before it had ever really begun. He had to get back to the stables and pack up his life.

It was time to move on. . . .

❖ 2 ❖

LATER THAT SAME morning, Bo Denton swung his legs over the side of the huge four-poster and sat up. He rested his elbows on his knees and dropped his head into his hands, groaning. He was only twenty-five, but like most jockeys, hard drinking and fast living were quickly taking a toll on him.

From behind him, a slender arm snaked out from underneath the covers and wrapped around his taut middle. "Mornin', honey."

He glanced over his shoulder and managed a smile. "Mornin', Trina," he said in his slow, easy drawl.

"You leavin' so soon?"

"I gotta get out to the stables and get my gear together. Rhinehart's funeral is today, and we're expectin' Bradley."

"Just because Luke Richards doesn't want to work for Bradley Rhinehart doesn't mean you can't." Katrina Kirby made a petulant face and propped herself up on an elbow, allowing the sheet to slip down to her waist, revealing lush, pink-tipped breasts. She pushed her long mass of blond hair away from her face so that it tumbled down her back in a waterfall of waves.

"There's a lot of things me and Luke don't see eye to eye on, but Bradley Rhinehart doesn't happen to be one of 'em. I can't stomach him any more than Luke can."

"Where will you go?"

"Raymond Miller wants me to ride for him. Most of his Thoroughbreds aren't as fine as Rhinehart's, but that big white yearling, Phantom, might do something over the next couple of years."

Reluctant to turn him loose just yet, Katrina leaned into Bo's back, brushing her erect nipples against his bare skin while her hand ventured south and went searching over the flat plane of his stomach.

Chuckling, he caught her hand. "Now, you know I ain't got time for any more of that, honey." He stood and looked down at her. "One of these days your husband is gonna come home early and shoot us both. Then won't that give the newspapers something to write about."

Scowling, she rolled over on her back. After a few moments her scowl melted into a wicked smile, and she pushed the sheet away, arching her back, striking a pose that was shamelessly enticing. She studied him, her sea-green eyes heavy-lidded with desire, as he shrugged into his shirt. Bo Denton was a handsome man—not very tall, smaller than the average male, but his shoulders were broad, his arms and back lean and muscled from years of riding horses, and she was as addicted to him as she was to the racetrack. If her husband ever learned of their affair, or of her gambling debts, she would be out on the street. Oddly enough, the risk of discovery only heightened her sense of excitement.

At thirty-five, Katrina was a beautiful woman who knew well the power of her charms, and she had no qualms about using her beauty to get what she wanted. What she wanted from Bo included more than just physical pleasure. She parted her legs the slightest bit, allowing him a provocative glimpse of the treasure he could have if only he would reconsider leaving her so early.

But Bo was not so easily enticed. "Not this morning, darlin'." He blew her a kiss, turned, and walked toward the door. He ducked just in time, hearing the hairbrush whiz past his ear a moment before it slammed into the door in front of him. Anticipating her next move, he chuckled and stepped out the door quickly, dodging the slipper he knew was sure to follow. It struck the door the second he pulled it shut behind him.

Chuckling, he made his way down the back stairs and out onto the rear porch, closing the door of the huge redbrick house on Third Street behind him. His affair with Katrina Kirby had begun two years before, two days after he'd met her at a social event held at the Louisville Jockey Clubhouse, and a month after she'd married Frank Kirby, a middle-aged widower who was one of Louisville's most prominent bankers and a founding member of the Louisville Jockey Club and Driving Park Association.

In the purple haze of early dawn, thoughts of Katrina dissipated, however, as he headed north up the street, past the many fine houses, all flanked with trees and lavishly designed flower beds. Most of Louisville's prominent folks lived in this section of the city, which was located south of Broadway. The houses were similar in design, principally brick with stone trim—Queen Anne style—but some were of Richardsonian Romanesque design.

At Main Street Bo crossed over to a small livery where he had stabled his horse for the night. He found the stable hand rubbing the sleep from his eyes. "Morning, Sam," Bo said with a smile.

"Morning, Mr. Denton," Sam said respectfully.

Bo paid the man and collected his horse, mounting him outside the livery. He rode through the awakening city and breathed in its vitality and energy. Streetcars clacked along the rails, and mule carts plodded down the streets. Vendors milled about, calling out their prices and setting up their wares along the walkways. Proprietors who owned or rented storefront space turned the signs in their doors to read: OPEN.

Louisville was located on the south bank of the Ohio River, beside the only falls in the river. The population was over 161,000, having grown considerably since it was founded in 1788. The city got its start as a transportation hub and was an important crossroads by water, rail, and highway. But since 1875 it had gained notoriety for something more—which was why Bo had left Texas to go there. It was the home of the Louisville Jockey Club and Driving Park Association. It was the home of the Kentucky Derby, Kentucky Oaks, and Clark Handicap, three major stakes races designed after the three premier races in England, the Epson Derby, Epson Oaks, and St. Leger Stakes.

Therefore, the city had become the center of Bo's dreams. He'd believed he could make a name for himself there as one of the best jockeys in the United States.

And he'd been right. The newspapers claimed he was one of the finest young jockeys a Thoroughbred breeder could employ, ranking him right up there with Isaac Murphy. Men respected him. Women loved him. Society embraced him.

He knew his father was disappointed that he had not stayed in Texas. His father had looked forward to the day his only son would work the ranch with him, but Bo had other plans for his life. Bo wanted to race horses.

He loved the roar of the crowds, the feel of the wind whipping against his face, the glory of being the hero who rode the winning horse across the finish line to victory.

It was a heady potion and one that he'd become addicted to ever since he'd won his first unofficial race back home at nineteen.

Benjamin Rhinehart's Thoroughbred stables were located east of the city, off Brownsboro Road. The stables and the surrounding land and buildings were impressive, the house a massive three-story white structure of Grecian design. A wide veranda wrapped around three sides of the house, and magnolia trees and rosebushes, now in full bloom, graced the outer perimeters of the manicured front yard.

The huge whitewashed stables and bunkhouse were in immaculate condition and located a good distance away from the house. A fenced-in paddock sat off to the right of the stables, and miles of lush green pastures rolled out behind.

To the left of the stables was a one-mile dirt track used for training. Beyond the training track, in the distance, the woods rose up tall and majestic with oak trees, tulip, sycamore, maple, and shimmering white pine.

Bo swung down off his horse and led him into the dark interior of the stables. The scent of leather, hay, and animals greeted him.

The stable hands were milling about, busy with their usual morning chores of feeding the horses and cleaning out stalls.

"Mornin', Mr. Bo," Ian Hanson said as he took the reins from the younger man's hand.

"Mornin', Ian," Bo returned with a smile.

Ian had worked for Benjamin Rhinehart for over twenty years. He was a small, wiry black man who was amazingly strong for his size. He, like most of Rhinehart's employees, had been loyal to the elder Rhinehart and was greatly saddened by his death. Because of Ian's small stature, he had also worked as an exercise rider for the Thoroughbreds. "You want me to brush him down and feed him, Mr. Bo?"

"I'd appreciate it," Bo said. He walked down the center of the barn and was greeted by a chorus of snorts and whinnies. He was surprised to see Eddie, a young man with dark brown hair and a perpetually serious demeanor, inside "the baby's" stall, shoveling out manure.

"Where's the colt?" Bo asked, his easy smile slipping.

Eddie looked up, then lowered his gaze to the floor. "You'd best ask Mr. Luke."

"Where is Mr. Luke?"

"In his room."

Bo walked to the back of the barn, then took a left and entered the open door of Luke's small room at Rhinehart Stables. A carefully made bunk was pressed against one wall. Against another wall stood a bureau with a mirror, a small bookcase filled with books, and a desk, whose top was cluttered with a scattering of papers and books. To the right of the door sat a potbellied stove. The walls were covered with an assortment of racing schedules and newspaper clippings about races and Thoroughbred champions from all over the country.

Luke stood with his back to the door, packing his belongings into a large trunk that stood in the far corner of the room.

"Where's the colt?" Bo asked.

"Gone," Luke said without turning.

"Gone?" Bo hooked his hands on his slim hips and stared at the taller man's back. "You serious?

Luke turned and leveled his blue-eyed gaze on his friend. "I followed through with Rhinehart's orders. The colt belongs to the Greene girl now."

"Holy shit," Bo swore softly, and walked over and sank down on Luke's hard cot. He glanced back up at Luke. "Bradley isn't gonna like this one bit!"

"Nope," Luke said matter-of-factly, "I don't imagine he is."

Tom Haines, a young man with pumpkin-red hair and a wide space between his two front teeth, stuck his head in the door. "You want me to put the harnesses on the yearlings, Mr. Luke?"

Luke nodded. "Just like always."

"Yes, sir," Tom said, and disappeared. Tom was a gentle, slow-witted young man, who at twenty possessed the mind of a ten-year-old. Rhinehart Stables had become his home nine years before, when he had wandered into the stables, looking for work after his mother died.

Bo propped his booted foot up on Luke's bed and leaned his shoulders back on the pillow, cushioning his head against the planked wall. "I sure was lookin' forward to taking a ride on that colt," he said wistfully.

A hint of a smile touched Luke's lips. He carefully folded a shirt and laid it in the trunk. "Yeah, I bet you were."

Bo cocked his head. "Think he could run?"

Luke's smile grew. "I guess we'll never know, but I sure had a feelin' 'bout that one."

Bo grinned. "Yep. So did I." He paused, then asked, "You gonna be visitin' him?"

"I don't plan to."

"I bet that sweet little girl wouldn't mind none."

"It wouldn't be a good idea. The horse is hers. I didn't ask her what she planned to do with him. I'd just as soon not know."

"Maybe you should have asked." Bo paused, his grin teasing. "If I remember right, she was a pretty little thing."

"The right man might think so." Luke's expression remained impassive, his tone disinterested.

"Well—" Bo paused a moment, studying his nails. "If you don't plan on lookin' in on the colt, maybe I should from time to time."

A picture of Bo talking and laughing with Darby Greene suddenly flashed through Luke's mind, and an odd feeling of discomfort caught him by surprise. It stumped him. He had no real interest in Darby Greene beyond the fact that she now owned the finest colt in Jefferson County. Irritated with himself, he shot Bo a disparaging glance. "She has a father who doesn't leave her alone for five minutes. I'd be careful if I were you."

Bo shrugged. "A father or a husband, what's the difference? I expect she's all grown up now and can make up her own mind."

"You could say that," Luke said, remembering the tempting swell of her firm young breasts pressing against her shirt.

Bo cocked his head and gave his friend a long, appraising stare. He and Luke had been working together as a team for more than five years, and their relationship had grown into one of mutual respect and affectionate sparring. "You got your eye on that little filly, Luke?"

Luke gave a soft huff. "She ain't my type."

"If I remember right, you said Katrina wasn't my type either."

Luke lifted his brows and widened his eyes. "And I was right. She's married to someone else, and you're the fool sneakin' in the back door every now and then. One of these days Frank Kirby's gonna walk in on you and shoot you both dead!" He delivered the lecture with such heartfelt conviction that Bo laughed out loud.

"So where you headed?" Bo asked, his mind veering off to other matters.

Luke shrugged a shoulder. "I don't know. Maybe back to New York. Maybe over to—"

"Where's my goddamn horse!" interrupted an angry voice from outside Luke's door. A second later Bradley Rhinehart appeared in the doorway.

Luke turned to face him.

"Where's the horse, Richards?"

Luke's expression was carefully blank. "What horse?"

"You know damn well what horse! Merry Molly's colt!"

Bo rose from the cot and stood beside his friend. He crossed his arms over his chest and widened his stance. If it came to blows, there was no question that Bo's loyalty stood with Luke.

"Answer me!" Bradley yelled, his gaze darting between the two men, his face growing purple with rage. Like his father, Bradley was a tall man with sandy brown hair and light brown eyes. He would have been considered handsome, but years of indulging himself with rich foods, along with too little activity, had aged him well beyond his years, causing his face to bloat and his middle to thicken.

A charged silence hung in the stables.

"Answer me, damn you!" Bradley demanded again.

Luke folded his arms over his chest and relaxed his stance. A tick pulsed in his cheek, but his deep voice was calm when he said, "Your father gave the colt to the girl."

"What girl?" Bradley's expression was incredulous.

"Darby Greene."

Bradley was all too well acquainted with who Darby Greene was. He was silent a moment. "That horse is my property!" he finally exploded.

"Not while your father was alive, he wasn't," Luke told him evenly. "Your father took care of the paperwork before he died. If you don't believe me, your uncle Nathaniel will verify what I've said when he reads the will this afternoon."

Bradley balled his hands into fists to keep them from trembling. He felt certain that his father had given the horse away to slight him. If the colt was anything like his Knightwind, he would have brought him a small fortune in winnings over the next several years. "You get that horse back, Richards!" he demanded, and jabbed a finger in the direction of Henry Greene's farm. "You go out to that goddamn farm and get that horse!"

Luke stared at him coolly while tension sizzled between them. "I'm afraid I can't do that, and even if I could, I wouldn't. I don't take orders from you, Bradley."

"You do now!" Bradley's complexion turned splotchy.

"No, I don't." Luke gestured to the nearly full trunk. "I resigned as of your father's death."

Bradley was silent a moment. "What do you mean, you've resigned?"

"I mean I quit."

"Same here," Bo added, breaking his silence.

The announcements had a drastic effect on Bradley's anger. He knew nothing about breeding and training Thoroughbreds. He'd never paid any attention to that facet of his father's business. He could not run the breeding farm in Fayette County or the training stables here without Luke Richards and Bo Denton. "Now, listen," he said amiably, managing a self-deprecating smile. "There's no need to be so hasty."

"Nothin' hasty about it," Luke said evenly. "The decision was made a long time ago."

"Surely we can work something out." Bradley held out his palms in supplication.

A wry grin touched the corners of Luke's mouth. "You and I can hardly stand to look at each other, Bradley. There ain't no way in hell we can run these farms together, and you know it."

Bradley turned to Bo. "Bo, I'll double your pay . . ."

Bo smiled. The offer was tempting, but he had never liked the younger Rhinehart either. "Sorry, Bradley. I'll be off the property with my gear by nightfall."

"That goes for me too," Luke said. He turned away and closed the lid of the trunk with finality.

Benjamin Rhinehart's burial was a simple, very brief affair, as was the reading of his will.

Luke sat in an expensive black leather chair beside Bradley. Across from them, seated at Benjamin Rhinehart's huge walnut desk, sat Nathaniel Rhinehart, Benjamin's lawyer and brother.

People found it hard to believe Nathaniel and Benjamin were brothers. Unlike his handsome younger brother, Nathaniel was a small, unassuming man with mouse-brown hair and pale blue eyes that were quite nondescript behind the thick lenses of his glasses. He was so thin that despite the fine cut of his clothing, his coat and trousers simply draped his bones like the well-worn rags of a beggar. At fifty-eight, he was two years older than Benjamin, and though he did quite well in his law practice, he'd long ago realized that he would never equal the success or have the social acceptance of his flamboyant sibling.

Benjamin Rhinehart's spacious study spoke of masculine elegance. The walls were paneled and polished. In the center of the varnished floor was a large Oriental carpet in deep shades of burgundy and green. A fireplace with an impressive mahogany mantel, stood between two massive bookshelves that rose from the floor up to the ceiling. Over the fireplace mantel hung a magnificent portrait of Knightwind, painted by Edward Troye, who was considered one of the finest artists of the time.

As the two men waited for him to begin, Nathaniel nervously cleared his throat. "Gentlemen," he finally said, shuffling through a thin stack of papers, "I offer my deepest condolences to you both. I understand your grief. I share it. As you both know, Benjamin was my only brother." He took a long, deep breath, and his gaze rested on Luke. "He wanted you to be present at the reading of his will. He thought very highly of you, you know." He paused and lowered his gaze to the papers he held in his hands. "As his lawyer, I attest to the fact that he was quite sound when he drew up his will. We went over it carefully several times in the past year, and he remained satisfied with the contents. So if you'll allow me . . ." He cleared his throat again, then lowered his gaze to the paper and began to read. " 'I, Benjamin Rhinehart, being of sound mind, bequeath to Darby Lynn Greene, the yearling colt out of the broodmare Merry Molly, sired by the stallion Knightwind.

" 'To my only son, Bradley, I bequeath the house, horses, and all properties of my breeding farm, located in Fayette County.

" 'And to my friend, Luke Richards—'' Nathaniel paused a fraction of a moment, interrupted by the soft gasp of surprise that escaped Bradley. "I bequeath the house, horses, and all properties of Rhinehart Stables, my Thoroughbred training farm located east of Louisville, in Jefferson County.

" 'My monetary assets are to be divided equally between the two men.' ''

Several moments passed while Luke and Bradley sat in shocked silence. The ticking of the clock upon the mantel seemed unusually loud, and to Bradley it was the cold voice of mockery.

Silent and numb, Bradley sat in the leather chair, his mind spinning. At thirty-four, he was Benjamin Rhinehart's only son and, by rights, he should have been his only heir. His mother, Sarah, had passed on shortly after his birth, denying his father any more children, for which Bradley had always been secretly grateful. He had had no use for siblings, nor for his uncle Nathaniel, for that matter.

Damn the old man! Bradley swore silently, his numbness turning into fury. He knew his father had always been disappointed that he had no real interest in the horses or stables. Instead of learning about the breeding of the Thoroughbreds, Bradley had taken up a different vocation: wagering on them, which was not so unusual in itself, except that he'd buried himself in debt countless times and would have suffered some very disturbing physical results had not his father paid off his debtors.

If that hadn't been humiliating enough, his father had all but cut him off financially six years before, allotting him only enough money for the necessities of life. Then he'd banished him to the smaller of his two farms, the one he used for breeding purposes, outside Lexington.

As he watched the two men digest the information, Nathaniel's gaze flicked from one to the other. "Do either of you have any questions?"

Bradley's eyes lifted to Nathaniel's. His dark gaze was hard and cold. "Is this some kind of a joke?"

Nathaniel coughed and pushed his spectacles up the short bridge of his nose. He squinted at the younger man. "I assure you it is not, Bradley."

"I see," Bradley said, and rose from his chair, his face mottling with suppressed rage. "Damn the old man to hell," he whispered with quiet venom. "And may you both join him there!" Then he turned and left the room, leaving the door gaping open behind him.

Luke ran a hand through his hair. His gaze was fixed on the man before him.

"Congratulations, Mr. Richards," Nathaniel said. He placed the papers into an envelope, then stood and offered Luke his hand.

Luke nodded. "Thank you." He rose from his chair, shook the lawyer's hand, then he, too, left the room.

He had work to do.

The stables and his horses were waiting for him.

A week passed, then two, and May became June.

The colt spent his first few nights in his new stall, whinnying furiously for his absent friends, but his appetite held strong, and Darby and Yancey saw that he was well fed.

By the second week Yancey had all but adopted the colt as his own. He seemed to know what needed to be done with him and when.

The colt had been broken to a halter, but within his first week at the Greene farm, Yancey managed to introduce him to the bridle and the bit. He walked the colt around a makeshift paddock until the two had begun to wear a path around the fenced area.

One morning, as Yancey and Darby led the colt out of the barn into the bright sunshine, he turned to Darby and said, "He's just about the finest colt I ever did see." He gave her a quick sideways glance. "What are you gonna do with him?"

Darby stroked the colt's sleek neck. "I'm gonna find a way to breed him. Someday I'm gonna buy him a mare. A mare worth breedin' him to."

Yancey's easy smile disappeared, and his whiskered face spoke his disapproval. "You can't just breed this horse." He looked at her as though she were addle-brained. "This ain't just any Thoroughbred, missy." He tipped back his droopy hat so he could nail her with his cool gray gaze. "This horse was born to run."

Darby looked over at Yancey, her brow puckering. "I know that, Yancey. But I also know what it takes to get a horse ready to race. I've been reading about such things since I was just a child, in case you didn't know it."

Yancey tried hard to suppress a smile. To him she was still a child, with her mop of dark curls and her full, dimpled cheeks.

They reached the corral that led to the small pasture that sufficed for Henry's six workhorses, two mules, and four cows. Darby lifted the latch on the gate, swinging it open. They led the colt inside the corral, then closed the gate behind, latching it securely. A bright yellow butterfly sailed in from the meadows and fluttered around their legs. "We'd need a trainer, a good trainer," Darby went on. "A jockey too." She thought a moment. "And not just any old jockey either." She nodded emphatically. "A real, honest-to-goodness champion needs a jockey like Bo Denton." Growing silent, she watched the butterfly light on the rusting plow that sat next to the barn.

Yancey raised one thick eyebrow and shook his head. "I always figured you had spunk, Darby," he said with a note of disappointment in his crusty voice. "I always figured if any of you girls had the spirit and the brains to git somethin' done, it'd be you. Don't you see, if you race him and he's a winner, breeding him will be easy. Every horse breeder in the state will be after him for stud. You'll be able to build your own farm around this horse. You'll be able to afford that filly you want for breedin'."

Darby was silent for a moment. Her hazel eyes took on a faraway look. "I'd love to race him," she admitted quietly, remembering the sight of Knightwind pouring down the track ahead of the other horses. "But Pa just couldn't afford to pay a trainer. You know that, Yancey."

The colt pawed the ground and shook his head, and Yancey tightened his hold on his halter. "Now, you just be patient, young fella," Yancey scolded good-naturedly. "You'll get to kick up those heels of yours soon enough." Yancey bent down and tugged a long, thin weed from the ground. He placed it in his mouth and chewed, his expression thoughtful. He looked over at Darby. "Maybe he wouldn't have to pay a trainer just yet."

Darby huffed and rolled her eyes. "People don't work for free."

"That's right, they don't," Yancey conceded. "Word has it Rhinehart left that young trainer the farm over yonder." He pointed in the direction of Rhinehart Stables. "I also heard the young jockey didn't go to work for Raymond Miller like he planned. He stayed on to ride for Richards. Heard Miller wasn't real happy about that either."

"So?" Darby said, confused.

"Maybe you ought to pay Richards a visit."

Her expression grew puzzled. "Why?"

Yancey gave her a look that said he didn't believe she

could be so dim-witted. "To hire him to train Blue to race, that's what for."

"Why would he want to do that? If it's true that the stables are his now, he has plenty of horses to train of his own. Why would he bother with my horse?"

"Because . . ." A crafty smile stole across Yancey's face. "If he's any kind of a trainer, and I hear he is, he already knew he had a champion in Blue, and I'd bet my eyeballs he wasn't real happy about givin' him up to the likes of you."

"What's wrong with the likes of me?" Darby asked, prickling, drawing herself up to her full height of five feet seven inches.

"You don't know nothing about raisin' a Thoroughbred, Darby Lynn."

She thought about that a moment. "I do. I read about it all the time."

"Readin' and doin' are two very different things. It's not so much what you know up here," he said as he pointed to his head, "it's what you know in here"—he placed his hand over his heart—"that counts when you got the best horses in the country running against each other. A good trainer can feel things about a horse that even the horse's owner can't. A good trainer has instincts."

"But I can't afford to pay Luke Richards—"

"Maybe you won't have to pay him till the horse runs his first race."

Darby frowned. "And what if he doesn't win?"

Yancey bent down and ran his hands over the colt's legs. Blue butted his head against Yancey's shoulder playfully. "Easy, boy," Yancey said softly. A lock of thinning hair fell down from beneath his floppy hat onto his forehead. When he looked back up at Darby, he was smiling. "He'll win, Darby."

There was a quiet confidence in his voice that puzzled her. She studied him in silence. She'd grown very fond of Yancey over the past four years. He'd drifted in out of nowhere one day and asked Henry Greene for work. Henry had hired him on and never regretted the decision. He'd become a second father to Darby, always looking out for her, scolding her often, yet covering for her whenever she was lax about doing her chores. Still, she knew very little about him beyond the fact that he was honest and dependable, somewhere around fifty years old, and he took an almost perverse pleasure in teasing Aunt Birdie by wearing that ridiculous old hat and not shaving his whiskers for days on end.

"How come you seem to know so much about horses?" she finally asked, her curiosity rife. When he didn't answer, she went on. "Where did you work before you came to work for my pa?"

His youthful gray eyes took on a hint of sadness, and he gave a soft snort and tipped his head back to watch a hawk ride across the blue Kentucky sky. "Never you mind 'bout that, little missy," he said with forced gruffness. "You just get yourself over to Rhinehart Stables and talk to that young trainer."

Darby took the colt's reins from Yancey. She slipped the bit from Blue's mouth, and he immediately kicked up his heels and shot off. He hopped about, then sprinted for a while before stopping to look at her over his shoulder. A huge horsefly landed on his front shoulder, and he nipped at it, then bucked wildly. Darby laughed and leaned her forearms over the top rung of the fence and rested her left foot on the bottom rung. Blue took off again, galloping into the wind, his shiny ebony mane whipping back from his neck.

"He's racing stock, Darby," Yancey said, and hooked his hands on his hips. "That horse wants to run."

Darby looked at Yancey, a smile deepening the dimples in her cheeks. "Would you be willing to bet on that?"

Yancey nodded. "I'd bet my life on it."

It was early the next morning when Darby walked into Rhinehart Stables.

The grooms and stable hands were busy with their chores, but they were so curious about her presence, they stopped

working to stare at her. It had been a long time since a female
had entered their domain, let alone a female who didn't look
like an ordinary member of her gender. She wore dark
britches, dusty black boots, and a tan shirt that was dented
on the shoulders by a pair of thick black suspenders.

Sensing their eyes on her, Darby stood in the center of the
barn, feeling awkward and uncertain. She wondered why she
had ever let Yancey talk into such foolishness. She felt certain
that Luke Richards would not be interested in her offer. He'd
think she was as simple-minded as Eda Mae Penney, who
lived up in the hills and claimed she saw haunts and demons
in broad daylight.

Go home, Darby Lynn, she said to herself, and was just
about to do that when Ian Hanson intervened.

"Mornin', miss," he called out. Darby swung back around
to face him. He walked toward her, a pitchfork in hand. His
partially toothless smile added an extra batch of wrinkles to
his already lined face. "You have business with someone
here?"

"I'd like to see Mr. Richards if I could," Darby said politely, gathering her courage.

Ian stopped before her. His eyes were even with hers. "He
ain't here right now, miss. He's out for his mornin' ride. But
I'm expecting him back directly."

"I see." She felt both relief and disappointment. Her confidence was leaking out of her pores by the second.

"Would you like to sit a spell and wait?" Ian asked kindly.
"We can fetch you a cup of coffee."

She offered him a smile, her dimples winking. "No, thank
you. But I'd appreciate it if you'd tell him that I was here."

Ian nodded. "I surely will, miss, if you'll leave your
name."

"Darby. Darby Greene."

"Well, well, well," said a very smooth, very male voice.

Darby turned, and her gaze collided with that of Bo Denton's. He walked through the door of the barn and all but
swaggered up to her, where she stood with Ian.

"If it isn't the lucky lady." His brown eyes, level with her own, were warm and friendly.

Flustered, she felt her face heat immediately. His gaze held hers, and his grin grew devilish.

"You got yourself one helluva horse, Miss Greene," he said.

"Yes, I know," she said quietly.

His eyes took a slow, intimate journey over her person, and, suddenly self-conscious, she glanced away.

"We hated to lose him."

Her gaze came back to his. "I don't blame you."

"I was looking forward to seeing what that colt could do."

She opened her mouth to respond, but the shrill whinny of a horse halted her as Luke rode into the barn and swung down from his horse.

Darby found her gaze riveted to him. His hips were lean, his long legs hard and muscular beneath his britches. As she stared at him she realized that he was every bit as handsome as Bo, though his dark good looks were a striking contrast to Bo's golden beauty.

Ian hurried to take the horse's reins.

Bo grinned. "We got company, Luke."

His stride strong and purposeful, Luke came over to where they stood.

"Miss Greene," Luke greeted Darby politely, studying her with cool disinterest.

"Hello, Mr. Richards," Darby returned.

"What can I do for you?" he asked, planting his hands on his hips.

She got right to the point. "I've come to ask for your help."

Luke felt a jolt of panic. "Is the colt all right?"

"Oh, yes, he's fine."

Relief flooded him. "Then what can I do for you?" he asked again, all business. He was eager to get on with his day.

Darby sensed his impatience, but Yancey's words echoed

in her mind: "I always figured you had spunk, Darby."

Determination stiffened her spine. Yancey was right. She did have spunk and, by golly, she was gonna use it. "I have a proposition for you, Mr. Richards," she said, her gaze direct and unflinching. She looked over at Bo. "Actually, I have a proposition for both of you."

❖ 3 ❖

Bo SMILED. "WELL, there's nothing I find more interestin' than a proposition from a pretty lady, how 'bout you, Luke?"

Luke's brows pulled together into a dark line above the bridge of his fine, straight nose. "It depends."

"I want you to train Blue to race," Darby said in a rush without flinching, then she turned to Bo. "And I want you to ride him. I want to race him in the Kentucky Derby and I want to win."

Silence fell. All activity ceased as the stable hands stopped working, having heard bits of the conversation.

After a few moments Bo crossed his arms over his chest and chuckled, then shot a curious glance over at his friend.

Luke shifted his stance, looked down at his boots, then back up at Darby. When he spoke his blue eyes were apologetic. "I'm afraid I'm not interested, Miss Greene."

"Why not?" Darby asked, refusing to accept his answer without an explanation.

He gestured to the many occupied stalls in the barn. "I have plenty of horses of my own to train, thanks to Benjamin Rhinehart's generosity."

Darby was not about to give up so easily. "I know you do. But my colt is special."

"She's right 'bout that," Bo cut in, earning himself a glare from Luke.

"Is it because Mr. Rhinehart gave me the colt instead of leaving him to you with all the others?" Darby pressed him. "Do you resent me for that?"

Luke thought about that a moment, then honestly said, "No. Of course not." But he did wonder why Rhinehart had given her the colt after all. He thought Rhinehart had wanted to save the colt from Bradley's misuse as well as repay Darby for what she'd done for him. But now he wasn't really sure what was behind his reasoning. Rhinehart knew that the colt had the makings of a champion. Had he left the colt to Luke, along with the other six yearlings, Luke would have trained him to reach his full potential.

"You know Blue is a winner," Darby said with conviction in her voice. "You know that even better than I do. If I can see his potential, surely you're even more aware of what he could do if he had the proper training."

Luke shook his head and opened his mouth to respond, but Bo laid a hand on his shoulder, staying him. "She's right, Luke, and you know it. That colt is a fine horse." He glanced over at Darby, then back at Luke. "Dammit, I think he might be the best we've ever had. He's bigger and stronger than even Knightwind was at his age. He's smart too. Maybe he's even faster . . ." He let the sentence hang and watched his friend struggle with indecision. He knew Luke ached to train him, to develop him into the winner his father had been. But he could also see that Luke was reluctant to accept Darby's proposition.

"Please, Mr. Richards, at least think about it," Darby begged, though it galled her to do so. She'd never begged for anything in her life, but then, she'd never wanted anything as much as she wanted to race Kentucky Blue. Her eyes pleaded with him. "I know you want to see him run every bit as much as I do."

Luke's expression remained unchanged, though he silently acknowledged that she'd hit a nerve. He owned six of the finest Thoroughbred yearlings in Kentucky, and three equally fine two-year-olds. But none of the horses excited him the way the colt had.

After a moment he lifted one eyebrow and narrowed his gaze. "And if I say no?"

Stumped, Darby's mind clicked. She decided to take a gamble of her own. She held his gaze. "Then I'll have no choice but to sell him."

Surprised, Luke felt his chest tighten with panic. If she sold the colt, he might be lost to him forever. With that thought in mind, he took silent measure of her. Surely she was bluffing. But he couldn't know for sure. "All right," he finally said. "I'll think about it."

"Thank you," she said on a huff of relief. "That's wonderful."

"I said I'd think about it," Luke warned, unable to quell the twitch of a smile that pulled at one side of his mouth. "I didn't say I'd do it."

But Darby was undaunted by his warning. She turned to Bo. "What about you, Mr. Denton?"

Bo gave her a lazy half-grin. "I'm with Luke. Whatever he decides, he decides for both of us."

"I see." She sobered and became all business. "I have to be honest with you both." Her gaze found Luke's once again. "I can't pay either of you till Blue wins his first purse, but when he does, I'll divide the winnings evenly with both of you."

Luke lifted one dark eyebrow. "Are you so sure he'll win?"

"Yes," she said quietly, and her face brightened into a beguiling smile. "I'd bet my life on it."

That night, sleep did not come easily to Luke.

He lay awake, long into the night, shifting on his hard cot in his small room. He listened to the gentle creaks and groans in the barn as it settled into sleep for the night, and he was comforted somewhat.

Although the big house was his, and he continued to employ Mrs. Brunsteader, Rhinehart's elderly housekeeper, to prepare meals for himself and his outfit, he chose to sleep in the stables as he'd always done, so he could be near his horses.

He felt a kinship with the horses. His horses were the only family he had ever known—the only things he had ever loved. He was used to being alone. Alone suited him just fine.

When he needed female companionship, he went out and found it, but it was usually only a temporary dalliance—a physical act of release, bereft of emotion.

But the horses were different; they were his children. He worried about every one of them, especially on the days they raced. He'd watched the stables closely after Rhinehart's accident. He knew only too well that it was not uncommon for unscrupulous grooms, hands, trainers, even jockeys and owners, to rig a race by injuring or killing a prospective champion. Some of the bigger farms had hired Pinkerton detectives to patrol their properties, but Rhinehart had always believed their greatest danger would not come from an outside competitor, but could come from someone within their own ranks.

Luke knew he was right. But he trusted all his grooms and stable hands. If he didn't, they would not be working with his horses.

It was not worry over his horses that kept him awake this night, however.

It was Darby Greene and her proposition.

God knew, he wanted to train the colt. He wanted that more than he wanted anything in the world. But it would take a great deal of time and money.

And he was scared.

He'd never had anything in his life, and he didn't know if he could hold on to it now that he did. Although Rhinehart had left him the house and stables, his funds were limited. As a trainer provided with room and board, he'd had plenty of money for himself, but things were different now. He had half a dozen stable hands and Mrs. Brunsteader to pay and feed, along with a stable of horses that had to be fed and cared for. The money Rhinehart had left him was a meager sum at best. Bradley had almost beggared his father with his gambling debts years before. And though Luke owned some of the best yearlings money could buy, a grand house, and one of the finest stables in Jefferson County, he had no breeders of his own and very little money left to buy them with. To continue to build Rhinehart's empire, he would have to turn his two-year-olds and his yearlings into winners and, when he retired them, breed them so he could build his own Thoroughbred farm. It could be done, and he would do it, but it would take time. First he had to concentrate on which of the horses held the most promise.

Which brought him back to Darby Greene and her colt. His instincts told him that the colt could be his champion of champions, the one above all others.

Knightwind had been a swift, powerful runner, but his legs had not been able to take the strain and pounding of the racetrack. If he had not broken down at the Derby, he would have easily taken the race, as he had taken all the others he had raced before.

Luke was thankful that the big stallion was past his racing prime. At least Bradley would not attempt to run him to death on a track.

But Darby Greene's colt held all the promise of Knightwind and then some. He was bigger and sturdier, promising the strength and endurance of his mother. Still, training the colt would be time-consuming. It would take him away from the other horses, and he would have to share his winnings with the girl.

With a soft sigh he turned onto his side. The cot groaned beneath his weight. From one of the stalls came a soft, comforting neigh and the crisp rustle of shifting hay.

In time Luke finally grew drowsy and began to drift off to sleep. But, oddly enough, it was not the colt's face he saw as he drifted off to sleep. It was the pert face of the young woman who owned him.

*　　*　　*

Two days later Luke and Bo stood on the back porch of Henry Greene's house and knocked at his door. Remus was sprawled out on the porch, fast asleep in a waning ray of afternoon sunlight. Luke reached down and patted the dog's head, and Remus slowly opened one bloodshot eye to see who had disturbed his nap.

Bo laughed, and Luke knocked on the door again.

It was a warm Friday evening. The air was light and sweet. In the distance the red sun melted into the hills, coloring the sky in shades of pink, gold, and lavender.

Aunt Birdie answered the door seconds later. "Why, hello, young man," she said with a twitchy little smile, recognizing Luke immediately.

"Hello, ma'am," Luke said. "Is your husband or Darby at home?"

Birdie smiled, then let loose with a merry trill of laughter. "Well, if my husband is home, he'd be surprised to know it, 'specially since he doesn't exist." She sobered some and kindly said, "I'm not Henry's wife. His wife passed on some time ago. I'm his sister, Birdie. You can call me Miss Birdie, if that seems fittin'. As for Darby Lynn, you'll find her out yonder, where she's been living these days with that colt and the shaggy old Yancey Latimer." She pointed in the direction of the small corral beside the barn.

"Thank you, ma'am," Luke said, and shot a glance over his shoulder at the corral. He turned back to Birdie and gestured to Bo. "This is Bo Denton, Miss Birdie."

"Well," Birdie said, opening the door a bit wider, "it is a pleasure to meet you, Mr. Denton. I've read a lot about you. Would you gentlemen like to come in and sit a spell? I'm expectin' Henry in from the fields anytime."

Luke smiled and shook his head. "If you don't mind, we'll just go on out and talk to Darby."

"Suit yourselves. Would you like a cup of coffee or a nice cold glass of lemonade?"

Bo flashed her his brightest, most charming smile. "I surely could go for a glass of lemonade, ma'am."

"Go on out, then, and I'll bring it to you in a minute."
Birdie closed the door and flew back into the kitchen while
the two men strode across the porch and down the porch
steps.

"Well, lookee there," Bo said as they approached the corral. There was a note of awe and respect in his voice. "I
guess if you don't train him, she's gonna give it a try herself."

Luke gave a soft huff of amusement. She'd been bluffing,
all right. She'd had no intention of selling the horse. "She's
got spirit. I'll give her that. But I doubt she knows what the
hell she's doin'."

When the two men reached the fence, they stopped and
rested their forearms on the top rung while they watched
Darby and Yancey lead the colt around in a series of figure
eights.

Bo cocked his head at his friend. "She ain't doin' so bad."

Luke remained silent.

Yancey noticed their presence first. "I told you they'd
show up," he said under his breath.

Darby's head snapped around, and her gaze collided with
Luke's. She felt an exhilarating rush of joy and relief. She'd
barely been able to sleep the last two nights, wondering about
his decision. She'd felt almost certain that Bo wanted to take
a chance on Blue, but she didn't know what Luke would
decide.

Darby waved, and the two men waved back.

"That's enough for today," Yancey said, and slipped the
bit from the colt's mouth. He turned him out into the pasture
to play, then he and Darby walked over to the fence.

"You came!" Darby said with unbridled enthusiasm. Her
eyes were bright, her smile contagious. "I'm so glad!"

"You drive a hard bargain, Miss Greene," Luke said quietly.

She turned to Yancey. "Yancey, this is Luke Richards and
Bo Denton."

Yancey held out his hand and shook hands with both men,

but his gray eyes were riveted to Luke's face with an awed intensity.

Luke leveled his gaze on the older man. "Did you try a saddle pad and surcingle on him yet?"

"Not yet," Yancey answered, regaining his composure. "I've been waitin' for you."

A small smile pulled at Luke's mouth, and he raised one dark eyebrow. "Is that a fact?"

Yancey nodded. "Yep. I figured you'd wanna do it your way."

Unable to help himself, Luke chuckled. "You were that sure I'd come?"

Yancey rubbed his whiskered chin and tipped back his old hat, his eyes squinty. "You'da been a fool not to."

Bo nodded emphatically. "That's what I've been tellin' him for two days."

"Hello, there," Henry called out from behind, joining them. He handed Bo a glass of lemonade, and Darby introduced the younger man to her father.

"Birdie said you were looking for me," Henry said to Luke.

"Yes, sir," Luke said. "I wanted to make sure you understood what your daughter had in mind for the colt."

Henry smiled and glanced at Darby. "She's twenty years old. I 'magine she's old enough to do what she wants, especially with her own horse."

"Yes, sir," Luke said, realizing the entire matter was between himself, Bo, and Darby. His gaze found Darby. "I'll train the colt," he said. "But there are conditions to my agreement."

"I'll ride him," Bo added, "as long as you agree to Luke's conditions."

Darby's elation deflated somewhat, and her expression clouded. "What are the conditions?"

"I want the colt back at Rhinehart Stables. I'll train him there, and he'll stay there. I have the training track, paddocks, and all the equipment I need."

Darby's eyes lost a little of their sparkle. "But I'll miss him."

Luke shrugged. "You can visit him from time to time."

"But I want to help." She looked from one man to the other. "I want to take part in his training."

"It's my way, or the deal is off."

Darby was silent a moment. Then she crossed her arms over her chest and set her jaw. "Then the deal is off."

Luke's heart kicked in his chest. He hadn't expected her to challenge his conditions. "Fine."

Darby held her ground and held his gaze.

"Now, wait a minute," Bo hurriedly jumped in, holding up his hands. He looked over at Luke. "It can't hurt to have her around. She can bathe him down and see to some of the extra work so that we don't have to pull the grooms and stable hands off the other horses."

His jaw set as stubbornly as Darby's, Luke's blue eyes locked with her hazel ones. In that moment they took silent measure of each other, and they both realized that this was only one of the many battles that would surface between them. Luke thought a moment. "All right," he said on a heavy sigh, his gaze still locked with Darby's, "you can help, but you leave the training to me and the riding to Bo."

Darby nodded. "Agreed." She glanced over at Yancey. "One more thing." Her eyes found Luke's again. "If my pa can spare him, I want Yancey to be there too. I want Yancey to help with his training. The colt likes him."

Yancey glanced over at Henry, who nodded. "I suppose I could spare him through a good part of the summer now that the crops are all in—"

"No!" Luke barked, and a tick began to pulse in his jaw. He turned to Henry. "I'm sorry for the interruption, sir." He looked back at Darby. "Nobody works with my horses but my own men. . . ." He let the sentence hang to see how she would react.

Once again her mouth puckered stubbornly, and anger flashed in her eyes. "Then forget the whole damn thing!"

"Darby Lynn," Henry reprimanded softly, though he was secretly amused by their sparring. They were an equal match for each other, and he was curious to see who would win out. But having raised her, he silently placed his bet on Darby. She may have inherited her mother's good sense, but she had also inherited his own stubborn nature. When she wanted something badly enough, she held on to the idea as a hungry dog would a meaty bone.

Yancey was not so amused. He saw Darby's dream crumbling. He reached out and laid a hand on Darby's shoulder. "Darby Lynn, you don't need to argue about thi—"

"Yes, I do, Yancey," she said with conviction. "I want you to be a part of this."

A long silence followed, broken only by the sound of the wind sifting through the trees. Then quite suddenly, as if he knew they were discussing him, the colt came flying up through the meadow. Seeing Luke, he let loose with a shrill whinny and trotted up to the group, pushing his nose over the fence toward Luke.

Luke reached out and rubbed his nose. "Hey, fella!"

The horse responded with a soft neigh.

"Looks like they've been takin' good care of you," he said grudgingly.

Blue snorted and searched Luke's palm. "All right," Luke said, walking toward his horse. He reached into his saddlebag and returned a few moments later with an apple. The colt snorted his excitement, and Luke offered him the treat. "Thata boy," Luke said as the colt took the apple and chewed.

"No wonder he's fat," Bo said under his breath.

Luke turned to Darby and Yancey. The tick had taken up residence above his right eye. "I'll see you both at the stables on Monday morning. Bring Blue." Then he turned and walked away, leaving Bo to follow.

Bo winked at Darby and handed her his empty glass. "Be there at dawn. He doesn't like to be kept waitin'."

*   *   *

Millie Johnson's jaw dropped three inches. She spun around in the polished pew in the Walnut Street Methodist Church on Sunday morning to get a better look at her friend's face. "Bo Denton's gonna race your horse?" she said in a whisper loud enough that nearly all the congregation heard her. "And Luke Richards is gonna train him!"

"Shhh," Darby said, and nodded.

"I don't believe you," Millie announced, and wrinkled her freckled nose.

"So don't."

"Bo Denton could race any horse he wanted."

"Well, he's gonna race mine," Darby stated confidently.

"Humph," Millie huffed, and fussed with the lace collar of her elegant white blouse.

In contrast to her friend's frilly garment, Darby was dressed in a simple blue dress that lacked any ornamentation. "You don't have to believe me," Darby whispered, "but it's true. You can ask Emma if you want."

Emma and Noah Sanders slipped into the pew beside Darby. Emma, like her father, was shorter than Darby, but her hair and eye coloring was a replica of Darby's. Instead of sporting the short curls her sister favored, however, Emma's hair was longer and was swept up into a fashionable arrangement upon her head. "You two might as well shout everything out loud. Your whispers are about as quiet as Aunt Birdie scolding Yancey and Eugene for being late to breakfast!" She pinned the two younger girls with a look of haughty disapproval.

"Oh, hush, Emma," Darby said, not bothering to keep her tone down. "Ever since you got engaged you've been putting on airs. If you aren't careful, even Noah won't be able to stand you much longer."

Noah was a big, soft-spoken man with pale blond hair and big brown eyes. He reddened with embarrassment, and Emma sniffed her disgust.

Millie leaned over the pew. "Is it true, Emma? Is Bo Denton really gonna ride Darby's colt for her?"

Emma shrugged. "I guess so. And Luke Richards is gonna train him. Papa was talkin' about it yesterday, so it has to be true."

"Golly," Millie whispered, sinking back down into the pew. She was truly impressed.

"Golly what?" Darby asked, though she knew exactly what Millie was thinking.

"Well, if you don't mind, Darby, I'd just purely love it if you'd introduce me. Papa took Mama and me to the Derby this past May, and I saw Bo Denton ride one of Benjamin Rhinehart's horses in the race. I can't remember what position the horse took, but I do remember thinkin' Mr. Denton was just devastatingly handsome." Millie rolled her eyes heavenward, pressed her palm against her amply endowed chest, and faked a delicious shudder.

"We're just business associates, Millie," Darby said on a dry note. Millie had grown up to be quite a beauty and an incorrigible flirt. Her flaming red hair was thick and lustrous, and her complexion, though slightly freckled, was smooth and creamy and fashionably pale. Millie had long ago forgotten her vow about not bothering with the male species. It seemed, to Darby's disappointment, that the male species was the only thing Millie did bother with these days. She was always off to one social event or another, and her list of beaus had grown impressively over the past several years.

Darby had no such list, and she'd never cared one way or the other. But today, for some odd reason, she was suddenly very aware of its absence.

"You'll be spending time together, though, and you're sure to become friends," Millie said, cutting into Darby's thoughts. "Men like you, Darby. You don't threaten them the way a real woman does."

Stung, Darby's gaze shot up to Millie's. Even Emma, who was usually the first to antagonize or insult her younger sister, threw Millie a harsh look.

"Gee, thanks, Millie," Darby said with a short little laugh, unable to keep the hurt note out of her voice.

"Oh, Darby." Millie tipped her head and smiled sweetly. She reached out and patted her hand. "You know what I mean."

Noah leaned past his fiancée and chucked Darby under her chin. "I don't know what she means. You sure look like a real woman to me, Darby Lynn. If I wasn't engaged to this pretty sister of yours, I'd be chasin' you all over the county."

Darby smiled. She liked both of her other two sisters' husbands, but Noah, who would marry Emma the following June, was easily her favorite.

Still, she knew Noah was just being kind. Men didn't chase after girls like herself. She liked barns and horses, britches and boots. She didn't know how to cook and didn't care to learn. She hated to sew, couldn't dance a step, and even when she wore a dress, it was obvious she wasn't the type for feminine fussing.

But she'd always liked who she was. Until lately.

She suddenly wished she were more like her sisters and Millie—feminine and pretty and intriguing.

Millie studied Darby's face for several moments, then her mouth dropped open in surprise once more. "Darby Lynn Greene, you want him for yourself!" she accused loudly, her big blue eyes widening with astonishment.

Darby felt every disapproving Methodist eye in the church turn her way. "Of course not," she whispered, blushing clear up to her hairline. Then she felt a condemning stab of guilt. Although she had never fully acknowledged her attraction to Bo Denton, she could not deny that it existed. She had been aware of him since the very first time she'd laid eyes on him.

"Mornin', ladies. Noah," her father said, saving Darby from further embarrassment. He turned sideways, allowing Birdie to slide into the pew beside Emma. Then he urged everyone to slide down to allow Ardis, her new baby boy, Jimmy, and her husband, James, along with Linette and her husband, Joe, to sit in the family pew. They all greeted one another with nods and smiles, then everyone turned their attention to the front of the auditorium and to the man who stood behind the pulpit, waiting to deliver the opening prayer, their preacher and Millie's father, the Reverend David Johnson.

On Monday morning, well before sunrise, Yancey and Darby led Kentucky Blue down Brownsboro Road.

When they reached Rhinehart Stables, the sun was just beginning to crest the hills, but Luke and Bo were already waiting inside the stable door, coffee cups in hand.

"You're late," Luke said tersely, then turned to Ian. "Take care of their horses."

"Yes, sir," Ian said with a nod. He smiled at Darby, then took hold of her horse's halter.

She swung down off her horse and pinned Luke with her gaze. "It's barely dawn."

"The days begin early 'round here." He took hold of Blue's halter. "Let's go, boy." He dismissed Darby, and Bo shrugged and turned back into the barn to get the needed equipment.

Luke looked over at Yancey. "We're gonna try the saddle cloth, the saddle pad, and surcingle on him today."

Yancey grinned and clapped his hands together. "Hooooee! He ain't gonna like it none. He ain't mean, but he's independent as hell."

"Yep, that he is," Luke agreed, and led the colt into a large stall. When Darby tried to follow Yancey into the stall, Luke turned to her and said, "It'd be best if you didn't come in. He may decide to fight, and there's barely enough room for all of us in here as it is."

Her eyes flashed fire, and she opened her mouth to protest, but he held up a hand, staying her. "There's nothing fun about training a racehorse, Darby," he said. "It's hard work and lots of repetition and patience. We don't take shortcuts. We don't take off for Sundays or holidays. We train regardless of the heat, rain, mud, or snow. Even then, only a small percentage of the best horses will ever make it to the Derby.

I intend for Blue to be part of that percentage. If that's your intention, too, then you need to follow my instructions and not question my decisions. I don't have time to justify everything I do. You may own this colt, but as long as I'm training him, he's mine. I'm not trying to exclude you. I'm only trying to do what's best for the horse.''

She stared at him a second, then closed her mouth. She was intelligent enough to know he was right. She wanted him to train her horse, and she had won the first battle. She was there, even if she was only watching, and Yancey was actually taking part in Blue's training.

Bo appeared a moment later, carrying a saddle cloth, a saddle pad, and a surcingle. His elbow subtly brushed her arm as he slipped past her into the stall. "Pardon me," he said, and smiled at her.

Darby's cheeks bloomed with color, and a slow tingle began down deep in her belly. Flustered, she lowered her gaze and stared at her boots.

Luke had not missed the exchange. He shot his friend a look of silent warning and inwardly acknowledged that training the horse would be an easy task compared to dealing with Darby's presence in his stables. Bo just couldn't help himself. There wasn't a woman alive, old or young, whom he didn't attempt to seduce, and Luke sensed that Darby Greene was as innocent about seduction as the colt was about what they had in store for him.

"Well," Bo said to Luke, playfully ignoring his glare of disapproval, "let's get on with it."

Yancey shut the door behind Bo, then reached over and double-checked the latch to make sure it was tight. He sent a reassuring smile at Darby, then, as though he'd done it countless times before, he went over to the colt and began rubbing him on the back and side, easing his strokes down toward the colt's fat belly. The colt stiffened and laid his ears back, and Luke took the saddle cloth from Bo.

"Easy, fella," Luke said. "This ain't gonna hurt one little

bit." He slid the saddle cloth up onto the colt's back and smoothed it down. "See there," he crooned in a deep, husky tone that Darby found oddly tantalizing. She found her gaze riveted to him as he took the saddle pad from Bo and laid it on top of the cloth, folding the front end of the cloth back over the pad. "Ahhhh, now, that's such a good boy. Yessiree, Blue. A good boy. All right, now . . ." He cast a glance over at Darby. "This is where he might get a little ornery." He pulled the surcingle over the pad and around the colt's ample girth. "Let's see if I can get this around your big belly, boy. Whoa," he said on a crooked smile as he fastened the surcingle. "Bo is right. You are one fat baby." Yancey smiled, and Darby giggled. The surcingle was not tight, but the colt had never had anything strapped around him before, and he let out a loud squeal of protest. When the offending object remained intact, he stamped his foot and tried to back himself into a corner, but Yancey and Bo kept a firm hold on his halter. He gave his head a hard shake and squealed a second time, this time even louder, and Luke scolded, "Now, that's enough, boy! You behave yourself!"

Unused to Luke's harsh tone, the colt went still, his eyes wide.

"Easy now." Luke stepped up to him and tightened the surcingle by one notch. The colt instinctively swelled his belly. Luke waited a moment and looked over at Darby. Her brow was furrowed with worry, and he felt a sudden need to ease her mind. "He's doin' just fine. Nothin' we're doin' is hurtin' him."

She nodded and tried to smile.

When the colt relaxed again, Luke tightened the surcingle a final time and backed away. Blue didn't like that one bit. He stamped his foot hard.

"Now, that's enough of that," Luke said, and took hold of the colt's halter. "Let's take a little walk and see if you don't feel better." He turned the colt around in the stall one time, and the colt followed perfectly, then Luke turned him around once more.

Yancey chuckled and shook his head. "He's doin' good."

"Is he?" Darby asked eagerly, leaning over the stall door. "Really?"

"He's doin' damn good, Darby," Luke said, a note of pride in his voice. He hooked one hand on his hip and studied the colt.

"Well, then, it's 'bout time we see how he likes a little weight on his back," Bo said. He waited for Luke and Yancey to get on each side of the colt and take a firm hold on his halter, then he moved to the colt's side. Luke leaned forward, grabbed Bo's left leg, and boosted him up so that he was lying across the colt's back, belly down.

For an instant Blue stood absolutely still, as if stunned, then he put his head down, bucked once, not too hard, took a few hops sideways, then quieted down. Luke turned him around the stall twice, and when the colt made no further objections to Bo's weight, Luke grabbed hold of Bo's left boot, allowing him to throw his right leg over and straddle the colt.

Darby held her breath while Bo waited for the colt's reaction. Luke stroked Blue's neck and praised him, watching for any signs that he might try to dump Bo. But Blue just stood there, his ears pricked forward, waiting to see what was coming next.

Luke and Yancey led the colt around the stall, letting him get used to Bo's weight. Then, after several minutes, Bo dismounted, and Luke patted the colt. "You done fine, boy." His deep voice was full of approval. "Real fine."

"He's gonna be a winner," Yancey said, taking off his hat and running a handful of fingers through his thinning hair. "I never, in all my days, worked with a horse like this one—"

Luke's head came up, and he shot Yancey a shrewd, questioning glance.

Yancey's smile slipped a little. "Well, compared to the field horses I usually spend my time with," he added quickly, "this baby sure is somethin' special."

"That he is," Bo agreed, and winked at Darby.

*　　*　　*

The next three days were replicas of the first one. The group spent hours inside the stall, going over the same procedure until they were bone tired.

On the fourth day they added the bridle and the saddle, minus stirrups.

That morning Bo swung himself up into the saddle, and Luke and Yancey left him alone in the stall to turn Blue in a series of slow figure eights, allowing the colt to get used to the feel of the bit on both sides of his mouth.

Blue got in a few good bucks, then quickly picked up on what was expected of him.

Luke and Yancey waited outside the door with Darby, in case of trouble.

On the fifth day they added the stirrups. On the sixth day they attached the martingale, or yoke—a leather strap that attached to the girth and ran between the front legs and split to attach to the reins, allowing the rider more control of the horse's head.

Darby was fascinated by the entire process. She went to sleep thinking about what they'd done each day and awoke every morning with a renewed sense of anticipation, wondering what Luke had planned for Blue that day. She wanted to learn everything about horse training; she wanted to understand everything Luke and Bo did with Blue. She studied Luke's facial expressions, his tone of voice, even his bodily gestures, and she decided that Yancey had been right. Book learning did not make a trainer. Instincts did. And Luke Richards had plenty of instincts.

By the time Kentucky Blue ran in the Kentucky Derby, she planned on having some too.

❖ 4 ❖

On the eleventh morning of Blue's training, Yancey dressed the colt in his gear and led him out of the stables into the early morning sunshine.

"Bring him over here," Luke ordered from where he stood with Darby inside a small corral.

It was the first time Blue had been outside the stables since his return to Rhinehart Stables, and Darby's stomach was jumpy with anticipation. She stole a glance up at Luke.

Feeling her gaze, he looked down at her. "We're gonna do the same thing we did in the stall. Only out here there's more room to work him." He paused, then asked, "Any questions?" There was a hint of amusement in his clear blue eyes. He'd come to expect her questions and, to his surprise, even looked forward to them.

"No," she said with a small smile.

"This is the easy part of the day. He won't mind this so much. But later on he might get a bit touchy."

Darby frowned. "Why?"

"He gets his first bath this evening, and that's gonna be your job. I'll help you with him the first couple of times, then it'll be up to you and Yancey to see to that duty every day after training."

Darby nodded.

"Blue isn't gonna appreciate it very much at first." Luke shoved his hands down into his pockets and grinned. "It's like everything else, it takes some gettin' used to." *Just like having you around does.* He turned to watch Yancey lead the colt out to them. "In a couple of weeks we'll take him out to the training track. We'll work him up to a mile. We'll walk him and jog him, let him canter a little, get him used to starting and stopping, to turning around."

Darby looked over at the abandoned training track. "I thought I knew a lot about horses, but I guess I don't."

"You do. More than most women do," Luke said with a note of respect in his voice. "But training a horse to race is a different business. I warned you that it was a lot of hard work."

She nodded. "I know you did."

"He'll be racing at Churchill Downs in the Spring Meets. If everything goes well, I want to race him in the Fall Meets too. By the time he's three, he'll be ready for the Derby. But we've got a lot of work to do before then."

A sudden sharp feeling of apprehension pricked her. "He'll be all right, won't he, Luke?" she asked, glancing up at him, her forehead creasing with worry. "I couldn't stand it if something happened to him."

He looked down at her and was struck by the urge to reassure her. His gaze slid quietly down to her breasts, resting there for only the briefest of moments. He caught himself, and his gaze skittered away. *What the hell is wrong with you, Richards?*

"Luke," she asked, her expression puzzled.

His gaze reluctantly came back to hers. "He's strong and healthy. He should be fine. If for any reason I think he's not one hundred percent, I won't run him. You have my word on that."

Relief flooded her, and her smile returned. "I'm glad you're training him."

"Yeah," he said softly, and averted his gaze once more. "Me too."

Yancey and the colt joined them. Bo came out of the stables a moment later, tapping a short whip against his high black boots, and wearing a helmet, short black pants, and worn silk shirt. "Howdy, folks!" he called out.

Darby eyed the whip with alarm. "You aren't gonna use that on him, are you?"

"Not today, I'm not," Bo said, and swung up onto the colt's back. He stuck his boots in the stirrups, and the colt gave a halfhearted buck, then settled immediately.

"You aren't gonna let him hit Blue?" Darby asked Luke, her expression one of disbelief.

"I don't allow any of my horses to be whipped," Luke said matter-of-factly.

"Then why does he have it?"

"So that the horse will get used to its presence. Sometimes when a jockey is heading down that last stretch of track, one little touch could mean the difference between winning the race or just placing well."

"I don't want him hit!" Darby exploded.

"There's a big difference between a touch and a whipping."

"I don't ever want him under the whip! Ever!" She crossed her arms over her chest and held his gaze stubbornly, refusing to back down.

Luke's gaze was as stubborn as her own. The tick in his jaw jerked twice, then traveled up to his right eye. "I thought we agreed to do things my way."

"We didn't talk about this!" Darby stated firmly.

"We won't hurt him," Luke said as patiently as he could manage, his temper escalating.

Her look of disgust sent an arrow straight to his heart. He felt as though he'd committed some unpardonable sin. Frustrated, he went nose to nose with her and jabbed an angry finger in Blue's direction. "Do you really think I'd let that colt be hurt?"

The easy camaraderie they'd shared just moments before dissipated as Darby remained silent and refused to break eye contact.

Sensing no impasse in sight, Yancey interceded by patting

Darby's shoulder comfortingly. "Nobody's gonna hurt Blue, honey. Luke wouldn't allow that. The whip is a jockey's tool. A good jockey rarely needs to use it."

Relaxing a bit, Darby broke eye contact, and Luke let the subject drop. He turned away from her. *God almighty! This whole damn thing was a bad idea. A very bad idea!* But it was not the argument over the whip that was bothering him, it was his own silent acknowledgment of his growing awareness of her.

For the next several hours Bo walked Blue in a counterclockwise circle while Luke barked out orders. Meanwhile, Darby and Yancey watched in silence.

Luke's mind was elsewhere, however, mulling over the feelings that had struck him earlier. Though he hated to admit it, he thought about Darby Greene a lot, and it worried him no small amount. He told himself it was because she owned the colt; he told himself it was because she was interested in his work, he told himself a lot of things. But he knew it was more than that.

He had expected a problem to come from Bo, but he hadn't expected one from himself. She's just a child, he told himself with self-recrimination. He had no right feeling anything for her. He didn't want to feel anything for her.

Disgusted with himself, he decided his attraction to her had a logical design. It had been a long time since he'd been with a woman. He'd suppressed his need beneath long hours of work. Acknowledging that fact, he promised himself he would venture down to the riverfront and visit Maybelle's Parlor as soon as possible. That would put an end to this foolishness. With that thought in mind, he forced his thoughts back to the duty of training his next champion.

Later that morning, when Blue was beginning to grow restless with the repetition, the four took a short break for lunch. Within the hour, however, Bo was back on the colt's back, changing direction, riding him clockwise. He was especially patient with the horse; it was important that the colt was comfortable walking in both directions.

The day wore on, and by the time the sun began to set, everyone was tired and irritable and more than ready to call it a day.

They trudged back to the stables in silence, but the moment they entered the open doors, they were greeted with, "Well, Darby Greene, I do declare you are the most difficult person in the entire world to find these days!" Millie Johnson sashayed up to greet them from inside the cool, shadowy interior of the stables. She spun her pink parasol around in a circle and cocked her head, her dainty foot tapping impatiently. "Well," she said when Darby just stared at her with eyebrows raised, "are you going to introduce me or not?"

Or not, Darby thought bad-naturedly, but gathered herself and turned to her companions. "Luke Richards, Bo Denton, this is Millie Johnson. My friend."

"Miss Johnson," Millie amended firmly with a wide flirtatious smile and plenty of emphasis on the "Miss." She extended her perfectly manicured hand toward the men.

Bo was the first to take her hand. "It's a pleasure, Miss Johnson." He sent her a long, lingering look that had caused many a young woman to forget propriety.

"Same here," Luke said politely, taking her hand and eyeing her with mild curiosity. He was well acquainted with the Millie Johnsons of the world. She was a practiced flirt, and given a few years, she might even rival Bo's Katrina at the game. He allowed his gaze to whisk over her form, taking in the fashionable pink frock that advertised her ample endowments.

"Gentlemen," Millie returned, batting her long eyelashes unmercifully. "The pleasure is all mine, I assure you."

Luke watched her fluttering eyelids for several seconds, then, unable to help himself, he asked, "Miss Johnson, do you have something in your eye?"

Astounded by the question, Millie blushed crimson.

Yancey choked on a cough of laughter.

Bo faked a sneeze and looked down at the ground.

Surprised, Darby's gaze swung over to Luke.

Millie hesitated a beat before replying, "No. Why do you ask?"

Poker-faced, Luke shrugged. "Just seems like you have a problem keeping your eyes open, that's all."

"Well, thank you for your concern, Mr. Richards, but I'm quite well," Millie said with a flustered sniff, then turned to Darby. "I've come to invite you to a benefit that the congregation of my father's church is sponsoring. It's a dance benefit really. My mother is in charge of everything," Millie added importantly. "All the ladies will have dance tickets, and any gentlemen who would like to dance with them will have to purchase their tickets. The proceeds will go to the orphan asylum on Green Street. I stopped by the farm to tell you and Emma about it. Emma said she'd come even though Noah was sure to buy all of her tickets so that she couldn't dance with anyone else. Linette and Ardis are coming with their husbands also. Everyone will be there, Darby"—Millie widened her eyes for effect—"even some of the members of the Louisville Jockey Club, who donated the use of their clubhouse for the dance as their own special contribution to the orphanage. The cause is a good one and will be supported by the community. I wanted to let you know about it so you'd have plenty of time to prepare. I know how you are about wearing dresses and all. Anyway, your aunt Birdie said if I wanted to talk to you I'd have to come out here." She held out her arms. "So here I am."

Ignoring Millie's thoughtless jibe, Darby decided the benefit dance was as good a reason as any for Millie to visit Rhinehart Stables. Millie wanted to meet Bo Denton and Luke Richards, and Millie usually got what she wanted.

"The dance will be held at seven, the first Saturday in August, at the clubhouse at Churchill Downs." She tipped her head and smiled sweetly. "You'll come, won't you, Darby? It just won't be any fun without you."

"Well, I—" Darby began.

"Besides, there's someone I want you to meet. Her name is Katrina Kirby." Millie missed the quick exchange of looks between Bo and Luke. "I met her at Mrs. Haberty's Millinery the other day. She knows an awful lot about Thoroughbreds and racing. Her husband, Frank Kirby, is a founding member of the Louisville Jockey Club, and she spends a good deal of time out at the track. We just happened to be talking, and I told her that Bo Denton and Luke Richards were going to be working with your colt, and she seemed most interested in meeting you. In fact," Millie said as she turned and beamed her brightest smile on the two men, "I'd simply love it if you'd both come. I'm sure she'd love to meet you as well."

Ian led a big chestnut gelding out of a stall behind them. The gelding hesitated, lifting his tail menacingly. "Come on now," Ian said gruffly, and tugged on the halter, forcing the horse to continue walking across the barn floor.

"Can I expect you?" Millie asked.

Luke shook his head and looked down at his boots. "I appreciate the offer, ma'am, but I don't think—"

"Of course we will," Bo interrupted, earning himself a glare from Luke.

"Oh, that's wonderful," Millie simpered, clapping her hands together. "I'll expect you both at seven sharp. Don't be late, or I may not have any dance tickets left for either of you." Her gaze found Darby once again. Her smile was bright with victory. "I suppose I should be on my way." She backed away, her gaze flitting coquettishly between the two men. She took one step back, then another, but the third step gave her pause as her left foot sunk into something soft and warm. For a moment she stood still as a corpse. Then a pungent smell wafted up to greet her, and she slowly looked down at her feet. Her pretty face crumbled into an expression of horrified repugnance as she lifted her dainty little high-heeled shoe from the pile of fresh horse dung and squealed, "Eeeeewww!"

Avoiding one another's eyes, Yancey, Luke, and Bo made a hasty departure, while Darby felt a twinge of sympathy for her friend. "Oh, Millie," she said tiredly, then she went in search of a something to clean off her friend's shoe.

*　　*　　*

Darby sat at the kitchen table, staring down into her cup of coffee. Lost in thought, she barely heard her father say, "I'm goin' out to wake Eugene. I'll be back shortly."

Birdie glanced over her shoulder and wagged a fork at him. "Tell that good-for-nothin' Yancey that breakfast is ready."

Henry nodded and went out the back door.

After several moments Darby looked up from her cup. "Aunt Birdie?"

"What, honey?" Birdie asked, glancing over her shoulder again. A loud pop exploded from the pan of sizzling bacon.

"Have you ever been in love?"

Birdie's eyebrows jumped, and her mouth worked wordlessly a moment. Stumped, she blinked several times, then blushed profusely. "Well, honey . . . why do you ask?"

Darby shrugged a shoulder and looked back down at her cup. "I just wondered, that's all." She paused, then tipped her head sideways. "I just kind of wondered what it was supposed to feel like."

"Well . . . My goodness gracious . . ." Birdie said, all in a flutter. She lifted the slices of bacon out of the pan and onto a platter, then took the skillet off the fire and wiped her hands on her apron. Taking a deep breath, she crossed the room and sat down at the table with Darby. "Do you want to tell me what's on your mind, Darby Lynn?"

"Well," Darby said, lifting her gaze, not sure how to begin. "It's just that I have these feelings sometimes." A deep furrow appeared between her eyebrows. "Do you think something's wrong with me?"

Birdie felt a swell of affection for her niece. *So, one of those two young men has sparked Darby's attention. Imagine that.* "No, honey," she said, shaking her head. "I just think you're growing up. You just took a little longer than your sisters did, that's all." Birdie patted Darby's hand. "There's nothing wrong with you, sweetheart. Feelings happen to all of us. You gotta be real careful, though. Sometimes love isn't what you think it is, and feelings can fool you." She paused a moment, then said, "To answer your question, yes, there was a time I thought I was in love."

"Really?" Darby asked, surprised.

Birdie's brown eyes twinkled with amusement. "Surprised you, didn't I?"

Darby blushed. "No. It's just—"

"That you can't imagine an old maid like me having a beau?"

"Oh, no, Aunt Birdie," Darby hotly denied, shaking her head. But both Darby and Birdie knew she had come very close to the truth. "It's just that you never talked about him before."

"There was never a reason to."

"Who was he?"

Birdie smiled, and her eyes took on a misty look of remembrance. "His name was Roland Wilson. Your father remembers him well, I'm sure. We all grew up together in Missouri. We attended the same school, the same church, shared the same friends."

"Whatever happened to him?"

Birdie paused a moment, and her smile slipped a little. "He married someone else."

Intrigued, Darby was silent.

"He married my best friend, Virginia Talbot."

Sympathy flooded her, and Darby reached across the table and covered her aunt's hand with her own. "I'm so sorry, Aunt Birdie," she said in a small, quiet voice.

Birdie straightened her back and smiled. She patted Darby's hand. "Oh, don't be sorry, darling. I'm not sorry at all. At least not anymore. Virginia did me quite a favor by stealing my beau."

Confused, Darby frowned. "Why do you say that?"

"Well . . . Roland and Virginia were barely married a year when he began to sneak out to the saloons and gambling houses down near the river. He continued to do so even after Virginia became pregnant. The years passed, and Virginia and Roland had three children. After a while he didn't even bother to sneak anymore, but grew quite blatant about his philandering. Everyone knew that he had become quite a scoundrel, drinking up every penny he made on his little farm, and Virginia often showed up in church with a fresh bruise on her cheek.'' Birdie shook her head. ''She and the children would have starved to death if not for her family and friends. It humbled her to have to accept anybody's help though. She was always very proud. She was easily the most beautiful girl in our group. But as the years passed, worry and heartache took its toll on her, stripping away her beauty. She grew old and tired before her time.'' Birdie smiled sadly. ''She came to see me one day to say that she was sorry she had taken Roland away from me. She said she believed God had punished her for her wickedness, for her disloyalty to our friendship.'' Birdie tipped her head; her eyes were moist. ''I told her God would not be so unkind to her or anyone. I told her she was punishing herself in staying with that awful man.''

''Is she still with him?''

Birdie nodded. ''Last I heard.''

''That's sad.''

''Yes, it is. It's very sad.'' Birdie reached a hand to Darby's cheek. ''But as to your question about me being in love—Roland was handsome and dashing. And when he left me, I thought my heart would break. But one day my mother, your grandmother, got tired of watching me mope around, and she sat me down and asked, ''What is it you love about that man?'' Birdie's smile brightened. ''And you know, honey, besides his handsome face, I couldn't name one thing that I loved about him. So I'd have to say, no, I've never been in love. Not really in love. 'Cause loving someone goes beyond loving the outer person. When you're really in love, you'll love the whole person, inside and out, for who they are, just as they are.''

Darby rose from her chair and came around the table to her aunt. She bent over and hugged her neck tight. ''I love you, Aunt Birdie. I love you so much.''

''I know you do, honey. I love you too.''

"Aunt Birdie?" Darby said into her aunt's nest of brown hair.

"What, honey?"

"The church is having a dance the first Saturday in August. It's gonna be held at the clubhouse at Churchill Downs."

"That's nice. Are you goin'?"

Darby pulled back and looked down into Birdie's eyes. "Do you think Linette or Ardis have a dress we could alter for me? I mean, everything I have is so, you know . . . simple."

Birdie pulled her close for another hug. "I'm sure we can find something suitable."

"Hey!" Yancey said, entering the kitchen. Behind him followed Remus, looking as tired and unenthusiastic as ever. "Where's my breakfast, woman?" he asked Birdie.

Frowning, Birdie stood and wagged her finger in an angry blur. "Don't you take that tone with me, Yancey Latimer! I'm not your woman, and don't you ever forget it! As for your breakfast, you'll get it when I'm good and ready! And you're not eatin' at my table till you get rid of that filthy hat! And get that lazy old hound dog out of my house! You know better than to let him in here!"

Yancey made a petulant face. "Aw, Birdie, honey, you know how I hate to take my hat off, and Remus is hungry."

"That dog don't move around enough to get hungry! And you know you won't get nothin' to eat in this house till you take that hat off!" She stomped across the floor and whipped it off his head, then whacked him on the shoulder with it before tossing it into a corner. She turned away, grumbling something about him being a disgrace to the male gender.

His expression as disgruntled as a small boy's, Yancey took a deep sniff.

"Now, sit down," Birdie ordered. "Do you want two eggs or three?"

Yancey pulled out a chair and plopped down, then looked over at Darby. "She don't pick on Eugene like she does me."

"Two or three!" Birdie asked louder.

"Three, for all the aggravation you give me!"

"Humph!" Birdie said under her breath while pouring him a cup of coffee. "Don't know why any man would be so touchy 'bout losin' his hair. Seems to me it'd be a blessin'. Less to fuss over."

"You wouldn't think so if it were you," Yancey said, running a finger through his wispy locks.

Darby stifled a giggle, and Birdie walked over to the table and handed Yancey a cup of coffee.

Yancey took the cup from her and bestowed on her a wide smile. "Why, thank you, pretty bird."

"Don't you pretty-bird me, you smelly old goat." She blushed crimson and whirled away, returning to the skillet that was heating over the fire.

Yancey winked at Darby. "I'm gonna marry that gal someday."

Birdie spun around. "Not in this lifetime you won't, Yancey Latimer!"

"They you'll die an old maid, Birdie Greene."

"Better to die an old maid than marry an old fool like yourself!"

Darby shook her head. The argument was familiar, the same every day. She rose from her chair and said to Yancey, "I'm goin' out to say good-bye to Pa. I'll saddle the horses. I'll be waitin' for you."

Yancey nodded, and Darby walked over to where Birdie stood by the stove. She gave her another hug.

"You be careful, Darby Lynn," Birdie whispered into her ear. "Remember what I told you."

"I will," Darby promised.

The next two weeks passed swiftly, and August rode in on a heat wave so fierce, it made July's temperatures seem more like February's. As the evening of Millie's social approached, Kentucky Blue, along with the other yearlings, was introduced to the training track. Blue did exceptionally well. He was, by far, the biggest and strongest of the yearlings, becoming a natural leader for the others, especially for a pretty little bay filly, Lady Effie, who'd formed an attachment to him.

Blue's disposition was so easygoing, his mere presence seemed to calm the other yearlings, whose squeals, jumps, and bucks posed a significant risk to them, should they get out of control and bolt.

Lady Effie was the smallest of the yearlings, but she was streamlined, with long, elegant-looking legs that suggested speed. She came from a long line of champions, and Luke had a feeling she and Blue would be his fastest runners. Effie was extremely shy and high-strung—so high-strung that Luke had yet to break her to the saddle.

It was Ian and Yancey who noticed that Blue seemed to have a quieting effect on her. When they told Luke about the phenomenon, he had Eddie put Lady Effie in the stall next to Blue's. Sure enough, Blue's presence worked wonders, and Luke and Bo broke her to the saddle within a week.

The evening of the dance finally arrived.

The air was thick and honeyed, and Darby felt an uncommon impatience to finish Blue's bath.

She was eager to get home and begin getting ready for the dance.

She knew Bo planned to go, but she didn't know if Luke would or not. She hadn't asked him. She didn't intend to. He'd grown especially distant with her, and the tenuous friendship that had begun to grow between them had faded into a memory.

She felt bad about that, so bad she wanted to tell him so, but every time she tried to talk to him, he cut her off coolly. Pride won out, and she eventually gave up the effort.

"So you're goin' to a party tonight," Yancey said, breaking into her thoughts. He sponged off Blue's legs and worked his way up the colt's sides. Blue didn't seem to mind the splashes down his back and legs, but he resented the intrusion under his tail, and he wasn't shy about letting Yancey know.

He was so much bigger and stronger than the other yearlings that he could do some serious damage if he decided to act up. After the last sharp kick to his shin, Yancey had learned to respect the colt's objections.

"I suppose so," Darby finally answered.

"You don't seem too eager 'bout the prospect."

"I am."

"Well, my goodness, you sure could fool me!"

"Oh, I am," Darby insisted, then paused. "It's just that I've never been too good at parties or dances."

"Aw, c'mon now. Young folks need to get out and shake a leg now and then."

Darby looked up at him. Her hazel gaze was vulnerable. "That's just it, Yancey. I can't dance a step. I'm as clumsy as old Remus is lazy. Besides," Darby said matter-of-factly, without a hint of self-pity. "Look at me. I'm hardly the kind of girl who gets her tickets all bought up."

Yancey snorted, and his brows dropped over his eyes. "Well, that's just pure foolishness, Darby Lynn!" he scolded. "You're as pretty as a ripe August peach. You're one helluva lot prettier than that empty-headed Miss Millie, who's so busy fluttering them eyelids of hers, she can't stay out of horse dung. So what if you can't dance? I'm sure some young fella would consider it a pleasure to teach ya!"

"I know I surely would," Bo said from behind.

Darby spun around to look at him. Her cheeks bloomed with color.

He pretended not to notice her discomfort and took her by the arm and pulled her toward him. "C'mon, pretty girl."

Darby's blush deepened. She shook her head. "I really can't—"

"Shhh," he said, and placed one hand on her waist. He took one of her hands in his, then placed her other hand on his shoulder and pulled her closer. "Just follow me and count one, two, three. One, two, three. C'mon. Count with me. One—"

"Two, three," Darby finished, and lowered her gaze to the floor so she could watch his feet.

"Sing, Yancey," Bo ordered.

Yancey humored him by breaking into a raspy rendition of "My Darling Clementine," while he continued Blue's bath with accompanying rhythmic strokes.

Smiling, Bo began to maneuver Darby around the stall.

Several of the stable hands stopped working and stomped their feet and clapped, adding their voices to Yancey's.

Hearing the commotion, Luke came out of his room. He walked down the center of the barn and stopped before Blue's stall. His expression unreadable, he crossed his arms over his chest and watched the two in silence. His gaze was riveted to Darby. Her dimpled smile was wide and happy, her eyes brighter than he had ever seen them. His gaze dropped to where Bo's hand rested at her waist. He felt a brief, uncomfortable stab of envy.

Darby stepped on Bo's toe, and he howled in pretended pain. Laughing, she cuffed him playfully on the shoulder. "I told you I can't dance. I nearly broke my brother-in-law's toe last year."

"You ain't doin' so bad," Bo said, and rolled his eyes in mock terror. " 'Course, my toes might have a different opinion."

Darby laughed again, and Bo spun her, and Yancey and the stable hands kept on singing.

After several moments Bo noticed Luke's presence, and he halted mid-step. Darby looked up, and her gaze locked with Luke's. She felt a flush creep all over her body, and she was suddenly very aware of Bo's hand at her waist. She stepped back, away from him, and Bo dropped his hand from her waist.

"Hey, partner," Bo said with a grin. "Want to give her a spin?"

Luke shook his head. "You're doin' just fine," he said with a tight smile. Then he turned and walked back to his room.

Darby's smile faded, and she let her arms drop to her sides.

"We'll continue the lesson later," Bo said, turning his attention back to her. "Save me a ticket tonight. And don't mind him." He hooked a thumb in Luke's direction. "He's got a lot on his mind these days."

Darby nodded and tried to smile, but the effort was wasted.

Yancey noticed her shift of mood. "Go on home and get ready for your dance, honey. I'll finish Blue."

"Thanks, Yancey," she said, and hugged his neck, then did the same to Blue's. "I think I will."

Birdie entered Darby's bedroom in a flutter. She was almost completely hidden behind yards of frothy, pale peach-colored material. She kicked the door shut behind her.

Darby watched her from her bath. Gazing at the garment, a surprised whisper escaped her. "Oh, my . . ."

She'd asked her aunt countless times about the dress, but all Birdie would say was "Don't worry. I'm working on something special."

Birdie spread the "something special" out on the bed with a smile of satisfaction.

"Oh, my," Darby said again, and stepped out of the water. She dried herself off, then slowly walked over to the bed and touched the dress with light fingers. "It's beautiful," she said softly, and turned to Birdie. "How did you—"

"Never you mind." Birdie cut her off gruffly, her expression as closed as a moonflower in the middle of a hot, sunny day. She wasn't about to admit that she'd spent a good bit on the dress, having bought it from one of Louisville's most exclusive dress shops. She'd done the same for each of Darby's sisters; she could do no less for her Darby Lynn. She turned to Darby and ordered, "Sit down now, and let me fix your hair, then we'll get you into this dress and see how it fits."

The door burst open, and Emma entered the room. Birdie turned to her and said, "Would you mind using my room to get ready in, honey? I don't want anyone to see Darby till I'm finished!''

Emma made a disgusted face, but said, "Oh, all right." She gathered her dress and the other things she would need, and backed out of the room, closing the door behind her.

Her stomach jittery, Darby submitted to her aunt's ministrations. Birdie started with her hair. Freshly washed, it curled stubbornly, but it had grown some over the summer. It hung almost to her shoulders now. Birdie swept the sides up and back from her face and secured them at an angle with two matching pearl-encrusted combs that had belonged to Darby's mother. She let the back of Darby's hair hang in a tumble of soft curls and combed her wispy bangs into a feathery border above her dark eyebrows. Then Birdie took a piece of red crepe paper, wet it, and rubbed it on Darby's lips and cheeks.

Satisfied with what she saw, she picked up the dress, shook it out, and ordered, "On with it!"

Moments later Darby stood before her aunt, feeling nervous and terribly conspicuous. Smiling, Birdie took her by the shoulders and turned her to face the mirror. "Honey, you're gonna knock the eyeballs right out of those two gentlemen of yours."

Darby's mouth fell open. She told herself she didn't give a hoot what Luke Richards thought. It was Bo she wondered about. What would he think when he saw her?

The young woman who stared back at her was a stranger. Her hair was a shiny dark halo of curls that framed a face flushed with excitement. Her cheeks were ripe and full, her mouth a pretty pink bow. The dress she wore was a lovely confection made of silk-welt gingham and lace, with a neckline that was cut considerably lower than anything she'd ever worn before. Darby stared down at the slight swell of her breasts. All that bare skin. And all of it hers. "My goodness," she whispered, amazed. The sleeves of the dress were full and puffy, the bodice simple in design. A wide peach satin sash wrapped around the middle of the dress and hugged her waist snugly. The upper part of the skirt fell gracefully over her slender hips, then flared slightly, shaped by five graduated slashes that began at her knees and through which frothy pale peach lace peeped forth.

"Oh, Aunt Birdie," she whispered, truly at a loss for words. "Thank you."

"You're welcome, honey." Then she turned to the door. "You can come in now, Emma!"

As though her ear had been pressed against the door in anticipation, Emma immediately entered the room. She was dressed in green silk, her shiny hair twisted up into a fashionable knot on top of her head. Seeing her little sister, she halted, her eyes big, her lips open. "Why, Darby," she said in astonishment. "You're absolutely lovely." She hesitated another moment, wordless and uncertain, then, skirts rustling, she walked across the room to the bureau and opened a drawer. She rooted through a box, then, finding what she sought, she turned and walked over to Darby. Her hazel gaze locked with her sister's, and her expression softened. "Millie's wrong, Darby. There won't be a man present tonight who won't think you're a real woman." She took her sister's hand and pressed into her palm a pair of pearl-drop earrings. "I was saving these for my wedding day. But I don't think anyone could look prettier than you do right now. I'd love it if you'd wear them for me tonight."

Stunned, Darby stared down at the earrings. Her gaze slowly lifted to her sister's. A big lump took up residence in her throat. "Thank you, Emma," she managed to say in a tremulous whisper.

Embarrassed, Emma huffed and gave her a quick hug. "Pa's waiting for you downstairs. Noah and I will see you later at the clubhouse." She lowered her dark brows and grudgingly added, "I suppose you can ride home with us, but if you lose my earrings, I'll make sure Eda Mae Penney puts a curse on you that will make all your teeth fall out before you're twenty-five!"

❖ 5 ❖

THE LOUISVILLE JOCKEY Club and Driving Park Association was founded in 1875 by Colonel Meriwether Lewis Clark, who was the grandson of William Clark, the explorer.

The racing track, grandstand, and clubhouse were built that same year.

The Louisville business community supported Clark's project enthusiastically, with the original 320 members of the Jockey Club raising $32,000. With that money Clark leased eighty acres of land three miles south of downtown from his uncles, John and Henry Churchill, and built a one-mile oval track, a grandstand that would seat two thousand people and was located on the southeast turn of the track, stables for four hundred horses, and a clubhouse for entertaining club members and guests.

In 1882 architect Charles Julian renovated the grandstand, turning it into one of the largest and most majestic in the country, with imposing towers of rare architectural beauty that rose sixty feet from the ground, and upon which flew colorful flags of all nations. Several other buildings stood nearby: a betting shed, which adjoined the grandstand, the judge's stand, a news reporter's stand that sat to the left of the judge's stand, and the stately clubhouse.

Henry Greene reined in his horses and brought his buggy to a stop in front of the clubhouse. The large square structure sat to the left of the grandstand amid a well-manicured lawn, complete with articulately designed flower gardens and bordered by a row of cedars.

Henry jumped down from his seat, and when Darby rose to do the same, he scolded her with "Now, just wait a dad-burned minute, young lady." He hurried around the buggy and held out his hand. "You're far too pretty to be jumping out of buggies that way, Darby Lynn."

Her eyes teasing, Darby tipped her head to one side. "Just 'cause I have a fancy dress on doesn't mean you have to treat me any different." But even as she said the words, she wondered if Bo would treat her differently also. Her stomach gave a nervous little jump of anticipation. "I'm no helpless ninny," she added, but took her father's hand nevertheless, allowing him to help her down to the ground.

A smile touched Henry's mouth. "I never thought of you as a ninny, Darby." He pressed a kiss to her cheek. "Have a good time, honey."

"I will, Papa."

"You sure you want to ride home with Emma and Noah?"

Darby nodded. "I'll be in the way, but they'll soon have a lifetime to catch up on all that kissing."

Henry chuckled, and she turned, picked up her skirts, and ran up the steps. As he watched her go, he was poleaxed by the realization that she had grown up, and he had not fully noticed it until that very moment.

His baby was a young woman on the verge of falling in love. He'd seen it in her eyes; he'd heard it in her voice. She would go on to a husband and a life of her own before too much longer, just as her sisters had done.

And that was how it should be, he acquiesced.

Reaching the door, she turned and waved to him, and he was struck anew by how much she resembled her mother. A wave of bittersweet nostalgia gripped him. He had not been so lucky to have had Laura with him for a lifetime. But the time they'd had together had been priceless, and she'd blessed him with four lovely daughters. He was a very lucky man. As would be the man who won the hand of his sweet

Darby. Smiling, he turned and climbed back up into the buggy.

The board of the Louisville Jockey Club consisted of an exclusive group of businessmen, one of which was Nathaniel Rhinehart, who had taken over his brother's position among the officers.

Many of the board members, including Nathaniel, were present at the benefit that evening, having donated the use of their clubhouse for the event.

Nathaniel Rhinehart watched the mingling crowd with detached interest. He stood within a small circle of his business associates, half listening to their conversation. His mind was elsewhere, rolling back to another place, another dance, a long, long time ago.

He'd been a young man then, twenty-four if he remembered right, and deeply in love with a beautiful young woman.

Sarah McKenzie—the woman who had become his sister-in-law. The woman who had become his brother's wife and Bradley's mother.

To this day he didn't know exactly how he had lost her. But he'd done so on a night very similar to this one.

Benjamin had been home from school for a few short weeks, and Nathaniel had urged him to attend the dance so he could introduce him to Sarah.

Nathaniel smiled grimly. He should have known better. Benjamin had always been gifted with a dazzling charisma that had brought him everything he had ever wanted.

And he had wanted Sarah.

Nathaniel shook off the painful memory and pushed his spectacles up onto the narrow bridge of his nose.

"I see Richards is here," Frank Kirby said to Nathaniel. Katrina Kirby's husband was a short, squat, middle-aged man with a fat nose and thick, graying eyebrows that formed a straight bushy line above his eyes.

Nathaniel turned to see Luke standing alone across the room.

"Fancy piece of luck, wasn't it, your brother leaving him the stables?" Frank added.

"Yes, indeed," Nathaniel said quietly. "My brother thought very highly of Mr. Richards." He paused a moment. "Pity though. I doubt the young man will be able to hang on to the property for any length of time."

Raymond Miller, a tall, balding, barrel-chested man outfitted in suit of fine wool check, raised a curious eyebrow. "You don't say?"

"My brother had very little left in the way of monetary assets, and what he did have was divided between Mr. Richards and his son, Bradley. Richards's expenses are high. I doubt he can withstand the financial strain of maintaining the stables. He has a team of stable hands to employ, several two-year-olds to race, not to mention half a dozen yearlings to feed and train."

"He could sell some of the yearlings," Kirby said.

Nathaniel nodded. "He could, but he won't. He values the animals as much as a man would his own children." He paused, then said, "If you'll excuse me, I should say hello." He turned and made his way through the sea of people. When he reached Luke, he extended his hand. "Richards. It's good to see you."

"Likewise," Luke returned.

"How's everything?"

"Quiet."

"That's good."

"That's the way I like it."

"I heard you have the colt back at the stables."

Luke stared at the man for several seconds before answering. "I'm training him, if that's what you mean."

"Ah yes." Nathaniel nodded and paused. "That's what I heard. May I ask how that happened?"

"Miss Greene wants to race him."

"And you?"

"I want to race him too."

"I see." Nathaniel ran a bony hand down the front of his

heavily embroidered vest. "That could be a very expensive project." His expression was as clear and innocent as a new piece of glass.

A disturbing tingle began in the pit of Luke's stomach. "You're right," Luke agreed, narrowing his eyes slightly. "It will be."

"My brother did not leave you much in the way of ready cash. How do you intend to finance this venture?"

Luke lifted one dark eyebrow. "Why do you ask?"

Nathaniel shrugged. His quiet smile was as unassuming as ever. "Just curious."

"I have some money of my own."

Nathaniel nodded. "Yes, of course you do. Well, I'm sure the colt will do very well."

Luke leveled a steady, skeptical gaze on the man. "He will."

Nathaniel gave an obliging chuckle. "You seem very confident about that."

"I am."

"Good luck, then. I'm sure all eyes with be on him come spring. Knightwind was the favorite of his day. He should have won the Derby. I'm sure his colt is every bit as impressive." He paused a moment, then said, "If you'll excuse me . . . I see someone I need to talk to."

Luke nodded. As he watched him walk away, uneasiness uncoiled within him like a thin river of smoke.

Darby entered the clubhouse and stood in the vestibule a moment, collecting herself. From where she stood, she could see into the main room. It was brightly lit and elegantly decorated with red and white streamers strung from corner to corner, across the high ceiling. The room was already filled with a score of handsomely clad gentlemen, some wearing black swallow-tailed jackets and starched white shirts, their ladies equally striking in a colorful array of silks and satins.

Although she was neither backward nor bashful, Darby felt a little out of place. She was suddenly very glad that Aunt

Birdie had been adamant about teaching her girls their social skills.

Darby knew many of the people present would be interested in meeting her, but she also knew why: She owned Kentucky Blue, Knightwind's colt. She was neither flattered nor hurt by the realization that it was her horse they would be interested in, not her. She was far too level-headed for that.

She was simply aware that her ownership of such a horse had elevated her social status considerably. Louisville's citizens spent a good portion of their time at the racetrack. They would be interested in the odds Blue would present with the bookmakers in the coming year. As Knightwind's colt, he was sure to generate a great deal of interest.

Rose Johnson, Millie's mother, peeked around the open doors of the main room and, seeing Darby, excused herself from a group of ladies in the receiving line and rushed to greet her. About ten feet away she stopped, and her mouth dropped open, her three chubby chins jiggling against her thick neck. "Darby, my goodness, if you aren't a sight!" she finally managed to get out. Rose Johnson was a sweet-tempered, comfortable-looking woman who smiled constantly. Gathering herself, her feet finally broke loose, and she lumbered across the floor to embrace Darby in a hug that made her ribs ache. "Well, if you aren't the prettiest thing I've ever seen! I'm so glad you came, honey. I've missed you. You haven't attended so much as one of our socials in the past two years, and I told Millie I just couldn't understand why."

Because I can't dance a lick, and I'm tired of feeling embarrassed about it, Darby thought, but all she said was "I've missed you too, Mrs. Johnson."

"Come on in, then. Let's see," she said, looking around the room. "Ardis and James are over there." She pointed to where the couple stood beside a linen-draped table laden with tiny little sandwiches, cookies, and a crystal punch bowl. "Linette and Joe are over there." She gestured toward a long

window that looked out over the grassy grounds. "I haven't
seen Noah and Emma yet, but I'm sure they'll be here soon.
And that's Katrina Kirby over there talking to one of your
gentlemen friends."

Darby's gaze found Bo. He looked as dashing as ever,
dressed in an elegant dark suit that fit him impeccably.

"Come, I'll introduce you to Colonel Clark." Rose Johnson leaned in and whispered confidentially, "He's the founder
of the Louisville Jockey Club and Driving Park Association.
I'm sure he would be quite pleased to meet the young lady
who owns Knightwind's colt." She took Darby's hand and
led her over to the group of men.

"Darby, this is Colonel Clark, Raymond Miller, Nathaniel
Rhinehart, and Frank Kirby." The four men eyed Darby with
polite curiosity.

"It's a pleasure, Miss Greene," Colonel Clark was the first
to say. He was a pleasant-looking man with a round face and
a huge, swooping mustache. "So you're the new owner of
Knightwind's colt."

"Yes, sir, I am."

Raymond Miller smiled down at her and said, "You're a
very fortunate young woman."

Darby returned his smile. "I realize that."

"Gossip has it that you intend to take the Derby in 'ninety-
two," Miller added.

"Absolutely," she said without a trace of cockiness.

"Well, good luck, then. You'll need it to beat my Phantom."

She inclined her head slightly. "I would say the same to
you."

The gentlemen chuckled and exchanged glances, amused
by her grace and confidence.

"Congratulations on the colt, Miss Greene," Nathaniel
Rhinehart cut into the conversation. His smile was thin but
steady as he took her hand in his own icy cold one. "I'm
pleased to finally make your acquaintance. I will always be
indebted to you for saving my brother's life."

"I'm glad I was able to help him."

"Miss Greene," Frank Kirby said, taking his turn. "How very nice to meet you."

"And you," Darby returned politely.

"Please excuse us, gentlemen," Rose said, rescuing her by pulling her away from the group. She turned to her and chuckled. "Darby Lynn, you're a treasure. I wish Millie had just a lick of your common sense. Speaking of that girl, you'll find her over there talking to Mr. Richards. Excuse me, honey," she said, and left, waddling back to her post.

Darby's gaze found Millie standing with Luke, her head tipped coyly to one side, her tiny hands gesturing animatedly. As though Luke felt Darby's presence, he looked up. Their gazes met across the room, hers uncertain, his dark and unreadable.

Remembering his earlier dismissal of Bo's offer to dance with her, she was stung again by a feeling of rejection. She lifted her chin the slightest bit. So what if he didn't want to dance with her, she decided. She didn't want to dance with him either.

They took measure of each other for several uncomfortable seconds, then he said something to Millie and began moving across the floor toward Darby.

Darby felt a terrible bolt of panic rip through her. She'd worked beside him almost every day for the past six weeks, but as she watched his approach, his easy, loose saunter coupled with an underlying confidence, she felt as though he were a stranger to her. His black boots were shiny; his dark evening coat and white shirt every bit as elegant-looking as Bo's. His shiny black hair was combed back from his forehead, but as always a rebel lock fell onto his forehead, calling attention to his striking blue eyes.

By the time he reached her, she felt winded, as though Francine had treed her all over again.

"Hello, Darby," he said in his deep voice. His gaze whisked over her quickly, and his eyes grew quietly admiring.

"Good evening, Luke," she returned, clasping her hands in front of her skirt.

"You look . . ." He let the sentence hang while he searched for the right words. He wanted to tell her how lovely she looked, but the words got tangled in his throat. Bo was much better at this sort of thing than he was, he silently conceded.

"Different," she finished for him, and glanced down at the pretty shoes Aunt Birdie had purchased to match her dress.

Amused, he shook his head and laughed. "No, it's much more than that. You look grown-up."

She felt the heat rise in her cheeks, and she wondered if he might be teasing her. She lifted her gaze to his. "I am quite grown-up, Luke."

He was silent a moment, and his expression sobered. "Yes, I can see that you are."

"Why, Darby Lynn!" Millie gushed, joining them. She dragged Bo and Katrina behind her like two leashed puppies. "I do declare, you don't look at all like yourself out of your britches."

Darby's cheeks flamed, and Luke felt a sudden annoyance toward Millie for her lack of sensitivity.

A long, low, wolfish whistle escaped Bo, earning him a sharp glance from Luke and a baleful glare from Katrina.

"Darby, meet Katrina Kirby," Millie rushed on, unaware of anything beyond herself.

"Pleased to meet you," Darby said with a smile.

"And you, Miss Greene," Katrina returned in a husky, sultry voice. "I'd love to hear more about your horse. My husband and I attend the races regularly. It's always nice to hear about a promising champion firsthand." She studied Darby from beneath her long, thick lashes.

"I think the band is about to begin," Millie interrupted, turning to face the group of men who had gathered at the north end of the room with their instruments.

In a very short time the room was filled with the lilting strains of a familiar, lighthearted waltz. Many of the gentlemen in the room hurried over to the ladies' committee table to purchase dance tickets.

Frank Kirby claimed his wife for the first dance. "Come, my dear. I've been looking forward to this all day." He held out his hand, and Katrina took her departure, allowing him to lead her out into the center of the room.

"Isn't that the most romantic thing!" Millie exclaimed, sighing. Her expression dreamy, she fixed Bo with a wide-eyed, questioning glance. Bo excused himself and went over to the committee table. He was back a minute later with a smile and an outstretched hand, which Millie wasted no time in accepting.

After several beats of silence, Luke turned to Darby. "I believe I have this dance, Miss Greene."

Darby's eyes rounded, and her brows lifted. "I beg your pardon?"

"This is my dance," he repeated, and held out his hand.

"You bought one of my dance tickets?" she asked, pressing a palm to her chest.

"Of course." A slight smile teased the corners of his mouth.

Flustered, she glanced down at the floor, then back up at him. "Why?"

His smile stretched and grew, reaching his eyes, causing the skin at the corners of his eyes to crinkle most attractively. He shrugged. "Because I wanted to." He took her hand, leaned in close, and whispered, "And because Yancey said he'd give me a hard time if I didn't."

She laughed and felt some of the tension drain out of her. She believed that explanation was much closer to the truth than his first answer had been. She placed her hand in his and allowed him to swing her out onto the floor. "I'm a terrible dancer," she warned, and looked down at his feet, trying to follow his steps.

"So am I," he said, though he moved with enviable grace.

"You are not!" she said after a few steps. "You're really very good. You're as good as Bo!"

He raised one dark eyebrow. *Well, that's something, Richards.* "So who told you you were a terrible dancer?" he asked, his eyes still smiling.

"No one had to tell me." Darby looked up at him. "When all of your partners are left limping after a round with you, nothing more needs to be said!"

Her expression was so sincere, he couldn't help but laugh.

"Did learning how to dance come easy for you?" she asked, curious as to how he had learned. He seemed so solitary, it was hard for her to imagine him frequenting events such as this one on a regular basis.

"No. It didn't come easy for me."

She tipped her head. "Do you have sisters who taught you?"

He shook his head. "No sisters. I learned at school in New York. In the orphanage really," he added matter-of-factly. "Where I grew up."

Surprised by his answer, she was at a loss for words. Her heart contracted with sympathy. After a few moments she gathered her courage and asked, "Do you have any family at all?"

"Not in the true sense of the word."

She felt a sudden swell of affection and appreciation for her sisters. "I'm sorry," she said in a small, quiet voice.

"Don't be."

"I guess I have wondered why you never talked about your family."

"I do . . . sort of," he said with a slow smile. "I have the horses. They're my family. And Benjamin Rhinehart was very good to me."

She was silent a moment. "Don't you get lonely?"

His expression sobered as he thought about that a moment. "I'm alone, not lonely."

Darby nodded. "I see. At least, I think I do."

They fell into a companionable silence, and the music played on. After some time Darby broke the silence. "Luke?"

"Hmm?"

"I've been wanting to say that I'm sorry."

"For what this time?" His smile was teasing once again.

"For making such a fuss about the whip."

He hadn't given the incident a second thought. The reason he'd been avoiding her was much more complicated and confusing than a simple disagreement over a whip. "Don't worry about it. It's forgotten." As he looked down into her face, time ceased, and he found himself wondering things, crazy things, dangerous things, things he had no business wondering about. His gaze slid down to her neckline, then lower to the milky rise of her breasts. His groin tightened. Reluctantly he lifted his gaze back up to hers.

His thoughts ran on, and their eyes clung. Her face became a curious mixture of confusion and hope. Something awkward began to happen to his heart. He tried to drag his gaze away but failed, even as he struggled against allowing himself to feel, to really feel something for someone at last. The moment wore on, and he realized she had a slight sprinkling of freckles across her nose and the prettiest eyes he had ever seen.

He was both relieved and disappointed when a moment later Bo tapped him on the shoulder.

"I believe this is my dance, Richards," Bo said with a wide smile.

Luke nodded and placed Darby's hand in Bo's. Darby felt a reluctance to go with him. For weeks she had hoped Bo would buy one of her dance tickets. Now that he had, it didn't seem to matter. She had little time to ruminate on the thought, however, for he immediately swung her out onto the floor.

In the meantime, Millie stood nearby, eyeing Luke hungrily, tapping her foot to the music. He did the proper thing and went over and purchased one of her tickets. When he returned, Millie immediately went to work on him, turning on her most dazzling smile.

Staring down at her, Luke lifted a skeptical eyebrow. "Miss Johnson," he said with a cocked eyebrow, "I believe I have this dance."

"I do declare, Mr. Richards," she gushed, affecting her most beguiling expression, "I am so glad you do!"

He spun her out onto the floor amid the countless swishing skirts. "So tell me, Mr. Richards," she said after a breathless second, "why don't you have a wife?"

He laughed. She was a pretty piece of lace, and she was used to teasing and tempting men. But she did not tempt him in the least. "Because, Miss Johnson," he answered, his tone quite serious, "I don't want one."

Meanwhile, Bo twirled Darby around the melee of swirling bodies. His unusually bright gaze was glued to her own. "You're becoming a mighty fine dancer, honey," he said, pulling her close, so close her breasts brushed the front of his coat. He leaned in and kissed her cheek, and she smelled the undeniable scent of whiskey on his breath. She felt a warning down deep in her belly, but she scolded herself for being so silly. This was only Bo, who teased her, whom she silently adored.

"It's gettin' warm in here," he said. "How 'bout we get some air?"

Without thinking, Darby instinctively looked around the room for Luke. Her gaze found him. He was dancing and laughing with Millie. "All right," she said, though she felt an odd twinge of discomfort.

Bo looped an arm around her waist and led her outdoors. They strolled down the walkway that led to the grandstand, the silvery moonlight pooling around them. The sound of music drifted out to them on the sultry night air. Here and there couples strolled along the grounds, while others gathered in small groups beneath flickering lanterns to chat and sip punch.

"All of your dance tickets were already sold," Bo said when they were finally out of earshot of everyone else.

Confused, Darby's brow puckered. "Are you sure?"

"Yes."

"Then how did you claim a dance?"

He grinned and winked. "I lied."

"Oh." She chuckled, not terribly surprised at his deception.

He led her over to the grandstand, then took her arm and turned her to face him. "You look lovely tonight, Darby."

"Thank you." She looked into his eyes, then nervously shifted her gaze to the sky, where the stars glittered brightly against the velvety midnight canvas. "It's so pretty out here, don't you think?"

"Oh, yes," he said, gazing into her face. "Very pretty." Almost the same height, they stood nose to nose. He clasped her upper arms and drew her closer. Her gaze came back to his, and they stared at each other another moment.

She waited with bated breath for that wonderful, thrilling feeling to grasp her.

But this time it didn't come.

He leaned into her, gently pressing her up against the wall of the grandstand.

Bo knew he'd had too much to drink. He'd begun drinking long before he'd arrived at the clubhouse, and he knew he was treading on dangerous ground. Luke would have his hide if he caught him trifling with Darby. He'd never verbally told him so, but something in his eyes said it very plainly nonetheless. But she was so sweet, and Katrina had become so demanding lately. Besides, it was all in fun. "You ever been kissed, pretty girl?" he asked, his voice thick and husky.

Darby felt the heat rise in her cheeks. "Of course."

"By a man?"

She swallowed and paused. "I guess. Sort of . . ."

Bo grinned. "Sort of?"

"Well, you know . . . my pa and my brothers-in-law . . ."

He chuckled. "That ain't real kissin'." He paused, then asked, "You wanna try the real thing? Just for fun?"

She was both excited and frightened by the prospect. "Well, I . . ."

He didn't wait for her answer, but leaned in and covered her mouth with his own. Once again she waited for that wonderful feeling to kick in, but it didn't. His lips were warm and wet. He increased the pressure of his mouth, and she felt the sudden heat of his hardening body pressing into her stomach. Mortified, she gasped, parting her lips, and he wasted no time thrusting his tongue inside her mouth, deepening the kiss with a practiced expertise. Shocked, she pulled back, bumping her head against the grandstand wall, her eyes confused.

"Like it?" he asked, his breath coming hot and fast.

"I'm not sure," she said honestly.

"Wanna try it again?"

Darby shook her head. She needed time to think. She'd anticipated this moment ever since the first time she had seen him. But now that it was happening, all she felt was awkward and embarrassed. He leaned in again, but this time she pressed her palms against his chest and gently held him away. "No, Bo, plea—" she started to say, but Luke's deep voice overrode her objection. "Darby, it's time to go."

Bo spun to face him, and Darby's gaze lifted to Luke's. Her cheeks burned with embarrassment.

"Emma was looking for you. She wasn't feeling well and was ready to leave. I told her to go on ahead, that I'd see you home."

The liquor having gone to his head, Bo felt an angry surge of heat flood his body at the timely interruption. "Maybe she's not ready to go yet."

"She's ready." Luke's hard gaze was unyielding. "Aren't you, Darby?"

Her tongue frozen, Darby's eyes flicked from one man to the other.

"I can see her home," Bo said, his brown eyes flashing.

Luke reached around Bo and took Darby's hand, pulling her out from behind him. Bo was his friend, and he knew him well. Bo liked his liquor and his ladies, and Luke had never cared about what Bo did when he wasn't on the back of one of his horses. Until now. Until it came to Darby. "You stay away from her when you're drinking," he said quietly. There was an unmistakable warning in his voice. "That's all I'm gonna say about this."

Bo drew himself up to his full height. "Well, hell, Luke, since when did you become her goddamned guardian?"

"Since right now. There are plenty of other women to trifle with. You don't need her."

Anger overrode her embarrassment, and Darby tried to pull her hand away. But Luke's fingers were taut and unyielding. "Quit talking about me as if I weren't here! I can see myself home just fine!" she finally managed to choke out.

"I told Emma I'd see you home, and I will," Luke said firmly. He didn't wait for any further objections, but turned and stalked off, keeping her hand clasped tightly in his, leaving her no choice but to follow him.

When they reached his buggy, she jerked her hand away from his and lifted herself up into the seat.

Bo stared after them for a brief moment, his anger fading as quickly as it had flared. Luke was right. There were always others. He shrugged and went in search of Millie.

The ride home was silent and tense. Fuming, Darby sat as far away from Luke as possible, keeping her arms crossed tightly over her chest. When they were almost home, she could hold back her anger no longer. She turned to him and said, "You didn't have to do that."

He stared straight ahead. "Oh, yes, I did."

"I am not a child, Luke!"

"Oh, no?" He laughed shortly. "Bo Denton would eat you alive."

"What do you care!" she shouted. "You aren't my father!"

He turned to face her, his expression hard. "No, but I'm the man you hired to train your colt!"

"What's that got to do with this?"

"If we're gonna win the Derby, we have to be a team— you, me, and Bo. To do that, I need you sound and healthy and level-headed. Not pregnant by some man who won't give you a second glance once he's had you."

Appalled, she stared at him openmouthed for several long

beats of silence. "How dare you say such a thing about me or Bo," she finally said in quiet astonishment. "He's your friend."

The moonlight cast milky shadows over the rugged planes of Luke's face. "That's right, he's my friend, but he's also a man." He sighed heavily, and his expression softened. "Darby, it happens. And to girls every bit as sweet as yourself." He paused for the space of several heartbeats, then said, "It happened to my mother. And I grew up in an orphanage, without her or my father because of it." He quickly turned his gaze back to the road, as though the admission shamed him.

She was so stunned, she didn't know what to say. She continued to stare at him and felt a surge of conflicting emotions. She was still angry with him, but not nearly as much as she had been minutes earlier. Beleaguered, she remained silent and returned her attention to the road ahead.

When finally Luke pulled the buggy to a stop in front of her house, she didn't wait for his help, but lowered herself to the ground and started off toward the porch steps.

Suddenly contrite, he caught up with her and took her by the arm, turning her to face him. "I'm sorry if I embarrassed you."

She looked up at him. "You did embarrass me."

Their gazes locked and held for several heartbeats, then his eyes trailed down to her lips. "Darby, you're so sweet. . . ." His voice was husky. He shook his head, fighting his own weakening resolve. "I just don't want to see anything happen to you that shouldn't."

A small furrow formed between her brows. "I would hope that you would give me credit for having a little common sense."

"Common sense can be forgotten when things start happening between a man and a woman."

Darby's cheeks felt hot. "I'm not ignorant, Luke. I know how things happen between men and women."

A wisp of a smile played along his handsome lips. "Do

you?'' he asked. Unable to resist, he reached up and stroked her cheek, then ran his thumb over her full bottom lip. "I'm not so sure."

She gazed up into his eyes, and her stomach jumped with anticipation. Then everything happened at once. His eyes darkened, and he reached for her, hauling her close. His head lowered, and he pressed his lips to hers with an urgency born of hungry denial. He kissed her with unwavering determination, thoroughly, deeply, tenderly, much differently than Bo had kissed her, running his tongue gently over her lips, urging her to open to him. When she did, his tongue, warm and sleek, toyed and taunted hers, teaching hers a dance as old as time.

The feelings he awoke in her were totally unexpected—a warmth, a tingling, a yearning for more. She encircled his neck and threaded her fingers into his thick black hair where it curled against his snowy collar.

When finally he lifted his head, she stared up into his blue eyes, her confusion about the entire evening deepening.

He reluctantly released her, and she touched light fingers to her lips. "Why did you do that?" she asked in a surprised whisper.

His expression was dark, unreadable. "Hell, I don't know. . . ." He shoved aside his coat and pushed his hand down into his trouser pocket, fingering the remainder of Darby's dance tickets.

She studied his face. "You didn't want Bo to kiss me . . ." She let the statement trail off.

"No," he said on a heavy sigh, and looked down at his boots. "I didn't want Bo to kiss you." His gaze came back to hers. Silence stretched between them for several moments. Then, because he did not trust himself to linger any longer, he turned and walked away.

He climbed up into the buggy and flicked his horses' reins, leaving her to stare after him long after he had disappeared into the inky night.

*   *   *

Bradley Rhinehart sat staring into the cold fireplace in a heavy brooding silence. He lifted the glass of fine bourbon to his mouth and quickly gulped down the contents, welcoming the warmth it brought to his stomach.

Fear was like a vulture, picking away at his bones, and he needed a measure of comfort, even if it came from a bottle.

He'd done it again. He was in trouble. Big trouble.

But this time his father was dead, and he had no one to turn to.

No one except his uncle Nathaniel . . .

❖ 6 ❖

NATHANIEL RHINEHART'S MODEST law office was located on Congress Street, about a block west of the county courthouse.

Two days after the benefit dance he was seated at his desk, when his nephew, Bradley, entered the front door without knocking, bringing with him a stifling blast of early afternoon heat.

Nathaniel looked up from the thick legal volume he was reading.

"Hello, Uncle," Bradley said, closing the door behind him. Using a limp handkerchief, he mopped at the oily veil of sweat on his brow and managed a shaky smile. His face was unusually pale and bloated, his suit wrinkled and stained.

Nathaniel's gaze was cool and questioning as he slowly closed the book. He adjusted his spectacles up onto his nose, then laced his hands together on top of his desk. "Hello, Bradley."

"Are you busy?" Bradley asked, his smile strained. He was well aware that his uncle was not nearly as generous a man as his father had been. Nor was he easily moved to sympathy.

"Not at the moment," Nathaniel answered, "but I'm expecting a client soon." He paused a moment, then gestured to one of the two chairs that flanked his small but adequate oak desk. "You may sit down if you like."

Bradley accepted the offer gratefully, lowering himself into the chair on his uncle's right, his bowler hat grasped tightly in his hand.

"How have you been, Bradley?" Nathaniel asked, eyeing the younger man with a mixture of curiosity and distaste. This was Sarah's child. Had things turned out differently, Bradley could have been his own son. Yet he felt no affection for the man. He never had, not even when Bradley was a boy. He was the one thing of Benjamin's that he had never coveted.

"Well, that's why I'm here, Uncle . . ." Bradley averted his gaze nervously and ran a hand through his unkempt hair.

A knowing smile touched Nathaniel's lips. He'd been expecting Bradley for weeks now.

"I . . . ah . . ." Bradley shifted positions in his chair. "I need some help. . . ."

Nathaniel leaned back in his chair and steepled the tips of his long, thin fingers. "I see." He watched Bradley squirm uncomfortably. "How much this time?"

"Not much," Bradley hurried to say. "Five thousand."

Nathaniel was silent a long while. Five thousand dollars wasn't all that great a sum considering that Bradley's gambling debts had all but exhausted his father's fortune by the time Benjamin had finally decided to cut him off. Nathaniel shook his head sadly and decided to deal his first card. "Five thousand dollars is a great deal of money."

"I'll pay you back." There was an urgency in Bradley's voice. "I'm good for it." His fevered gaze flicked over his uncle's face, searching for some trace of empathy.

Nathaniel inclined his head slightly and gave a short little laugh, then dealt his second card. "How? You have nothing to pay me back with."

"I'll make it back. You'll see. My luck is about to change. I can feel it!" Bradley mopped at his forehead again.

"I believe I've heard that very statement before. Many times, in fact, when you said it to your father." Nathaniel toyed with him as a cat would a mouse. "I'm afraid you're into a bit of a bind this time, son." He added "son" and felt a delicious shiver of justice sluice through him.

Bradley's expression grew alarmed. He pressed forward in his chair. "You don't understand, Uncle! If I don't pay what I owe, they'll kill me this time!"

Nathaniel heavy-lidded gaze was as sympathetic as stone. "Oh, I understand that very well. I'm well acquainted with your friends."

Bradley was silent a moment. His eyes grew suspiciously damp. "Please help me . . . you're all I have . . ."

Nathaniel stood and walked over to stare out the window at the busy street. Streetcars clacked by and passersby strolled along the crowded walks. The corners of Nathaniel's mouth turned down. Louisville was full of simple-minded, weak people like Bradley. People like Frank Kirby and his faithless wife, Katrina. People like Luke Richards and Bo Denton and poor, feeble-minded Tom Haines. He smiled inwardly. Everyone had their Achilles' heel. Everyone had something to lose. That realization only fed his sense of justice. "I'm sorry," he finally said, "but I cannot make you a loan, Bradley."

"Please," Bradley repeated, feeling hope slip away.

Nathaniel turned to face him. His eyes were like granite. "I *can* help you, however."

Some of the fear left Bradley's eyes as his expression became wary and sharp. "How?"

"I'll give you the five thousand you need. Today, in fact. But in turn you must sign over Rhinehart Breeding Farm— the property, the house, all of the horses."

Bradley's jaw dropped in disbelief. "You know the farm is worth ten times that! Knightwind alone is worth a small fortune."

"Exactly."

Bradley stood. "No! That farm and those horses are all I have."

Nathaniel shrugged a bony shoulder. "It's your decision."

"That's robbery!"

Nathaniel's expression hardened, and the quiet, unassuming expression he usually wore was as absent as though it had never been. "What you did to your father's estate with your gambling debts was robbery also."

Shocked by his uncle's ruthlessness, Bradley was silent a moment, weighing the risk of his refusal. He had one other option. He could accept the challenge to enter Knightwind in a match race against Phantom, Raymond Miller's young stallion.

He knew Knightwind was well past his prime, but Miller was not concerned with that fact. He and the bookmakers were eager to see one of the greatest and most famous horses in Kentucky run again—so eager, in fact, that Miller was willing to risk his own future champion in an unofficial match race.

The older stallion was still strong, Bradley silently reasoned. Even if Knightwind lost the race, he could make money if he placed his wager wisely. Of course, Richards would be furious if he found out. But the event could be kept relatively quiet. Even if Richards did find out, it would be too late for him to intervene.

The decision made, Bradley's eyes lost their look of desperation. He placed his bowler upon his head. "I won't give up the farm."

Nathaniel shrugged. "The stallion won't win, and you'll eventually lose the farm anyway." He smiled complacently. "Why not keep it in the family?"

Caught off guard by the fact that Nathaniel knew about the race, Bradley's confidence wavered. "Knightwind was retired too early. He can still run. He might even win."

"I wouldn't bet on it."

Bradley stalked to the door and yanked it open. He turned to his uncle. "The farm is mine!"

Nathaniel smiled. It was a hard, cold smile. "Not for long."

August sizzled to an end, and September slid in on a trio of rainy days.

Three weeks had passed since the night of the dance, and

this warm, misty morning was the first since Blue's training had begun that Darby set off for Rhinehart Stables without Yancey. She missed him already. He'd acted as a buffer between herself, Bo, and Luke, easing the awkwardness that had hovered over them since the night of the dance. But harvest was drawing near, and Henry needed both Yancey and Eugene at the farm.

When Darby arrived at the stables, she swung down off her horse and gave him up into Ian's capable hands.

Luke greeted her with a stiff nod. "Let's get to work. You're to do Yancey's job until he gets back."

"Fine," Darby said, and followed him into Blue's stall.

Bo came up behind her and nudged her with his elbow. "Morning, honey," he said, and smiled, then went off to gather Blue's equipment. Though he still teased her, she'd noticed that there was a certain restraint to his teasing that had not been present before the dance. Emma had told her he'd been seen paying court to Millie on occasion. Oddly enough, Darby was unmoved by that disclosure.

None of the three had ever talked about what had taken place the night of the dance. In fact, both men acted as though nothing had ever happened.

But Darby knew better.

She could not forget her argument with Luke, nor could she forget his kiss. The memory haunted her dreams, causing her to toss and turn long into the night, deepening her confusion about him.

She did not trust her own feelings any longer. She had thought it was Bo she was attracted to, but now she did not know what she felt for either man.

"I'll hold him steady," Luke said, breaking into her thoughts. He reached for Blue's bridle.

Darby met his gaze with her own. "I can tack him up by myself." She was well aware that no one aided Yancey with the chore.

"I'll help you this time," Luke insisted, his eyes cool and distant. "You can get him ready by yourself tomorrow."

"Here you go, Darby," Bo said, returning with Blue's gear.

She studied Luke's face, hoping to see that slow, lazy smile touch his mouth and ride up to his beautiful blue eyes. But it didn't come. Disappointed, she averted her gaze and took the saddle cloth from Bo's outstretched hand.

September passed, and Darby surprised herself with how adept she became at tacking up the horses. She was flattered when Luke asked her to tend to Lady Effie as well, since the little bay filly in the stall next to Blue's would not cooperate with anyone. Ian, Tom, and young Eddie made it clear they would just as soon shovel horse manure all day long than tend to the high-strung filly.

But Luke had a soft spot for her, and Darby knew it was an honor that he trusted her to be her groom.

Darby's affection for Blue grew, as did her affection for Lady Effie. The filly had wide, intelligent eyes and perky ears, and though she nipped and butted at times, Darby refused to be intimidated by her. It wasn't long before it was obvious that Lady Effie preferred Darby over everyone, even Luke.

October arrived, bringing gray skies and a raw chill to the air. Kentucky Blue, along with some of the other yearlings, was now galloping the track. While the other yearlings were wanting to pull up, Kentucky Blue and Lady Effie were coming back fresh, ready to take off all over again.

Luke was pleased but cautious. Running, competitive running, would come later on. He was still uncertain of the colt or the filly's speed capabilities and did not wish to push either horse too far.

Much could happen before spring. Three of the babies had already popped a couple of splints, and their progress had all but halted.

Splints appeared as a swelling on the bone usually just below the knee. They were an inflammation of the connective tissue between the cannon bone and the fourth metacarpal. If a splint was severe, it cost the horse downtime. The horse had to be taken out of training and rested.

Luke wanted both Blue and Effie ready for a match come spring. He couldn't afford downtime with either of them. If his instincts were correct, they were the best he had.

Although there was much to be done before either horse would be ready for a real race, he could see they grew more comfortable running the track every day.

He wished he could say the same about his own response to Darby's daily presence in his stables. He fought his growing attraction to her, but she was always on his mind, even after she'd gone home at the end of the day. He saw her in his sleep, dressed in britches and suspenders, with her rich dark hair mussed and her plump cheeks flushed with excitement. He saw her as she was the night of the dance, lovely and vulnerable, looking up at him with hope and expectation in her eyes. He awoke in the morning, aroused and frustrated. He wanted her. He'd wanted her the night of the benefit every bit as badly as Bo had. Maybe even more so. He was no better than Bo, he decided—just a little more cautious. Darby Greene deserved the best a man had to offer, a man who was not afraid to lose his heart to her.

Luke was not that man.

"How are they doing?" Darby asked him early one frosty morning as they stood along the fence line. Ian was on Lady Effie, and Bo was on Kentucky Blue. The two riders galloped the horses down the back straight of the track.

"Good," Luke said quietly. "Blue is bigger, stronger, his stride longer, but the filly is plenty fast too. Blue could easily outrun her, even though Bo is holding him back, but he paces himself to Effie's stride." He gave a soft huff and shook his head. "I never saw a couple of horses take to each other like those two."

Darby smiled and without thinking said, "Maybe they just know they belong together."

An uncomfortable silence fell between them as it had so

many times over the past several weeks. She could stand it no longer. "Luke?"

"Hmm?" He turned and stared down at her. She was close enough that he could smell her. She smelled fresh and clean. Dangerous. He wondered if she knew the effect she had on him, then decided she didn't. Her eyes were guileless, innocent of anything except confusion as to his continued coolness.

"Are you ever going to talk to me again?"

"I'm talking to you now." He was teasing, but the smile never reached his eyes, and it saddened her.

"You know what I mean. You've hardly said more than two words to me since the benefit dance."

He was silent a long while. "It's best that way."

"Why?"

He read the confusion in her expression and was tempted to try to wipe it away. But he knew the barrier it presented was needed. It represented safety for him and for her. He did not want to feel anything for her. He did not want her to feel anything for him. He'd spent his entire life without attachments. He could walk away from any job, at any time, and the only thing he would leave behind would be his horses. That was hard enough. But Darby was different, and somehow he knew if he allowed himself to care for her, losing her would be much more painful than the loss of any animal. And lose her he would. For no human being had ever been a permanent part of his life. "We need to stay focused on our goal," he said in answer to her question.

"What is our goal?" She knew only too well, but she had to ask, hoping that in hearing the words they would help her understand and would ease the unexplained heaviness in her heart.

He turned his gaze back to the galloping horses. "To win the Derby."

"Mr. Luke! Mr. Luke!" Tom Haines yelled from behind, commanding their attention. He came running toward them, his unruly pumpkin-colored hair flopping wildly in the wind.

By the time he reached them, he was winded, his face a picture of fear and agitation.

"Take it easy, Tom," Luke said, placing a hand on the younger man's shoulder. "What is it?"

"It's Knightwind, Mr. Luke!" Tom said between ragged breaths. "I was in town gettin' supplies just like you told me, and I heard men talkin' and placing wagers. Mr. Rhinehart is gonna race Knightwind against Miller's big white colt in an unofficial match today!"

Luke's face registered his surprise and shock. "Jesus," he whispered, and ran a hand through his hair. "Miller's gonna race Phantom?"

"Yes sir!"

"That colt isn't much older than Blue. He could ruin him."

Tom shook his head, still fighting for his breath. "Don't matter to Mr. Miller. Word has it Phantom is strong and fast, that he'll beat Knightwind, then he'll take Kentucky Blue at the Derby in 1892."

Luke's brow creased with worry. "Knightwind's leg can't take the pounding." But Luke also knew the great stallion would run if given the chance. He would push himself beyond endurance, regardless of pain or injury, just as he had the day of the Derby. He wouldn't give up. He wouldn't quit. Once he was on the track, Knightwind did not understand defeat. That was why Luke had retired him. The horse would have eventually died on the track.

Luke's expression hardened as fear squeezed his heart. "Where is the race taking place?"

"At the training track on Raymond Miller's farm off Bardstown Road."

Luke's mouth tightened into a taut line. Without another word he broke into a run. After several yards he hollered over his shoulder, "Flag down Bo and tell him to meet me at the stables!"

Stunned, Darby studied Luke's receding back for a moment, then broke into a run herself, following him to the stables. Outside the stables she heard him yell for Eddie to fetch Toby.

Darby went directly to her own horse and saddled him.

Within seconds Bo came running into the stables on foot, having handed Blue into Ian's care. He went directly to his own horse and saddled him.

Luke and Darby were in their saddles within minutes. Bo was just a few beats behind. Luke looked over at Darby. "Where do you think you're going?"

"With you."

"No, you're not."

Irritated with them both, Bo cut into their argument. "We don't have time to argue 'bout this. Tom says the race is set to begin in less than an hour!"

The three rode hard. When they reached Raymond Miller's farm, a substantial crowd had already gathered at the track. In the center of the crowd was Bradley Rhinehart and Raymond Miller, along with several bookmakers who were taking wagers.

Bo was surprised to see Katrina Kirby among the onlookers. Luke was not surprised at all.

What did surprise Luke was the presence of Nathaniel Rhinehart. To Luke's knowledge, Nathaniel had never shown any interest in his brother's horses or in the sport of Thoroughbred racing.

Her heart pounding, Darby followed Luke and Bo, her gaze riveted to the two magnificent horses already on the track. Their riders were astride them. Knightwind was as stunning as ever. He was as majestic and full of life as she remembered him. He tossed his shiny black mane and pawed the ground. He knew he was going to run. Again. At last.

Phantom was every bit as impressive. Not yet two years old, he was almost as big as the black stallion. His powerful legs were long and lean, his coat a spotless brilliant white.

Darby was awed. This beautiful horse would be one of Blue's competitors. Though the white stallion was older than

Blue by months, they would both be three the same year. They would both run in the Derby.

Luke was off his horse in a heartbeat. He stormed toward Bradley Rhinehart, his expression thunderous. Bo was right behind him. ''What the hell are you doing, Rhinehart?'' Luke bellowed, bearing down on him.

But his question was never answered. The flag dropped, and the two horses bolted from their positions.

''No!'' Luke hollered, shoving his way through the crowd. ''Stop the race!''

But there was no stopping anything. Both stallions had been trained to run, and run they would. The riders rose high in their stirrups and bowed low over their horse's necks.

The crowd began to scream encouragement, and Luke forgot about Bradley, his feet frozen to the ground, his gaze riveted to the track.

Knightwind and Phantom were fighting head to head, but it was obvious the black stallion was struggling furiously for the lead. His jockey brought the whip down hard on his hindquarters, and he bolted forward. A deafening roar rose from the crowd, and Luke's heart pumped painfully. Knightwind rounded the first turn, his head stretched forward. He held the lead down the backstretch and through the next turn, but as the two horses thundered toward the cheering crowd, a quick sharp sound, like the snapping of brittle wood, reached Luke where he stood, and his worst fear became a reality.

Then Phantom was in front by a length, then two.

The jockey astride Knightwind leaned back in his saddle in an attempt to rein in the powerful horse, but Knightwind ignored him. He ran as though oblivious of his injury. He was racing again. This time he would not give up. He ran and ran and ran until the exposed bone of his left leg burst through the muscle and skin, until he could run no more. Then, midstride, he went down, the sound like an awful roll of thunder, giving his rider only a fraction of a second to roll away from him.

The crowd hushed, and the track became as still and silent as a graveyard.

Heartsick, Luke and Bo broke loose, and they pushed their way through the crowd and onto the track, where the stallion lay on his side, winded and lathered, his three good legs still churning, determined to keep running, as though he still thought he could win the race.

"Goddamn you, Bradley," Luke whispered, staring down at the horse. "Goddamn you, goddamn you." His eyes stung; his vision blurred. He slammed his eyelids shut tight against the ugly sight of Knightwind's mutilated leg. When he forced his eyelids open, he turned to Bo and said, "Get my rifle." His voice was husky.

His gaze as somber as Luke's, Bo turned to do his bidding.

Standing behind them, Darby felt her throat thicken with tears. Without thinking, she reached up and placed her hand gently between Luke's shoulder blades, hoping to offer him some measure of comfort. She ached for him, for the beautiful stallion, for what Luke would have to do to ease his suffering.

"Now, wait just a goddamned minute, Richards!" Bradley Rhinehart said, charging them from behind and taking Luke by the arm. "That's *my* goddamn horse! I'm not gonna let you shoot him! We can fix him up and still use him for stud!"

Before he knew what hit him, Luke's fist smashed into Bradley's face, sending him sprawling onto his back in the dust.

"You're an ass, Bradley!" Luke's blue eyes were glacial. "There's no fixin' this horse."

"He's right, Rhinehart," Joshua Landers said, joining them. "This stallion is as good as dead." He reached out and placed a gentle hand on Luke's shoulder. "I'm sorry, son." Joshua Landers was the veterinarian who had cared for Knightwind when he'd injured the same leg five years before. He had heard about the race and felt compelled to attend, hoping his services would not be needed.

Raymond Miller clamped his fat cigar in his teeth and caught Bo by the arm as he passed by. "My offer still stands,

Denton. You can jockey for me. Phantom is going to take the Derby in 'ninety-two. You could ride the champion.''

Bo gave the man a hard look. "I'll stay with Richards, and I'll ride the champion.''

Miller shrugged and turned to the crowd. His face jubilant, he raised his arms high into the air. "Phantom is the winner! Collect your winnings, gentlemen!''

Some of the crowd cheered, but most of the spectators were somber and silent. This was not sport to them. They turned away, eager to be gone before the great horse was put down.

His stride swift, Bo fought his way back through the crowd to Luke's side and handed him his rifle.

"Take Darby back to her horse,'' Luke said without looking at her. "She doesn't need to see this.''

"You want me to do it?'' Bo asked, his brown eyes sympathetic.

Luke shook his head. "I should do it.'' He dropped down on one knee and gently stroked the horse's sweat-soaked neck. "You did good, boy. Real good.''

Hearing Luke's voice, Knightwind lifted his head, pricking his ears forward. He neighed softly and tried to focus his gaze on Luke, while Luke fought the urge to hug the stallion's neck.

Bo gently took Darby's arm. "C'mon, honey.''

With one last look at Luke and the fallen stallion, Darby turned away. When she reached her horse, the shot rang out, sending a reverberating echo out into the wind and shivers rippling through her body. She buried her head in Bo's shoulder and cried.

A hissing lantern sent shadows dancing into the corners of the stables. The stable hands had retired to the bunkhouse hours before. A shroud of melancholy had hovered over the workers long into the evening.

It was well past midnight, and Luke knew he should get some rest also. But he could not sleep. Instead, he stood outside Blue's stall, stroking his neck, grieving the loss of the colt's father.

Luke had been Knightwind's trainer for only one year, but, as always, he'd formed an attachment to the great stallion.

Knightwind had been the most beautiful horse he had ever worked with. Fast and spirited, the stallion's only flaw was that his leg had not proved strong enough to withstand the pounding stress of the racing track.

Luke hugged Blue's neck and pulled him close, then leaned his forehead against the colt's neck. The colt neighed softly and blinked his heavy lashes. "Don't you break down on me, Blue," Luke said softly. Darby would never forgive him if something happened to the colt. He'd seen the look of horror in her eyes when he'd returned to her and Bo after putting Knightwind down. He could only imagine how she would have looked at him had Knightwind been Kentucky Blue.

In the stall nearby, Lady Effie snorted then neighed softly. Blue's ears pricked forward, and his head turned toward her. With a responding nicker, he abandoned Luke and turned so he could reach his head over into her stall. Effie lifted her head to his; Blue lowered his head obligingly, and the two horses stood quietly together.

With a heavy sigh Luke turned and walked through the shadows to his room and sat down on his hard cot. It creaked beneath his weight. With Darby's face still haunting him, he dropped his head into his hands and rested his elbows on his splayed knees.

He stayed that way for a long time, listening to the comforting sounds of the horses shifting on the hay in their stalls.

Then, sensing Darby's presence, he looked up.

She stepped out of the shadows and into the doorway of his room. Her slender silhouette was framed by the soft glow of the flickering lantern that hung on a hook from the ceiling. She walked toward him, scattering bits of hay with her soft footsteps. She wore a light blue shirt tucked into a clean pair of britches, and her little nose was shiny from a fresh washing. "I was worried about you," she said quietly, stopping several feet in front of him. "I came back to see if you were all right."

Luke tried to force the vulnerability from his face, but the effort took more strength than he had. He rubbed a weary hand over his face, then lowered his arms and let his hands dangle between his knees. "I'm fine."

Her hazel eyes were red from crying. "I know how hard this has to be for you."

His dark brows arched above his blue eyes. "Looks like it's been harder on you." He averted his gaze and said, "I'm surprised you even want to talk to me."

"It wasn't your fault."

He nodded. "I know that, but somehow it still feels like it."

She dropped her gaze and was silent.

He stood. "Days like today go with the job. What happened to Knightwind could happen to Blue too, you know." His voice was harsher than he intended it to be. "If you can't handle it, say so now."

She'd thought about that very thing all evening. Was she strong enough? Blue was more than just a racing horse to her. He was hers, and she loved him. But she also knew her dream of breeding horses might never be a reality if she didn't race him. Without looking up, she nodded and quietly said, "I can handle it."

He paused a moment, then shifted his stance, anchoring his hands on his lean hips. He could smell her from where he stood. Her clean scent curled out and wove a tantalizing web around him. He gave her a long look. His entire body awoke, thrumming with the need to touch her. He was all too aware that they were alone, and that their aloneness brought danger. "Your father will be fit to be tied if he wakes up and finds you gone."

"He'll never miss me." She stole a glance up at him and couldn't stop the smile that lifted one corner of her mouth. "I'll be back in bed before he ever wakes up. Millie and I used to raid old Widow Simmons's watermelon patch at midnight when we were girls.''

The innocence of the admission brought a smile to Luke's mouth. For the first time in weeks, the smile reached his eyes. She thought it was the most beautiful thing in all the world.

He chuckled and saw her once again as the lanky tomboy she'd been when he'd first met her. "Yeah?"

A soft little laugh escaped her. "Yeah."

"I have a hard time imagining Millie doing such a thing."

"I have a hard time remembering Millie doing such a thing."

Their eyes clung.

Darby tipped her head slightly. "But you don't have a hard time imagining me doing it, do you?"

"Not at all."

They both laughed, but their laughter soon faded as their gazes held fast and something very compelling happened. They stood still as shadows, studying each other while time ticked on, and their pulses thrummed, and common sense sifted away like smoke on the wind.

"Darby," he said, his throat tight. "You'd better go."

Her lips dropped open, but no sound came out, nor did her feet move. His ebony hair glistened in the lamplight, and she thought he was remarkably beautiful despite the fatigue etched in his face. Her soul trembled; her heart hungered, but for what she did not know. But she somehow sensed that he could feed her hunger.

She realized at that moment what Aunt Birdie had been trying to tell her about feelings, about how misleading they could be, and she knew that the feelings she'd had for Bo had never been anything more than a schoolgirl crush.

It had been Luke who had drawn her all along, with his steady strength and summer-blue eyes, since the first day he had looked down at her while seated on Toby.

With a groan he closed the distance between them and reached for her, dragging her into his arms. She did not resist him, but went up against him with a sigh, as though it were the most natural thing in the world for her to do. His mouth was on hers at once, searching, tasting, teaching. . . .

He stepped backward, pulling her with him, his mouth still locked on hers, then together they sank down onto the cot. He turned her onto her back, gently dropping his full length on her. His weight pressed her down into the thin mattress. He rose up on his elbows, afraid of crushing her, and toyed with her hair, pushing it back from her face, dropping a series of moist light kisses across her lips, chin, and nose, until she could stand it no longer.

"Oh, please," she whispered. She lifted her arms and encircled his neck, pulling him down onto her fully once more.

His kisses grew rugged and wet while his hands stroked her, moving over the length of her body, learning all the hollows and curves, sending waves of desire pulsating down to her core. He found her breasts and cupped them with gentle reverence, his thumbs riding up over her nipples in a light caress. She shivered and moaned.

Her hands moved over the hard planes of his back, reveling in the way his body differed from hers. He was warm and hard and smooth. She felt the need to see all of him, to touch him everywhere.

For Luke this was torture. His groin ached. He pressed his hips into hers, burying his head between her breasts. She cradled him close and listened to his harsh breathing, then shivered when he lifted his head and sucked her breasts through the taut, thin cotton of her shirt. She gave herself up into a wave of desire, rocking her hips with him, even when one of his hands rode down her ribs to her waist, over her hip, and found the moistness between her britches.

He held her tight, curling his fingers into her, and she felt a hot tingling ignite within. "Luke," she whispered, pressing herself into his hand. "Please . . ." she begged, aching for release.

Quite suddenly he went still and expelled a ragged breath, then dropped his face into her shoulder, "Jesus," he whispered, then rolled to his side, panting, dropping one arm over his forehead and one hand across his groin.

She lifted her head and looked at him. "What's wrong?"

He didn't answer her until his pulse had settled. "This is crazy."

"Why?"

"You know why."

But she didn't know why. Not really. "I don't understand."

He heard the confusion in her voice and turned his head to look at her. Her hair was mussed, her lips swollen. He reached over and gently grazed her cheek with his work-roughened hand. "I'm not for you, Darby. I don't think I'll ever want anything permanent with any woman. I like my life just the way it is."

She swallowed, trying hard to understand, trying even harder to hide the hurt his words had wrought. She felt the awful weight of his rejection.

His steady blue eyes held her gaze. "I'm trying to be honest."

With a shaky sigh she turned away and lifted herself up off the cot. "I suppose I should thank you for that," she said very quietly, then she squared her shoulders and walked out of his room.

Harvest came, then drew to a close, and a chill rode in on the wind. The Kentucky hills blazed with a magnificent display of color. The trees in the forests wore their bright leaves proudly, and though the mornings were frosty, the afternoons were warm and golden.

Yancey was free again to participate in Blue's training, and Darby was glad. His easygoing nature eased the tension between Darby and Luke somewhat. They avoided each other's eyes and barely spoke. When they did communicate, it was usually through Yancey or Bo.

It was just as well that the days at Rhinehart Stables were long and hard. Darby went home tired, too tired to care about

anything except getting a good night's sleep. But her dreams
were troubled, riddled with kisses and caresses, eyes the color
of the purest summer sky, and the ominous thunder of hooves.

December brought colder days and a light dusting of snow
which clung to the ghostly limbs of the now-barren trees.

Christmas was quiet and restful. Luke told Darby and Yancey to take the day off. Yancey spent the day doing his best
to provoke Aunt Birdie, and Darby did her best not to think
about Luke spending the day alone. Henry had asked both
him and Bo to dinner, but they had both declined.

January brought more snow and a shortness of tempers.
Luke grumbled about the training track being a sloppy mess;
Bo grumbled about Luke's grumbling. Yancey grumbled
about them both.

All of the yearlings, regardless of when they'd been foaled,
had birthdays and automatically became one year older on
January first.

And as February drew to a close, Luke decided it was time
to ask more of his new two-year-olds. It was time to see if
they had any speed. . . .

❖ 7 ❖

THE EARLY MORNING air was cold and crisp, the training track hard and dry, just as Luke hoped it would be.

All of the two-year-olds had had their turn on the track, except for Kentucky Blue. Most of their times had been good.

Luke was pleased.

He was especially pleased with Lady Effie's time.

By the end of April, she, Kentucky Blue, and some of the other two-year-olds would be racing in the Spring Meets.

Effie was small, but fast and strong, holding her own against the larger colts. He believed she would do well matched against fillies her own age next year in the Kentucky Oaks. The Kentucky Oaks was the sister race to the Kentucky Derby. It was a grand event, modeled after England's premier filly race.

But the Derby and the Oaks were still over a year away, and now it was time to see what Kentucky Blue could do on the training track.

Luke, Yancey, Darby, and several of the stable hands stood along the north edge of the racetrack, watching Bo trot Blue up and down the track, warming him up.

The colt's nostrils blew frosty white spirals into the chilly air. He held his head high, his ebony mane blowing wildly in the wind. The gray winter clouds parted, and the sun peeked out, sending fingers of golden light down to warm the heads of those who watched the colt, their anticipation building.

Darby felt a rush of pride. Kentucky Blue had grown considerably since the day Luke had brought him to her. Luke said he was even bigger than his father had been at his age, but more streamlined. His legs were long and powerful, his body hard and lean and muscled. He was no longer the fat roly-poly baby he'd been when she'd first seen him.

His brow tight with tension, Luke glanced down at his stopwatch, then back up at Bo. "Get him ready!"

Bo nodded and maneuvered the colt to his starting position on the track.

Her nerves on edge, Darby glanced over at Yancey. He smiled and winked at her, then patted her hand where it rested on the fence.

"Remember," Luke yelled, "don't push him!"

"I won't!" Bo hollered back. "But he's gonna go like hell, Luke! I'm telling ya! He's been waitin' for this!"

Yancey nodded and turned to Luke. "He's right. That colt's chompin' at the bit to run. I just hope Bo can pull him up."

"If anyone can handle him, Bo can," Luke said with quiet confidence, then lifted his arm high into the air. Watching him, Bo rose up in his stirrups, the front half of his body lowered over the colt's neck.

His stopwatch ready in his other hand, Luke nodded and, with one swift movement, yanked his arm down to his side.

Kentucky Blue broke beautifully.

His opening strides were smooth and long, almost dreamlike.

Bo felt a rush of exhilaration. The colt seemed to float beneath him. He rolled along, his powerful legs churning faster and faster, until Bo felt the cold air burn his face. He felt the horse's power beneath him, all the energy waiting to be turned loose, and he realized for the first time in his riding career that he was not in charge. Kentucky Blue was now the boss.

Realizing that, Bo tried to pull him up, knowing Luke would have his hide if he didn't. But Blue was having none of it. He fought for his head, rounding the first turn, then he pounded down the backstretch, streaking into the second turn at a speed that almost unseated Bo. He barely had time to regain his balance when the horse poured down the homestretch, whizzing past the stunned crowd.

Bo finally managed to slow him up enough to catch his breath, then he talked to the colt till he calmed, finally pulling him up before they reached the first turn once again. "Wheweee!" he hollered, then turned the colt around, trotting him back to where the group waited.

Luke looked down at his watch, then up at Bo. His expression was grim. "What the hell did you think you were doing? I told you not to push him, to hold him back!"

"I tried!" Bo yelled down at him. "Ain't nobody gonna hold this horse back if he wants to go!"

They glowered at each other for a tense moment, then a ghost of a grin caught at Bo's face. "So what'd he do?"

Very slowly, a hint of a smile tipped up one side of Luke's mouth. "One forty-two."

Bo's eyes got big. "Whoa!" he hollered, his grin becoming full-blown. Kentucky Blue's time was faster than many of the Derby's finest champions. And this was only his first run, and amazingly the big horse had not even broken a sweat.

Yancey shook his head. "That colt sure is somethin'!"

Ian came up behind them. "You bet he is!"

Darby turned to Luke. Her face was flushed with joy and relief. She forgot the tension between them and went up against him, hugging his neck. "He did good, Luke! He did good! I just knew he would!"

Caught up in the excitement, he, too, forgot himself. He laughed and gave her a quick, hard squeeze, lifting her off the ground and swinging her around in a circle. "You bet he did!"

When he lowered her to the ground and released her, their gazes locked and held for several silent heartbeats, until the

silence between them stretched into awkwardness. Her hazel
eyes searched his blue ones, yearning for an end to the distance he'd put between them.

But even as she stared up into his face, the invisible wall
rose back up into place.

She blushed and averted her gaze while he fought the urge
to reach out and pull her back into his arms.

Instead he turned and climbed over the fence, turning his
attention to Blue's legs as he checked for any sign of injury.

In an effort to ease her discomfort, Yancey put an arm
around Darby's shoulder and squeezed. "You're gonna have
that horse farm someday, Darby Lynn," he promised. "And
everything's gonna turn out just fine, you'll see."

She managed a smile and pressed a kiss to his grizzled
face. "I know it will," she said with much more conviction
than she felt.

Word traveled fast from farm to farm, and it wasn't long
before Kentucky Blue's name was on everyone's lips.

When Raymond Miller heard about the black colt's aston-
ishing first run, he felt the first quiver of discomfort. He had
not been threatened by the colt's existence until that moment.
Phantom was strong and fast, but he had yet to touch Kentucky Blue's time. That left two things Miller could hope for:
Bo Denton could be bought, or Kentucky Blue would break
down like his father.

Standing beside the window in his office, Nathaniel Rhinehart turned a cold stare on the young woman who was seated
in the chair in front of his desk. "I'm afraid I'm losing my
patience with you, my dear. Your payment is long overdue."

Katrina Kirby toyed nervously with her purse strings. "I'll
get you the money, Nathaniel. But I have to wait until Frank
is out of town. I can't possibly get to my jewelry until then."

Nathaniel sighed heavily. "Your little addictions are going
to ruin you one way or the other." He paused, choosing his

words carefully. "What would your husband say if he knew how much of his hard-earned money you whittled away at the track while he was out of town?" Nathaniel's voice was soft and mellow, but his threat was clearly evident. Nathaniel had known Frank Kirby for years. Although Frank Kirby was not above placing an occasional wager on a promising horse himself, Frank was a frugal man who did not approve of squandering money foolishly.

Pretending to be unruffled by the threat, Katrina didn't even look at him as she waved a hand carelessly in the air. "I doubt he'd say very much." She gave a soft of huff of laughter. "Frank loves me far too much to deny me anything."

"Ah, I see," Nathaniel said thoughtfully. "Does he love you so much that he would allow you your little dalliance with the handsome young jockey?"

Katrina's head snapped up. She drew her breath in sharply and narrowed her jewel-green eyes. "What are you talking about?"

"*Tsk. Tsk. Tsk.* Come now, my dear. Everyone knows. Everyone except good old Frank, that is."

She rose from her chair, her face white with fury. She did not love Frank Kirby, but she needed him. She needed his money and she enjoyed the ease and respectability marriage to him had brought to her life. She wasn't about to return to the past, to the seedy little house along the riverfront where she would have to endure the sweaty touch of so much as one more boatman. She lifted one well-defined eyebrow. "Are you threatening me, Nathaniel?"

"Oh, certainly not, my dear," he said, his voice silky-smooth. "Let's just say I'm giving you an incentive to pay your debt."

A cynical little smile touched her beautiful mouth. "My friends told me you could be trusted."

"And I can be," Nathaniel assured her, slowly closing the distance between them. "You see"—he laid a cold palm against her cheek—"if you can't come up with the money right now, you can pay your debt in another manner."

Katrina's gaze narrowed. She tipped her head, and her smile grew bitter and knowing. She reached out and fingered his lapel. Slowly her hand trailed downward to the waistband of his trousers. Her touch was practiced and adept. "What is it you want, Nathaniel?" Her voice was low, seductive.

Nathaniel chuckled and caught her hand, holding it steady for a moment before he firmly removed it from his person as though it were a revolting object. His gaze locked with hers, and his nondescript pale blue eyes grew cunning behind his spectacles. He laced his long fingers together in front of his coat. "Don't flatter yourself, my dear. It's not you I want. But I do need something from you. Not now. But when the time comes, I want you to remember—you owe me. . . ."

Yancey Latimer was tired of waiting. He'd been hot for Birdie Greene since the first day he'd laid eyes on her. Where others found her dull, he found her bright. Where some thought her plain, he thought her lovely. He loved the sheen of her pretty brown hair and the soft floral scent of her skin. He loved the depth of her big brown eyes.

He adored her.

And now she'd up and accepted an offer to ride to church with that fussy old coot, Walter Walcott, who had a full head of hair and owned that little pig farm down the road.

Jealousy burned hot within Yancey's breast. As he thought about the new development, he decided he'd been patient with Miss Birdie long enough. He'd teased and taunted her, allowing her time to get used to him being around, sensing she did not trust easily. But four years had passed, and he figured she ought to be mighty used to his being around by now.

Still, she wouldn't let him get anywhere near her.

Well, by golly, it was high time he melted that ice block she had stored up underneath her skirt. He took a sip of his coffee and stared at her small, shapely backside and decided to make his move. "Birdie Greene," he said, "if you get any prettier, I just don't know what I'm gonna do."

Still half asleep, Eugene coughed his disgust and sucked in

his false teeth as they slipped, threatening to fall out of his mouth. "Can't you come up with anything better than that, Yancey?"

Birdie spun around, her expression furious. "You're right, Eugene! I heard him say that very thing to the Widow Simmons last Sunday after church!" She pinned her dark gaze on Yancey and sniffed. "You're nothing but a faithless flirt, Yancey Latimer!" She shook her spoon at him so hard, oatmeal went flying off into the air and landed on top of Remus's head, waking him from his nap. The dog yawned, his long tongue uncoiling slowly.

"Why, Birdie, I do believe you're jealous," Yancey accused in a slow drawl, wiggling his eyebrows wickedly.

"I am not!" she denied hotly.

"She is," Eugene said, switching alliances as easily as a juggler does eggs. He let out a loud guffaw, and his teeth plopped out onto the table, earning him a harsh, disapproving glare from Birdie.

"Eugene, put your teeth back where they belong!" She shook her head in disgust. "Between your teeth and Yancey's filthy hat, it's a miracle anybody has an appetite around here." She spun around to stir the bubbling pot of oatmeal.

His expression that of a disgruntled child, Eugene picked up his teeth and put them back in his mouth, while Yancey leaned back in his chair and narrowed his gaze. "But I mean it when I say it to you, pretty bird."

"Humph!" Birdie huffed without turning.

He unfolded himself from his chair and crept up behind her.

She sensed his presence and whirled, raising her spoon, ready to bean him. Anticipating her move, he wrapped his arms tight around her, pinning her arms to her sides, and planted a wet kiss smack-dab on her lips while she squirmed and stared up at him, wide-eyed and flabbergasted.

"Hooooeee!" Yancey squealed when he finally released her. He agilely ducked her swatting spoon. "Now, tell me if ol' Walter can kiss you like that, honey!"

"Ooooooo!" Birdie squealed, her cheeks bright with embarrassment. "I'm gonna clobber the daylights outta you!" She lurched at him, swatting at him like he was a pesky fly. He shot off, laughing uncontrollably, and she chased after him. Around and around the table they ran, not missing a step even when Eugene hollered "Ouch!" as one of Birdie's badly aimed swats came down on his head, splattering him with flecks of oatmeal.

Darby stood at the bottom of the stairs, watching the three with interest. Henry joined her. They exchanged looks of bemusement and shrugged.

"At least Walter Walcott is a decent, God-fearin' man!" Birdie hollered at Yancey's back.

Yancey dipped and swooped his hat up from the floor, swerved sharply, then shot straight for the back door. "Just 'cause he's God-fearin' don't make him decent! Walter fears just 'bout everything! I imagine God scares him too!" He shot a quick look over at Darby and bolted through the door, pushing it wide, banging it against the outside of the house. "C'mon, Darby Lynn. Blue's waitin'!"

Her spoon still tightly clenched in her hand, Birdie was right behind him, but she stopped short of chasing him out into the yard. She stood on the porch, oblivious of the frosty February air, her breath coming in cold spurts. She pressed light fingers to her burning lips and tried to still her fluttering heart. She hadn't been kissed like that in twenty-two years. Twenty-two years! *Well, my goodness gracious . . .*

"Come over later," Millie whispered to Darby across the pew the following Sunday morning after the Reverend Johnson had delivered the closing prayer.

"I'm not sure I can," Darby said. "I have to get out to the stables."

"Please come, Darby."

One look at Millie's face told Darby something was wrong. "But—"

"Please. I have something I really need to talk about."

There was an earnest plea in Millie's eyes that had never been present before, one Darby could not ignore.

Darby had been so busy with Blue that except for church on Sunday, she'd barely seen Millie over the winter months. And despite Millie's tactless and sometimes insensitive comments, Darby missed her. "All right," she said, unable to bear Millie's dejected expression a moment longer. "I'll stop over after dinner, before I go out to the stables."

Millie's house sat on Magnolia Avenue, just a short distance away from Central Park.

The congregation of the Walnut Street Methodist Church loved their reverend and his jovial wife and saw to it that his salary included a house worthy of their devotion.

The large, elegant two-story house was of Victorian design, complete with a lovely bay window, two turrets, and a wide porch that wrapped around three sides of the house.

As Darby stood on the porch and knocked on the Johnsons' door, the brisk February wind cut through her wool coat and britches.

Rose Johnson answered her knock almost immediately. "Why, hello, Darby," she said warmly, ushering her into the brightly lit house. "Millie's up in her room waiting for you." She took Darby's coat and steered her toward the wide staircase, then left her to see herself up to Millie's room.

Millie's bedroom door was open. Darby peeked in. The walls were covered with a satiny rose-print paper. A bureau, a lovely four-poster bed, and a full-length mirror that hung on an oak frame graced the gleaming varnished floor. Seeing her, Millie got up from the bed and rushed toward her, taking her hand and drawing her into the bedroom. She closed the door shut tight behind her. "I'm so glad you came!" She pulled her over to the bed and pressed her down onto the pink and white bedspread, then sat down beside her. "I need to talk."

A slight frown marred Darby's smooth brow. "What is it, Millie?" While she waited for Millie to speak, she studied her. There was something different about her, though Millie was as pretty as ever. Her blue eyes were bright, her cheeks flushed with color. Her shiny red hair was pulled back from her face and arranged in a high twist on the back of her head. She wore a white shirtwaist and a long, slender black skirt. It was no wonder Bo was attracted to her, Darby thought without a trace of envy, knowing it was common knowledge that they'd been courting regularly.

"I don't know how to begin," Millie finally said, raising distraught eyes.

Darby shrugged and smiled. "The beginning would probably be as good a place as any."

Millie smiled sadly. "Darby, you were always so smart." She paused a moment, then said, "You would never get yourself into such a predicament." She paused a moment, then said, "You know I've been seeing a lot of Bo Denton?"

Darby nodded. "I heard that you were."

Millie shrugged one shoulder. "I would have mentioned it to you before now, but I felt so guilty. I wasn't sure if you had been interested in him yourself. I didn't want to hurt you. I didn't want you to think I stole him away from you. I—" She dropped her gaze and fidgeted with her hands. "I saw him kiss you the night of the benefit dance. I followed Luke when he came looking for you."

"I see," Darby said, and felt a swift surge of affection for Millie. The change in Millie was becoming. She appeared more mature, less dramatic, more sensitive.

Darby reached out and patted her hand where it lay on the bedspread. "Don't feel guilty. It was only one kiss, and it meant nothing to either one of us."

"Really?"

"Really."

"Swear it," Millie ordered, tipping her head and narrowing her eyes much as she used to do when they were children, telling each other wildly exaggerated stories.

Darby pressed a palm to her chest and smiled. "I swear it."

Greatly relieved, Millie sighed. "Oh, well, that makes me feel so much better."

"Why?" Darby asked on a soft huff of laughter.

"Because," Millie said, standing, glancing away, unable to meet Darby's steady gaze.

Alarmed, Darby stood and took Millie's hands in her own. "Whatever is it, Millie?"

Millie lifted her gaze to Darby's. Her blue eyes were suddenly mature beyond her twenty-one years. "Oh, Darby. I think I'm pregnant with his baby."

Darby's hands lost their grip on Millie's and slipped limply to her sides. She sank back down onto the bed, her lips dropping open. Luke's words of warning about Bo flashed through her brain. "Oh, my . . ." was all she could think to say.

"You must think I'm horrible," Millie said plaintively. "I know it's a sin. At least Mother and Father and the church would say it is, but it didn't feel that way when it was happening. . . ." Her distressed voice trailed off.

Remembering her own weakness in Luke's arms, Darby understood completely. What they had done together in Luke's room had felt good and right and so very wonderful— not at all sinful. In fact, had Luke not stopped what was happening between them, she might be the one making a confession to Millie. "Oh, Millie, I don't think badly of you. Honest I don't."

"You don't?"

"Of course not."

Millie plopped down on the bed beside her. "I don't know what to do."

"Are you sure about this?"

"Well, not positively, but I'm late by several weeks. . . ."

Darby was silent a moment. Aunt Birdie's story about Roland Wilson flashed through her mind. If Bo married Millie, would he treat her like Roland had treated his wife? Darby's steady gaze held Millie's, and her heart ached for her. Millie deserved so much better. "Do you love him?"

Millie shrugged. "I don't know. I suppose I thought I did,

but I'm not so sure now." She lifted her palms. "A baby, Darby. I'm not ready for a baby. I'm too young. I want to dance and play and travel someday. . . ."

Darby took Millie's hands in her own and held them gently on her lap. She thought about her sister Ardis, who was only two years older than Millie and herself. Ardis had been more than ready when her own baby boy had been born. But Ardis and Millie were two very different people. Darby wondered how she would feel if she were pregnant with Luke's baby. Oddly enough, the thought did not bring a feeling of distress. "Have you told him?" Darby asked quietly.

Millie's eyes filled with tears, and she shook her head. "Not yet. I thought I'd wait another week or so."

"Do you want to marry him?"

Millie shrugged. "No. Yes." She lifted her hands. "I don't know. I suppose I'd have to. Mother and Father would insist on a marriage."

Darby swallowed thickly and hugged her friend close. "It'll be all right, Millie," she comforted softly. And she desperately hoped it would be.

March rode in on a ray of sunshine, bringing the first light breath of spring.

Training picked up, and the month passed swiftly.

April dawned, and it was time for the Spring Meets.

Lady Effie took third place in her first Spring Meet. Luke's three-year-olds placed second and fourth in theirs. The purses they brought eased Luke's financial worries somewhat.

Then, at last, the day of Kentucky Blue's first race finally arrived.

Luke and his crew spent the better part of the morning inside the stables at Churchill Downs, chasing off newspaper reporters who called out questions like "Is it true Kentucky Blue's first run on the track was faster than his father's?" "Is Knightwind's colt going to take the Derby next year?" "How do you feel being the owner of such a horse, Miss

Greene?'' ''Is it true that you and Mr. Richards are romantically involved?''

That question in particular caught Darby by surprise, but Luke fielded the question expertly, along with all the others, while he tried to keep things as calm and quiet as possible for Blue.

When it was time, he and Darby and the rest of their outfit left the stables and went to the track, where they stood in silence, watching Bo trot Blue around, warming him up.

The track at Churchill Downs was in good shape—hard and even and fast. Luke was thankful. He glanced down at Darby and felt his heart kick in his chest. She looked undeniably lovely with her plump cheeks pink from the cool morning air, her dark hair blowing back from her face. ''Relax,'' he said quietly, sensing her tension.

She glanced up at him. Her knuckles were white from gripping the top rung on the fence. ''I'm trying.''

Yancey joined them. ''He looks good.''

Luke nodded. ''Yep, he does.''

''Odds have him at nine to two.''

A slow grin touched Luke's mouth. ''Better put a little something down on this race, Yancey. This is the last time you'll ever see odds like this with Blue. After today everyone will know he's a racehorse.''

Out on the track, Bo jogged the big colt along and forced himself to collect his thoughts. He was good at what he did, even when his mind was troubled. And his mind was troubled plenty. He'd seen Millie the previous night, and she'd told him of her suspicions. He felt a surge of guilt and remorse. He liked Millie fine, even felt a certain affection for her, but he did not want to marry her or anyone else. He enjoyed his freedom. He could not imagine walking the straight and narrow as Millie's husband, as the Reverend Johnson's son-in-law. He should have left Millie alone. The responsibility of a wife and child just didn't fit into his lifestyle. But he was not without a conscience. He could not continue to live in Louisville and ignore the fact that a young woman was pregnant with his child. Besides, for all her flirtatiousness, Millie had been an innocent. She no longer was, thanks to him.

He pushed thoughts of Millie to the back of his mind and tried to focus on the horse beneath him. He had a race to win. And win it he would.

He rode up to the group and pulled Blue to a stop. He swung down off Blue's back and grinned at Darby. "Hey, honey."

Darby forced a smile. "Hey, Bo." She was worried about Millie, and she wondered if Millie's suspicions had proven true. She wondered if she'd said anything to Bo yet. He seemed as lighthearted as ever, as handsome as ever dressed in his finest jockey silks with his halo of sunny hair falling down into his eyes. Though she no longer felt the giddy attraction she'd once felt for him, she understood Millie's predicament. Bo Denton, with his teasing brown eyes and white smile, would always be attractive to the ladies. Darby felt a rush of sisterly affection stir within her breast for him. She loved Millie, but Bo was special to her too. He had always been in her corner, urging Luke to accept her offer of training Blue, urging Luke to allow her and Yancey to take part in his training.

"Watch out for that big chestnut stallion," Luke said, breaking into her thoughts, inclining his head toward a horse over by the starting line. "He looks rowdy."

Bo glanced over at the horse. He was an impressive animal with a burnished coat of chestnut gold. His head was large, his movements graceful. But Bo saw what Luke was warning him about. The stallion's eyes had a tense, savage look. "I'll keep plenty of distance between him and Blue."

Luke nodded. "I don't see Phantom."

"I heard Miller had taken him to the tracks up north for a while. I doubt he'll match him against Blue before next May. He wants to build the tension for the Derby."

"Just as well," Luke said quietly.

The sound of excited voices reached them as the grand-stand filled with people. Well-dressed men and their fashionably dressed ladies placed their wagers with the bookmakers, then took their seats, eager to see what their favorites would do.

Luke, Bo, and Darby stood a moment in silence, letting the fresh air clear their heads and calm their minds. Then Luke turned to Bo and said, ''You know what to do out there.''

Bo nodded. ''You bet.''

Luke reached down and lifted him up onto Blue's back in one fluid motion. He slapped Bo's thigh in a gesture of camaraderie, and Bo turned the big black colt toward the post.

Bo felt Kentucky Blue's reckless energy beneath him. The colt was uncharacteristically nervous, and Bo had a hard time holding him steady as the other five horses and their riders found their positions on the starting line.

The big chestnut gelding fought against his bit, trying to edge his way over to Blue. Blue laid his ears back and screamed a whinny in challenge. Bo wrapped a hand in Blue's mane and braced himself for the start. His face was buried in his neck, eyes front, knees pressed against his shoulders. He was so busy keeping an eye on the chestnut stallion that he missed the flag drop.

And Blue broke poorly.

He was two big jumps behind the other five horses. But before Bo even had a chance to collect his thoughts, Blue caught up to the other horses. The jockey on the chestnut stallion cast a glance Bo's way and tried to maneuver his horse over to where Blue hugged the inside of the track.

It was a shrewd move, Bo knew, meant to intimidate him. But Kentucky Blue was oblivious of the threat. Focused on winning, he stretched his neck forward, and in seconds he and the chestnut stallion left the other four horses behind. The chestnut stallion leapt sideways, charging Blue, striking his foreleg with his hoof, drawing blood immediately. Blue stumbled, and Bo clung tight, fearing the worst.

The crowd gasped, and Darby squeezed her eyes shut.

But Blue found his footing almost immediately and, with

one powerful thrust of his body caught up with the other stallion.

Silent as a statue, his expression unreadable, Luke watched the horses thunder down the backstretch. The crowd cheered, and Darby held her breath. Then she felt Luke's big, rough hand wrap around her own. Her eyes opened, and her heart blazed with warmth at the comfort his touch brought.

Blue and the chestnut stallion fought for the lead while Bo fought to keep Blue under control. The chestnut stallion charged him again, his nostrils flared, his teeth bared, but Blue was ready for him this time.

As though he were propelled by a sudden bolt of lightning, Blue shot forward, leaving the chestnut stallion behind. He streaked into the homestretch, alone now, his graceful stride gathering speed, becoming as swift and smooth as rushing water over a falls.

A deafening roar rose from the stands as the spectators stood. Even those who had bet against the black colt were cheering for him now as he thundered down the stretch, past the finish line, winning his first official race by five full lengths.

Bo jogged him back to the winner's circle. Blue was not breathing heavily, and there was still no sweat on his heavy frame. He just looked curious, his eyes wide, his ears flicking back and forth as he listened to the loud noises coming from the crowd.

Luke and Darby ran to his side. Luke bent down to look at the bloody wound on his leg while Darby fought the urge to fidget.

"Is he hurt bad?" she asked, worry evident in her tone.

After a few seconds Luke shook his head. "It looks worse than it is. It's only a superficial wound." He looked up at her and smiled his own relief. "He'll be fine." Luke stood and patted the horse's shoulder. "You did good, fella." Then to Bo he nodded and said, "Good job, Bo."

Bo grinned down at him and with his usual cocky confidence, said, "Of course."

*   *   *

Bradley watched from his seat in the grandstand, his anger building to a volcanic pitch. As Kentucky Blue crossed the finish line, his anger became a bitter bile in his throat, almost choking him.

He'd placed his wager against the colt, certain he would not be able to best the big chestnut stallion.

But he'd been wrong. Again. And now he'd lost all that he'd won when he'd bet against his own horse, Knightwind.

He was in the hole again, and he did not have a way to climb out of it this time.

He felt hatred for Luke Richards burn hot in his breast. The colt should have been his. The winning purse should have been his. Richards had no right to any part of his inheritance any more than his uncle had, no matter what his father had had written into his will.

Seated above Bradley, perched on the edge of his seat like a great bird of prey, Nathaniel Rhinehart watched the revelry with interest and rubbed his chin thoughtfully.

It was almost time, he decided. A divided camp would most assuredly fall. . . .

❖ 8 ❖

LATER THAT EVENING, back at Rhinehart Stables, Kentucky Blue's winnings were divided. The purse had totaled $1,010.

Luke shared a portion with his grooms and stable hands, and Darby paid Yancey.

Joshua Landers came out to the stables to take a look at Blue's leg. The veterinarian's prognosis confirmed Luke's. The wound was not serious. He cleaned and bandaged Blue's leg, extended his heartfelt congratulations for his victory, then went on his way.

In the calming shadows of the coming twilight, Darby stood with her arms resting over the gate to Blue's stall. She watched Blue clean up his feed. Despite the vigors of his first race and his wounded leg, he was as perky as ever. In the stall next to him, Lady Effie neighed softly, waiting for him to finish.

The stables were quiet, the flickering lanterns casting pools of light throughout the barn. Yancey, the stable hands, and grooms had gone into town to celebrate the victory. Exhausted, Darby was ready to go home too.

"Hey, Darby," Bo said as he walked by, his coat slung over his shoulder. "Why don't you go home and get some rest?"

She sent him a reserved smile. "I'm going in a minute."

Bo halted and turned around. "Darby, what's wrong?"

She stared at him in silence, and he knew.

He paused, uncharacteristically uncomfortable with her. His handsome face looked weary beyond his twenty-six years. "It's about Millie, isn't it?"

Darby blushed and looked down at her dusty boots.

Bo shifted his weight. "I suppose you think I'm quite the scoundrel."

Darby glanced up at him and honestly said, "No, I don't. But I am worried about Millie."

Understanding her concern for her friend, he nodded. "Well, don't be. I intend to do right by her. I'm going to ask her to marry me."

Darby was both relieved and hopeful. "Oh, Bo, I hope you'll be very happy."

His eyes smiling, he took her hand, leaned in, and kissed her cheek. "I'm always happy, Darby, you oughta know that by now."

Coming out of his room, Luke caught the intimate exchange between them, and he felt a swift bolt of jealousy rip through him.

"See ya, honey," Bo said, turning to leave, giving her hand a squeeze. He saw Luke walking toward them. "Night, Luke," he called out, then sauntered out of the barn into the growing darkness.

His emotions still turbulent from the race, Luke joined Darby. They stood together in silence for several moments, looking at Blue, then Darby glanced up at him and quietly said, "Bo's going to ask Millie to marry him."

Surprised, Luke raised his brows.

"She's going to have his baby."

That statement did not surprise him nearly so much as her first statement had. "I see" was all he could think of to say. For a brief moment he wondered if the news distressed her. Did she have feelings for Bo?

But the sudden memory of her lying beneath him on his bunk flashed through his brain and answered that question for him. He remembered her swift, hot response to his touch, and desire uncurled within him.

He stared down at her. She was so damned pretty. Her hair was mussed and gleaming like dark satin in the soft glow of lamplight. He studied the soft curve of her plump cheek and fought the urge to reach out and touch her. If he did, he was afraid he wouldn't be able to stop. He wanted her. Each and every day he wanted her. He couldn't get close to her without wanting her.

As though she read his mind, Darby looked up at him, and for one moment time ceased, and they both remembered the night she had come to him. They silently acquiesced how easily the very same thing could be happening to them that was happening to Bo and Millie.

Luke's gaze held hers. Darby watched the change in his eyes. The blue intensified to a deep shade that took her breath away. Her heart picked up a beat. Something warm and fluid drifted through her body.

The truth of their attraction for each other hung in the charged air. Slowly he reached up and slid his fingers into her hair, lifting her face as he lowered his. "I'm sorry," he said as his lips whispered over hers.

She didn't know what it was he was sorry for, and she didn't want to know. It didn't matter. He traced the tip of his tongue along her lower lip, and she parted her lips in invitation. She stretched up into him, deepening the kiss, tangling her tongue with his. He pulled her close, and a low, rough sound of arousal rumbled deep in his chest. He tasted her, the mellow sweetness of her, and felt her soft breasts melt into his body. His groin tightened and throbbed with the need for release.

She gave herself up to his touch, helpless to stop the feelings he evoked in her.

Luke let his own feelings take him while his hands took a slow journey over her slender body, molding her up against him. His hands cupped her bottom, bringing her tight against his aching member. Then his hands rode up over her hips to her breasts. He lifted them, held them, caressed them through her shirt, his thumbs rubbing lightly over her nipples. She moaned deep in her throat, and he lifted his mouth from hers, his heart beating out a tremulous warning. He stared down into her face. She was so sweet, so innocent, so uninhibited in her passion. He knew he could take her right there, standing up against the stall door. But it would have been wrong. She deserved so much more, and he knew his heart could not give it to her.

He found the strength to lift himself away from her.

"Don't stop," she pleaded, her arms locking tight around his neck, her breath coming hot and fast.

He gazed down into her limpid eyes, and common sense prevailed. "Darby . . ." He spoke her name on a warning.

"Please . . ." she whispered.

He shook his head regretfully. "We can't."

"Why?" Her eyes were confused.

"Because. I'm not for you."

"Why not?" she cried, her voice tinged with hurt.

"Just trust me."

"I do. That's why I'm here. That's why I let you touch me. That's why I touch you," she said in a distressed rush, her wide hazel eyes filling with tears. "Luke, I love y—"

"Don't, Darby. Don't say it."

"But—"

"No, don't!"

"What are you afraid of, Luke Richards?" she asked, her expression pained. She dropped her arms to her sides and took a step back from him.

"Of you. Of loving you," he said quietly, honestly.

"But why?" Her brow tightened with frustration.

"Because I don't know how to love you back. Because I really don't want to love you. Because someday if I can't make a go of this farm I'll move on." He stopped, realizing he had never fully voiced his fears even to himself. "I'm a horse trainer, Darby. That's all I know how to do. I go where the work is. I don't want anything to hold me back. I don't want to feel guilty about leaving someone behind." He set his jaw in stubborn resignation.

She studied his handsome face in silence, her expression one of hurt and confusion as she realized the folly of allowing herself to care for him. Tired and frustrated, she took a deep, shaky breath, dropped her gaze in defeat, then turned away from him and strode toward the open barn doors. She held her head high and kept her back stiff with resolve.

"Darby . . ." Luke said, lifting a hand to her back. "I am sorry . . ."

When she reached the doors, she stopped for a brief moment and, without turning to him, she quietly said, "You're a coward, Luke Richards, and I'm the one who's sorry. I'm sorry for you."

Later that night, restless and lonely, Luke let himself into the big house. The spacious, tastefully furnished rooms were the same as they'd been when Benjamin had been alive, although Luke had had the furniture covered for protection. He lit a lamp and, carrying it with him, he walked through the house, listening to the sound of his boot heels clicking across the gleaming oak floors. He felt the quietness echo around him. He still felt no desire to live in the house himself. It did not feel as though it was his. He doubted it ever would.

He paused in the doorway of the parlor. The cold, unlit fireplace gaped at him, like an empty eye socket, beneath a handsome mantel that boasted a fine example of hand carving. A sudden picture flashed through his mind. A picture of Darby, sitting in the room, dressed in britches, reading to a passel of plump-cheeked, dark-haired children who looked just like her. He imagined the sound of their voices and laughter, and he felt lonelier than ever.

He shook his head and laughed a short, cynical laugh. "Jesus, Richards . . . what's happening to you?"

"Is that you, Mr. Luke?" Mrs. Brunsteader called out, appearing a moment later in the hall with a lamp held high in one hand while the other clasped her robe tight over her long, billowing white nightgown.

"It's me, Mrs. Brunsteader," he said, sorry to have disturbed her.

"Are you all right?" she asked, concern in her voice.

"Yes, ma'am. Just restless, that's all."

"Heard Kentucky Blue won his race."

"That he did."

"Well, congratulations!"

"Thank you."

"Darby must be plenty pleased about that."

"She is," Luke answered with a wisp of a smile.

"She's a sweet thing, that girl is."

Yes, she is, Luke thought, feeling his chest tighten. He missed her already. Darby was right. He was a coward.

Mrs. Brunsteader paused a moment, studying his face. "Are you hungry, Mr. Luke?"

He lifted a dark eyebrow and gave her a crooked grin. "Are you?"

She smiled and puffed out her ample chest, glad to be needed. She missed the presence of another human being in the big old house and welcomed a chance to cater to her new boss. She'd always harbored an affection for the young trainer. He reminded her of her youngest son. "Well, I could do with a little somethin', now that I think about it. Come on," she said, leading the way into the kitchen. "I have a nice big ham in the icebox we can carve up for sandwiches. . . ."

Millie and Bo were married the second Sunday in May. The wedding was a small, hurried, subdued affair, as the Reverend and Mrs. Johnson felt time was of imminent importance. Millie wore a simple long white dress, and Bo wore a dark suit and white shirt. They were a handsome couple, but when they greeted their few guests, Millie's smile was forced, and Bo's was strained.

The Reverend Johnson performed the ceremony, his expression one of rife disappointment, while his usually cheerful wife wept softly into her lace-trimmed handkerchief from where she sat in the family's front pew.

Darby, her family, and Luke attended. After the simple reception, everyone wished the handsome young couple well, then took their departure.

Though Darby saw Luke daily, their conversation was stilted and strained. She had grown tired of his rejection. She was tired of hoping he would return her affection. She would not be so willing to go into his arms again.

That night, despite a gnawing fist of guilt churning in his gut, Bo left Millie to cry into her pillow inside the little house he'd let in Louisville, and he rode across town to see Katrina.

Katrina sighed, and her eyelids slipped shut as a smile crept across her lovely face. Her expression was one of sated victory. She wrapped her fingers in Bo's golden hair and her long legs around his lean hips, and laughed deep in her throat as he convulsed against her, finding his release.

She'd been furious with him when she'd heard of his impending marriage to the Johnson girl. But her fury had been spent in his arms since then. His presence at her door this night, the night of his wedding, reassured her that he would be back whenever Frank was out of town. He would continue to share the pleasures of his body and the wealth of his wagering tips with her.

Spent, Bo rolled to his side. He threw his arm over his eyes and sighed. A picture of Millie, with her lovely red hair spilling out onto her pillow as she slept, flashed through his mind. He turned to see Katrina staring at him, her green eyes heavy-lidded with renewed desire. Her hand drifted down to caress his naked thigh, but he pushed her away and stood.

He wanted to go home.

Nathaniel Rhinehart stood in the parlor of his new house. The house was quite familiar. He had grown up there. He watched as Bradley gathered the last of his things from the desk in the small but tastefully furnished study. Bradley's expression was dark, his resentment so obvious and palpable, Nathaniel could almost taste it.

It did not distress him, however. He was only claiming what should have been his in the first place. The house that sat on Rhinehart Breeding Farm in Fayette County had once been his parents' home. As the oldest son, it should have been handed down to him, but because he'd shown no interest in the horses his parents had loved, they'd left the farm to Benjamin, compensating Nathaniel with what they felt was a comparable monetary gift.

Benjamin had been very successful with the farm and with breeding the horses, and by the time he'd married Sarah, he'd been able to afford to build her a new house on property he'd purchased outside of Louisville.

Nathaniel's gaze found Bradley again. "Don't worry, Bradley. You can always come back for a visit."

Bradley glared at him. "I'll rot in hell first."

"Oh, you probably will. Eventually, that is," Nathaniel said, his smile thin. It had been quite easy to break the younger man. All he'd had to do was wait for Bradley's gambling to get the best of him, and waiting came easy for him. Nathaniel had spent his life waiting for a chance to right life's wrongs.

Bradley grabbed his wrinkled coat from where it lay over the chair, and stalked across the floor, stopping before his uncle. Nathaniel handed him the check. Bradley looked down at it. It was for $7,500—a pittance really. Barely enough to cover his gambling debts and keep him in food and drink over the next several months. His eyes came back to Nathaniel's. "Tell me one thing. If you wanted the goddamned place so bad, why didn't you just write it into my father's will? No one would have known."

"I'm afraid you're wrong about that. Your father had many friends, and he made it common knowledge what he intended to do with his estate in the sad event of his death." Nathaniel forced his expression into one of contrite innocence. "He wanted to make sure matters were taken care of as he intended them to be.'' Nathaniel sighed heavily. ''You'd almost think he didn't trust me, wouldn't you?'' He laughed shortly. It was an ugly sound. ''Despite what you think, he really did love you, Bradley. *Tsk. Tsk.* Foolish man. You were never any more worthy of his love than he had been of our parents' unwavering devotion. They always preferred him over me, you know. From the very day he came into this world.'' He shook his head. ''Parents can be so blind when it comes to their offspring.'' He sighed heavily. ''But back to the subject at hand. I really had very little influence over your father in regard to his will. The only thing I was able to convince him to do was to give the Greene girl Knightwind's colt.''

''Why would you do that?'' Bradley couldn't help but ask.

Nathaniel tapped his long fingers against his trouser leg. His smile went flat. ''Think about it, Bradley. Think long and hard, and maybe someday your whiskey-soaked brain just might figure it out.''

Emma and Noah's wedding day arrived as May crept to an end. Unlike Millie's rather morose ceremony, Emma's wedding was a happy, lovely affair held at the Walnut Methodist Church at three on a warm, bright Saturday afternoon.

Emma looked radiant, dressed in a gown of ivory satin with trimmings of white point Venice lace. She had swept her hair up into a lovely puffy arrangement on top of her head, and she wore the pearl drop earrings she had lent to Darby the night of the benefit dance.

Darby thought her oldest sister had never looked more beautiful.

Noah was as handsome as Emma was beautiful, clad in an elegant dark suit and starched white shirt.

After the ceremony the reception was held out on the gaily decorated church grounds.

Luke attended, as did Millie and Bo. Only four months along, Millie was still trim. She was as lovely as ever, but Darby detected a sorrow in her eyes that had never been present before. She wanted to ask her about it, but she was afraid of the answer.

Bo joked and teased with everyone as usual, but Darby noticed his laughter was sometimes a bit too loud and raucous, as though the effort to be funny was difficult for him these days.

Darby stood beside a sniffling Aunt Birdie, watching a four-man band take their places beneath the shady arms of a huge oak tree out on the spacious lawn.

"Don't cry, Aunt Birdie," Darby said, and gave her tiny aunt a hug. "This is a happy day."

With that Birdie only sniffled louder. "One more to go, and all my girls will be gone."

"Gone where?" Yancey said, joining them.

"On to husbands," Darby said dryly, knowing she was the "one more to go." She also knew that she was not likely to be going anywhere and that her aunt was wasting her tears.

Yancey smiled down at his two favorite ladies. He was aware that he looked surprisingly dapper dressed in a neatly pressed dark coat and trousers, a flawless white shirt, and shiny black boots. His floppy hat gone, his thinning hair was slicked back from his forehead. His usually whiskered jaw was shaved as smooth as a gourd.

He bent down and kissed Darby's cheek. She looked like a fairy princess, dressed in a slender-fitting butter-yellow gown that hugged her tiny waist and flowed gently over her hips. Her shoulder-length hair was caught up from her face and hung freely in soft loose waves, with wispy bangs framing her brows.

Yancey's clear gray eyes found Birdie. His gaze grew openly admiring.

She wore a simple, elegant lavender dress that emphasized her girlish figure. Her shiny brown hair was caught up in a high twist on the back of her head, and her cheeks were pink from excitement. Her luminous brown eyes were red from crying, but Yancey thought her tears only made her more adorable.

The band started to play, and Yancey winked at her and held out his hand. "How 'bout a dance, pretty bird?"

She gave him a disparaging glance and was about to refuse him, but Darby nudged her and said, "Oh, go on, Aunt Birdie. What can it hurt?"

Birdie shot her a frown that said Darby would find out what it could hurt later, but she placed her hand in Yancey's and allowed him to swing her out onto the lawn.

Yancey held her at a respectable distance, whirling her carefully among the many swaying couples. "How'd you get so pretty, Birdie Greene?" he asked quietly. "That's what I'd like to know."

She gave a disdainful huff and lifted her big brown eyes to his face. No one, to her knowledge, had ever thought she was pretty.

"You look prettier than morning dew does on a rose," he went on, his gaze warm on her face. "I mean it, Birdie. I never in my life thought anyone looked prettier than you do this very moment."

Their gazes locked and held, and Birdie's lips dropped open, and something very wonderful happened. She felt her face heat and her heart begin to melt.

He steered her away from the crowd and behind the trunk of a big tree. Once they were safely hidden, he looked down into her eyes. "I want to kiss you more than I want anything in the world. Can I, Birdie?"

The fact that he'd asked for her permission had an amazing effect on her. She felt an intense rush of affection bloom for him. Her heart thrummed within her tiny breast, and her hands shook. He took her silence for acquiescence and lowered his head, touching warm lips to her open ones. He kissed her slowly, tenderly, his mouth working a mystery she had never known as his hands found her head and cupped it as though it were the most precious treasure in all the world.

When he lifted his head, her eyes were wide with wonder. She was breathless, tingling all over from head to toe. "Well, my goodness . . ." she said for want of anything else to say.

Yancey pulled her up against his chest and held her tight, loving the feel of her little body pressed up against his hammering heart. How odd and wonderful that life had given him one more chance to love.

The music threaded out to them, along with the hushed buzz of conversation, but they stood pressed together for the space of several heartbeats. Then, when she'd finally collected herself, she glanced up at him and smiled a very wicked, very teasing smile. "You're absolutely right. Walter Walcott does not kiss like that."

Darby stood alone, watching her aunt and Yancey disappear behind the tree, her smile one of gentle amusement. Yancey was in love with Birdie, that much was clearly evident. The sight of them together warmed her heart. She wished Bo would look at Millie the way Yancey had looked at Aunt Birdie. She sighed heavily. She wished Luke had looked at her that way. A year had passed since he'd come into her life, bringing Blue to her. She was no longer the wide-eyed, innocent tomboy who had thought she was in love with the dashing jockey. She had learned that love and attraction, though their faces were similar, were really very different. Not only was she attracted to Luke Richards, but also she had fallen in love with him. She had fallen in love with a man whose steady hands and kind nature could gentle horses, a man who treated his employees and friends well and fairly, a man who for all his goodness could not love her.

As though bidden by her thoughts, he appeared at her side, coming up from behind. "Hello, Darby," he said quietly.

She turned to him and smiled, but her smile was cautious and hesitant, not spontaneous and full-bloomed like those she'd once bestowed on him. That realization made him sad.

"Hello, Luke," she returned politely. He looked devastatingly handsome, his eyes bluer than ever, his dark suit simply cut but fitting his tall, broad-shouldered frame impeccably.

"Emma looks lovely."

Darby nodded and glanced over at her sister, where she

stood smiling up at her new husband. "She certainly does."

Luke was quiet a long while. "You do too, Darby."

She glanced down at the lush green grass, not trusting herself to meet his gaze. "Thank you."

"Would you like to dance?"

She lifted sad eyes to his. "No, thank you."

Her refusal cut him deeply, far more than he ever imagined it could. He dredged his mind for a reason to linger at her side, hoping for a topic he could turn into a conversation. But nothing came.

A tall young man with light brown hair and a wide, white smile worked his way through the crowd to where Darby and Luke stood. He was dressed in the latest fashion, a checked wool suit, under which he wore a white shirt with a wing-tip collar, banded by a black silk tie. "Hello, Darby," he greeted her warmly.

"Hello," Darby returned, her surprise evident in her voice as recognition dawned. "Jeffrey?" she said in question.

He laughed. The sound was full and rich. "It's me."

She smiled. "How have you been?"

"Fine." He nodded. "Just fine."

"How's school?"

"I'm done and home for good. I'm finally ready to set up practice in town."

Jeffrey Morgan was three years older than Darby. His father owned a modest farm two miles south of Henry Greene's. His oldest sister, Elizabeth, was Emma's best friend. Jeffrey had been away at school the past several years, studying medicine just as his father had always planned for him to do.

Jeffrey turned to Luke and extended his hand in a gesture of open friendliness. "I don't believe we've met."

Luke shook the younger man's hand. "Luke Richards," he said in greeting.

"Jeffrey Morgan. I've heard and read plenty about you. My father tells me you're training Darby's horse."

Luke nodded.

"I'm an old friend of Darby's," Jeffrey said, then laughed

disparagingly. "Well, sort of. Our sisters are friends, and Darby used to pound the daylights out of Edgar Cawley for me after school. Even though I was older, she was tougher." He looked over at her. "But you've changed, Darby. You've grown up. You look, well . . . wonderful." His gray-blue gaze was openly admiring, and Luke felt a stab of jealousy burn deep in his gut.

Darby returned his smile, noting the change in Jeffrey as well. He had been as smart as a whip as a boy, but so small and awkward that bullies had picked on him constantly. She'd often felt sorry for him and had come to his rescue. But time had obviously righted things for him. He was tall and broad-shouldered now, and really quite good-looking. His radiant smile exuded a confidence that made him appear much older than his twenty-four years.

"How's Millie?" Jeffrey asked, casting a glance over at the attractive couple.

"Married," Darby answered. "Just recently, to Bo Denton, the jockey."

"Ah . . ." Jeffrey said, his gaze coming back to hers.

"Oh, I'm fine," Darby said, missing his point completely.

Jeffrey laughed. "I can see that." He paused and lifted one eyebrow meaningfully.

Surprised, Darby felt her cheeks heat. "Oh . . . well . . . no," she said on an embarrassed huff of laughter. "I'm not married."

"Got a beau?" Jeffrey asked boldly, shifting his gaze from her to Luke. He was no longer the shy, bookish young man who could barely put two words together.

Darby dropped her gaze, her heart beating wildly. She felt Luke's gaze on her face. Slowly she lifted distressed eyes to Luke's and wished her answer could be different. "No," she said quietly, "not really."

As he stared down at her, Luke flinched inwardly, knowing the pain he felt was of his own making.

Obviously pleased by her answer, Jeffrey's smile widened.

He held out his hand, palm up. "Then how 'bout a dance for old time's sake?"

"Oh, I . . ." Darby shook her head, ready to refuse.

"If you'll excuse me," Luke said, turning away, feeling the need to escape, feeling jealousy explode within him like an exploding stick of dynamite. He could not watch Darby place her hand in the handsome young man's. He just couldn't.

Jeffrey nodded. "Nice to have met you, Richards," he said good-naturedly.

Because she liked Jeffrey, and because she was hurting, and because she needed a diversion as much as Luke did, Darby placed her hand in Jeffrey's and allowed him to lead her out among the other whispering skirts.

Luke left the gathering and did something he hadn't done in a very long time. He headed straight for the riverfront. When he reached the large gray clapboard house that sat on the corner of Water Street and Jackson and sported the sign MAYBELLE'S PARLOR, he swung down from his horse and tethered the reins to a hitching post that flanked the building.

He went inside and was greeted almost immediately by Maybelle, who was dressed as primly as a schoolmarm and was fifty years old if she was a day.

"Why, hello, Luke," she greeted him brightly, patting her flawlessly arranged black hair.

"Hello, May," Luke returned, doffing his Stetson.

"It's been a while."

"I've been busy."

"So I've heard."

"Is Lucy in?" He knew what he needed and he didn't want to waste time getting to it.

Maybelle nodded and lifted one thinly plucked eyebrow. "I'll let her know you're here. Help yourself to a drink," she said, gesturing toward the open doors of the spacious parlor. She turned toward the wide, curving staircase and left him.

While he waited for Lucy, Luke went into the parlor and

poured himself a stiff shot of whiskey, then sat down in a wing-back leather chair where he could watch the staircase.

Lucy came down the stairs a half hour later, tying the belt of her frilly, filmy red wrapper around her waist. She sidled up to him. She was young, full-figured, barely twenty-five, and pretty, with a frothy mass of pale blond hair.

She bent over and kissed his cheek, giving him an expansive view of her ample endowments. "Luke, I've missed you. It's been well over a year."

A small smile touched one corner of his mouth. He was quite sure Lucy said much the same thing to all of her paying customers.

"Word has it you've got another big winner in Knightwind's colt. I've read all about it in the *Courier-Journal* and the *Times*."

"We'll see," Luke said.

She straightened and hung one hand on her hip. "Want to go upstairs?"

He stood. "That's why I'm here."

She turned, and he followed her up the staircase.

Once they were in her room, she closed the door and removed her wrapper. She wore only the barest of lacy undergarments. She pressed up against him and wrapped her arms around his neck. Lifting her face to his, she waited for him to kiss her.

But he didn't. He just couldn't.

Her breath smelled like smoke. Her skin smelled musky, tinged with the scent of stale perfume. He thought of Darby, who smelled so fresh and clean and pure, and any desire he tried to ignite for Lucy died before it ever flickered into a flame.

He apologized and paid her anyway, then left, feeling even worse than when he'd arrived. He rode out of Louisville, trying to concentrate on his horses, on the coming meets, on all that had to be done in preparation, but all he could think about was Darby—Darby and that nice young man, Jeffrey Morgan, who was so obviously smitten with her.

*   *   *

Luke was about a mile away from home when he noticed the sky. It was brightly lit in a blaze of gold, as though dawn were attempting to break over the hills in the dead of night.

It took a few seconds for realization to hit him, but when it did, it hit him with force. "Oh, my God," he whispered, then dug his heels into Toby. Propelled by adrenaline, he rode hard, toward the telltale orange glow, while terror arced a wicked path through his heart.

✦ 9 ✦

LUKE'S HEART HAMMERED. His chest hurt.

As he rode over the last hill, the acrid smell hit him, and his worst fear became a reality as Rhinehart Stables came into full view.

The stables were ablaze.

The flames shot up through the hayloft and already ate at the sides of the stables.

He kicked Toby hard and raced onward through a haze of fear and dismay.

The stable hands had already formed a line from the well to the stables, passing buckets of water. Mrs. Brunsteader stood on the lawn, shouting orders like a military leader.

"Did you get the horses?" Luke yelled from a hundred yards away, leaping off Toby before he had even pulled the horse to a stop.

"Ian's tryin', Mr. Luke!" Eddie yelled out, his young face streaked with grime and sweat.

Luke raced for the barn, but Tom Haines grabbed him from behind and held on tight. "Don't go in there, Mr. Luke! Please, please don't . . ."

Luke shook him off roughly.

"Please, Mr. Luke!" Tom tried again, his expression one of fear and panic.

Luke ignored him and yelled at Eddie. "Get a bucket of water over here! Dump it on me! I'm goin' in!" Eddie obeyed, dumping a bucket of water over him, and from some-where out of the confusion came Yancey, Henry, Eugene, and Darby.

Unable to sleep, Darby had sat staring out of her bedroom window long into the night. Just before midnight she'd seen the first golden flickers in the sky and had awakened her father and Yancey.

"Don't go, Luke!" Henry hollered, and grabbed Luke's elbow as he ran by. But Luke yanked his arm away and plunged on toward the stables.

Meanwhile, Yancey took a bucket of water from Tom's hands and dumped it over his head, then raced for the stables on Luke's heels.

"Where's Blue?" Darby screamed, and tried to follow them, but Mrs. Brunsteader grabbed her around the waist and held tight. "You can't go in there, honey!" she hollered. "You just can't!"

Luke dashed through the open stable doors. He ran through the sea of smoke, his eyes stinging. "Ian! Ian, where are you, goddammit!" His horses were in a panic. The sound of their shrieks of terror and the thumps of their hooves mingled with the roar of the flames.

The beams above were already in cinders, falling to the floor around him. He dodged them and pulled his coat up over his mouth, so he could filter the smoke that had already begun to burn his lungs.

"I'll get the horses!" Yancey yelled, suddenly beside him. "You find Ian!"

Yancey plunged ahead to Blue's stall. A chunk of flaming debris fell in front of him, blocking his path. He sidestepped it and swung Blue's gate open. Inside his stall, Blue screamed a whinny and paced frantically. He hung his head over the rail, trying to reach Lady Effie. "Come on, boy!" Ian yelled, and tried to take hold of his halter. But the colt lifted his head into the air, away from him, balking, refusing to be led out of his stall.

It took Yancey a moment before he realized why. Then he

spun and went to Lady Effie's stall, throwing the door open wide. "C'mon, girl!" he hollered, and tried to chase her out. The high-strung filly sidestepped in terror. She reared up, striking the stall walls with her hooves. "C'mon, now, girl!" Yancey yelled again. Frightened, she finally bolted from her stall. She ran three good leaps, then locked her legs and turned back around toward Blue's stall. Yancey waved his hat wildly in front of her face, trying to force her to turn around, but even as he did, a large flaming beam fell from above, striking her on the forehead, hitting her with such force that it brought the little filly to her knees. Yancey kicked the beam away, swatting out the flames on the right side of her face, then he pulled roughly on her halter, finally forcing her to her feet. "Git! Hyah!" he yelled, chasing her through the flames and out into the yard. Then he turned and ran back into the stables for Blue.

Meanwhile, Luke searched for Ian through watering eyes. The sleeve of his coat caught on fire, and he slapped out the flames, squinting through the wavering waves of heat. He swabbed at his eyes with his other sleeve and threw open the stall doors as he passed them, hoping the horses would find their way out.

Just as despair began to rob him of his strength, he finally found Ian.

He was on the floor in the back of the stables, in front of the last stall door, his left leg twisted at a weird angle and pinned beneath a smoldering beam. "Jesus, Ian," Luke said, lifting the beam off him, scorching his hands in the process.

"Get the horses out," Ian said, his voice a mere whisper.

"Not till we get you out, old man," Luke said, and hauled the smaller man up over his shoulder. He bolted for the doors, hearing the haunting, helpless cries of his horses calling out to him.

He got Ian outside and lowered him gently to the ground, then yelled, "Somebody get a doctor out here for Ian!" He turned and, as though in slow motion, he watched the left side of the barn collapse into an orange shimmer of sparks.

Frantic, Darby was at his side, tugging at his sleeve. Her face was streaked with dirt and tears as she grabbed at him, her fingers digging into the hard muscle of his forearm. "Please don't go back in there, Luke," she pleaded. "Please . . ."

"Blue's still in there," he said, his eyes red and tearing, "and so are my other horses. I don't have a choice. You know that, Darby." His gaze steady, he lifted her hand from his arm, then turned to Eddie and grabbed another bucket of water, sloshing the contents over his head.

Sucking in his breath, head bent low, he ran back into the flaming inferno. Five feet into the stables, he felt a sharp jolt to the back of his head, and he fell to his knees. A haze of darkness threatened to overtake him, but he fought against it, forcing himself to his feet. He stumbled toward Blue's stall. He heard the colt's frantic whinny and Yancey's voice. "She's safe now, Blue! C'mon! It's yer turn!"

Luke lurched into the stall and took hold of Blue's halter. "Grab him on the other side! We'll run him out together!"

Around them hay ignited. The huge colt reared and fishtailed, but the two men hung on, refusing to let loose of his halter. They forced him through the stall door, then plowed onward toward the open doors, the muscles in their arms aching from the strain of trying to drag the big horse. Lady Effie's whinny cut through the crackling noise of the flames and, hearing her call out to him, Blue's legs finally broke loose, and he all but dragged the two men out of the stables in a gallop.

Darby rushed to greet them. She hugged the colt's neck and pressed her face to his muzzle, her throat filling, tears streaking down her cheeks. "Oh, Blue," she sobbed. "Oh, Blue . . ."

Her gaze locked with Luke's. She wanted to throw her arms around his neck and once again beg him not to go back into the stables, even though her heart was breaking, even as she listened to the terrified, fading cries of the horses still trapped within the hungry flames.

Luke and Yancey spun, ready to go back in for the other horses, their hair and eyebrows singed, their faces streaked and dirty. But before they could take another step forward, an awful roar arose, and the night was lit by a blinding brilliance as the entire roof of the barn crashed downward, exploding into an awesome shimmering spectacle.

Luke knew there was no going back in.

He knew there was no saving the other horses.

Heartsick and exhausted, he stood with his arms hanging limply at his sides, watching the flames dance and flicker against the midnight sky, watching his entire world disintegrate into a swirl of ashes and black smoke.

Darby came up behind him. Together they stared dully at the devastation, helpless to do anything to stop the tragedy. She reached over and took his hand, desperately wanting to offer him a measure of comfort.

He winced at her touch, and she turned his hand over and saw his burnt palm. ''Oh, Luke,'' she whispered grievously, fresh tears stinging her eyes. She took his other hand and turned it over as well. ''Your hands. You need a doctor.''

The townsfolk began to arrive by the wagonload, having seen the telltale glow on the horizon.

Men shouted orders, and women climbed down out of the wagons. A red fire wagon pulled by a team of horses clanged by. The stable hands ran to greet it, unwinding the hoses, stretching them out, getting in place to man the pumps.

''You better get a veterinarian out here, Mr. Luke!'' young Eddie yelled. ''There's something bad wrong with Effie!''

''I'm already here,'' Joshua Landers answered, swinging down off his horse and reaching for his bag. He strode straight for little bay filly, who was throwing her head wildly and stumbling around aimlessly.

Leading Blue by the halter, Darby and Luke turned away from the stables and walked over to Joshua Landers and Lady Effie.

Blue lifted his head into the air and called to her, then

maneuvered his body around so he could be near her. Sensing his presence, she calmed somewhat.

Luke and Darby waited in silence while the veterinarian examined the frightened horse.

"How bad is it, Josh?" Luke finally asked.

Joshua Landers lifted distressed eyes to Luke. "Her face is badly burned, and she's suffered some serious damage to her eyes, especially the right one." He paused a moment, his face a picture of compassion. "I'm sorry Luke . . . I hate to say it, but I don't think she can see anything out of the right eye."

Luke dropped his chin to his chest, shaking his head. Darby's heart ached for him and for Effie. Joshua Landers laid a hand on Luke's shoulder, then busied himself with cleaning Effie's wounds. He put a salve on her burns to ease her discomfort and cleaned out her eyes as much as possible, taping a large patch over the right eye to protect it from the smoke and ashes floating through the air.

Luke turned to Henry and Yancey, who joined them. His tone dead, he said, "Would you take Effie and Blue home with you?"

"Of course," Henry said without hesitation.

Luke's gaze found Darby. She looked small and vulnerable, but he sensed her strength. He wanted to go to her, pull her close, and seek comfort in her arms. But he didn't. He had no comfort to offer her in return. He had nothing to offer her in return.

Yancey took Darby by the arm. "C'mon, honey. There's nothing more we can do here. Let's go home and calm these horses down."

Darby's gaze held Luke's. She did not want to leave him. She wanted to reach out to him, to tell him that everything would be all right. But the words did not come.

Her gaze shifting between them, Mrs. Brunsteader took Darby's hand and kindly said, "You go on home, honey, and take care of the horses now. Get some rest. I'll take care of him." She nodded at Luke.

Exhausted, Darby did as she was bidden, her hand locked on Blue's halter as though she would never let go. She turned away and led him through the crowd, with Yancey and Henry leading Effie behind her.

Bo galloped into the crowd and swung down from his horse. He frantically searched the throng for Luke. Finding him, he ran to his side. "I'm sorry, Luke," he said quietly.

Luke nodded and, using the back of his hand, wiped the sweat and soot from his eyes. "Yeah, me too."

Bo cast a glance toward Darby, Kentucky Blue, and Lady Effie. Reluctantly he turned back to Luke. "The other horses?"

Luke shook his head. "They didn't make it," he whispered thickly, dropping his chin to his chest, squeezing his eyes shut tight.

Bo was silent a long while. "How did it happen?"

Luke shrugged. He opened his eyes and looked at Bo. "I don't know." Silence, then, "Not yet."

"It could have been a simple accident," Bo said, understanding his meaning.

Luke glanced over at the burning pile of debris. "It could have been." But something in his voice told Bo he didn't believe it for a minute.

"Are you all right?" Bo asked, his expression one of concern.

"I will be. Ian's hurt, though. He needs a doctor."

"Old Doc Adams is tending to him now. He was right behind me."

"Good," Luke said, his tone weary.

They stood together in despairing silence, trying to make sense out of the senselessness of it all, wondering where to go from here. After some time Mrs. Brunsteader took charge and said, "I suppose this means you'll be staying in the big house for the time being, Mr. Luke." Her kindly old face was compassionate.

"I suppose it does, ma'am."

"Well," she said on a heavy sigh, "that's one good thing."

It was barely dawn the next morning when a knock sounded at Henry Greene's door. Darby, Yancey, and Henry had gotten home from Rhinehart Stables an hour before, and no one except for Eugene and Yancey had even bothered to try to go to bed.

Numb and exhausted, Darby was upstairs in her room, soaking in a hot tub of water, while Birdie busied herself in the kitchen, scratching together some breakfast for the weary crew.

Birdie answered the door, her eyes red-rimmed from sleeplessness.

Sheriff Harvey Roth stood on the porch, hat in hand. "Is Henry around, Miss Birdie?"

Having heard the knock, Henry Greene joined his sister at the door. "Hello, Harvey. What can I do for you?"

Harvey shifted his weight, obviously uncomfortable with the business at hand. "I'm lookin' for Yancey Latimer, Henry."

There was a note of regret in Harvey's voice that sent a wintry warning down Birdie's spine.

Henry frowned his confusion. "What do you want with Yancey?"

"I have some questions to ask him as to his whereabouts last night."

"Why?" Henry asked, his puzzlement growing.

"I'd rather talk to Yancey, if you don't mind, Henry."

Henry was silent a moment as his mind clicked. Then he hooked his hands on his hips and without preamble said, "Well, I can tell you where he was. He was at my daughter's wedding for the better part of the afternoon, then he was over at Rhinehart Stables for most of the night, fighting the fire along with the rest of us."

Harvey nodded. "I understand that. But I'd like to know where he was between the time he came home from your daughter's wedding and the time that the fire started, which Mr. Richards estimates to be somewhere around midnight.''

Henry shrugged. ''I 'magine he was in bed like the rest of us.''

''Yes, well, I'd like him to tell me that himself,'' Harvey said, his tone firm.

Bemused, Henry narrowed his eyes. ''Did Luke send you out here?''

Harvey glanced down at his dusty boots, then back up at Henry. ''No. To tell you the truth, Luke Richards don't know nothing 'bout this visit, although I did talk to him just a short while ago. All I can tell you is I'm following up on a lead that was passed on to me by someone else.''

Henry gave him a hard stare. ''Now, you listen here, Harvey. I don't know who your source is or what you're gettin' at, but Yancey Latimer risked his life last night to save my daughter's and Luke Richards' horses.''

''Now, Henry, don't be gettin' yourself all fired up that-away.'' Harvey lifted his hands in supplication. ''I'm not implying anything. I just want to ask Latimer a few questions, that's all.''

A tense moment passed while Birdie's heart stopped beating, and Henry worked hard to rein in his temper. Yancey Latimer was one of the finest men he'd ever met—hardworking, dependable, honest. ''All right,'' Henry finally said, deciding to put an end to this foolishness. ''I'll go get him for you.''

His suspenders hanging in limp loops at his sides, Henry stomped down the steps and strode across the dew-soaked lawn to the bunkhouse. He knocked once on the heavy wood door, then entered the small building that Eugene and Yancey shared for their sleeping quarters. Eugene was sound asleep on his cot, burrowed under the covers, snoring peacefully.

''Yancey?'' Henry called out, opening the door wide enough to let the sunlight slant across the wooden floor. His gaze swept the room. Yancey's cot was neatly made and Yancey was nowhere in sight.

Oddly enough, neither were any of his belongings.

* * *

Later that afternoon Nathaniel Rhinehart stood beside Sheriff Harvey Roth on his late brother's porch and knocked at the door.

Mrs. Brunsteader answered the knock and reluctantly ushered the two men into the tiled hallway.

"I'm here to see Mr. Richards," Nathaniel said, his tone one of cool superiority.

His tone did not impress Mrs. Brunsteader in the least, however. As fond as she was of her former employer, she had equally disliked his brother. She raised her eyebrows and stated, "He's sleeping."

"Wake him."

"No, sir, I won't do that." She puffed herself up like a chicken fluffing her feathers for battle. "He just got into bed and he needs his rest. You'll have to come back later."

"I'll have to insist—" Nathaniel began.

"That's not necessary," Luke said from the top of the stairs. "It's all right, Mrs. Brunsteader. I'm awake." Clad only in a clean pair of britches, his bandaged hands hanging at his sides, he slowly made his way down the wide-curving staircase.

She turned, plunked her hands down on her generous hips, and arched him a pointed look of disapproval. "You shouldn't even be out of bed. You with them awful burns."

He tried to give her a reassuring smile, but the effort was wasted. "I'm fine, ma'am, really."

"And there's no need to be callin' me 'ma'am' any longer." She shot Nathaniel a disdainful look and lifted her nose. "I work for you now." With a sniff of dismissal she turned and lumbered away, her dislike and disrespect for Nathaniel Rhinehart plainly evident.

"What is it, gentlemen?" Luke asked when he reached them, his expression one of weary confusion. Then to the sheriff he said, "I didn't expect to see you back so soon."

"Well . . ." Sheriff Roth said, "Mr. Rhinehart has something you oughta take a look at."

"Allow me to extend my sympathy about your misfortune, Mr. Richards," Nathaniel said on a silky note. "*Tsk, tsk.*" He shook his head. "Terrible thing, isn't it? Those poor, poor animals. What a horrible way to die."

Luke studied him in silence, a weird discomfort churning in his belly.

Nathaniel affected a compassionate smile and handed him a yellowed newspaper clipping. "I thought you might be interested in this."

Luke looked down at the clipping. The date on the newspaper read June 10, 1862. The New York headlines read: *Missing Young Trainer Suspected of Arson.* Then, underneath in smaller print: *Well-known Thoroughbred trainer Yancey Larson is wanted for questioning about the suspicious fire that completely destroyed the stables and killed nine horses at Barclay Farms, where Larson has been employed over the past five years. . . .*

Luke read no further and lifted his gaze, handing the clipping back to Nathaniel. "What does this have to do with anything?" His tone was carefully controlled.

"I've done a little checking up on Yancey Latimer," Nathaniel answered matter-of-factly. "Oddly enough, he and Larson have very similar physical descriptions." He paused a moment, cocking his head to the side. "Don't you find that a bit odd?"

A tick began to pulse above Luke's right eye. "Not particularly."

Sheriff Roth cut in and said, "That's not all, Mr. Richards. I rode out to the Greene farm this morning to ask Latimer some questions, and he was as gone as gone could get. He's up and packed up all his belongings and lit out."

Luke crossed his arms over his wide bare chest and looked from one man to the other. "What are you trying to say, gentlemen? That Latimer set the fire last night?"

"It's a distinct possibility," Nathaniel said.

Trying to control his rising anger, Luke shook his head.

"Not to me, it isn't. Yancey Latimer is as good a man as there ever was."

The sheriff took a deep breath, then asked, "How well do you know the man, Luke?"

"Well enough," Luke answered quietly. His gaze shifted to Nathaniel. "Better than I know you, Rhinehart."

A thick silence fell, and Luke's eyes became cold chips of blue ice. "I'm a bit curious about something myself, Rhinehart. Just how the hell did you manage to get that clipping so damn fast? The fire hasn't even been out for six hours."

His composure cool and collected, Nathaniel raised his brows innocently and pushed his spectacles up the narrow bridge of his nose. "I make it my business to know things. Especially when it comes to people connected to my late brother's holdings." He paused a moment, then went on. "Take you, for instance . . . I know you grew up in an orphanage. That you were abandoned by a mother you never knew. Your father could have been any man on the street for all you know about him. You don't even know your real name. Luke Richards was the name the nuns picked out for you."

"What's your point, Rhinehart?" Luke asked tersely.

"My point is this," Nathaniel went on. "The farm is a big responsibility. You're not cut out for this life, my boy. You're a horse trainer, not a Thoroughbred breeder. There is a difference, you know." He paused a second. "I came to offer my help—"

"And how would you do that?" Luke asked, cutting him off.

Nathaniel smiled benevolently. "I would be willing to make you an offer on the farm, relieve you of the burden, so to speak, now that you've lost all of your horses. . . ."

In the past several hours Luke had thought about that very thing, about giving up, calling it quits, selling out and moving on, but thoughts of Darby had intruded. He'd made her a promise, a promise to train her horse to win the Kentucky

Derby, and he had never broken a promise to anyone in his life.

From somewhere within, Luke felt a surge of strength kick in, and his expression hardened with firm resolve. "I didn't lose all of the horses, Rhinehart. Thanks to Latimer, I still have Kentucky Blue and Lady Effie, although she suffered some injuries."

Nathaniel's eyes revealed nothing of his surprise.

Luke's gaze bored into the older man's. "Thank you for the offer, but I'm not interested."

Nathaniel was silent a moment. "I see. Well . . . I do hate to see you in such dire straits. I could make you a loan so you could rebuild your stables if that would be more suitable to your needs."

"No, thanks," Luke said without hesitation.

"Are you quite sure?" Nathaniel asked, narrowing his gaze.

"I've never been more sure of anything in my life."

"Well," Nathaniel said, and sighed softly, "I hope you're not making a mistake."

"I'm not," Luke answered quietly, then dismissed both men by opening the door and seeing them out.

The burns on Luke's hands would heal, as would Ian's broken leg.

But sadly enough, Henry rode out on Tuesday to tell Luke that Josh Landers had been right about Lady Effie.

The beam that had landed on her head had burnt her badly. She was completely blind in her right eye and partially blind in her left. By racing standards, Lady Effie was ruined. She would not run in the coming Fall Meets. She would not race in the Kentucky Oaks next year as a three-year-old. Lady Effie would never race again. Her days as a champion were over before they'd ever really begun.

Though the news saddened him greatly, Luke was grateful that she had survived the fire. He knew he could breed her, and breed her he would. She came from a long line of champions. He loved her, and he would see that she had a comfortable, happy life.

The morning of his visit, Henry sat in a rocking chair next to Luke on the wide front porch, his expression troubled. He looked out at the blue-tinged Kentucky hills and said, "About Yancey, Luke. I don't know what to think. But I gotta say I just don't see Yancey doin' this terrible thing."

"It's all right, Henry." Luke shot him a reassuring smile. "I can't either."

Henry frowned, his leathery face wrinkling into an expression of total bemusement. "Why do you think he took off that way?"

"I don't know," Luke answered thoughtfully. "I guess he'll have to tell us when he comes back."

"You think he will?"

Luke nodded. "Yes."

"Well, I sure as hell hope so," Henry said, thinking of Darby and Birdie, whose eyes echoed their hurt at his hasty, wordless departure.

The week drew on, and Mrs. Brunsteader fussed over Luke like a mother hen, changing his bandages daily and feeding him till he thought he would burst. He found that living in the house was not so bad and decided he would continue to do so even after he rebuilt his stables, at least for the time being.

He knew rebuilding would take some time. His funds were low, and neither he nor Ian were physically up to the job. That left only a handful of stable hands, and he knew he would have to let them go. He could no longer afford to pay them.

Before dawn the following morning, he called them together and said, "You all know I don't have the work to keep you busy anymore."

Understanding his predicament, several of the stable hands left to seek work elsewhere. But Tom, Eddie, and Ian—propped up by his crutches—said they'd stay on for room and board. They said they believed in Kentucky Blue and what he could do. They said they believed in Luke too, and that they could wait for the coming Fall Meets to collect their wages.

Later that afternoon Bo came by and told him he felt the same. He said he had a little extra money put by, and he had no intention of riding any other horse but Kentucky Blue across a finish line.

Luke slept a little better that night, and Saturday morning, to his surprise, Henry Greene and several of the surrounding farmers banded together with some of the local horse breeders and their jockeys, trainers, and stable hands, and showed up at his door. By dusk that evening, Luke had new stables.

The week after the fire passed in a dull haze for Darby. She grieved Yancey's disappearance, along with the loss of Luke's horses and Lady Effie's injury. She didn't know what to think about Luke where Blue was concerned. She didn't know if he would continue Blue's training or whether, as some folks speculated, he would give up and sell the farm.

What she did know was that her dream of building a Thoroughbred farm of her own was not dead. It would never die.

She knew her father had gone to see Luke, to tell him about Lady Effie. When she asked him if Luke had said anything, Henry just told her to be patient—he was sure Luke would be out to see her once he'd had time to think things through.

So she tried to be patient and she tried to keep busy. She helped an unusually quiet Aunt Birdie with the chores around the house, and she rose early every morning and led Blue through his figure eights. She changed Effie's bandages daily just as Doc Landers had taught her, and she spent long hours talking to the filly and Blue in an effort to ease her own loneliness.

But the days drew on endlessly nevertheless. She missed the daily routine of the stables. She missed working with Luke, Bo, and Yancey, along with the rest of the outfit.

On Saturday afternoon, a week after the fire had taken place, Jeffrey Morgan rode out to see her.

She was out in the corral, walking Blue, her mind rolling back to the sunny day a year ago when Luke and Bo had come to tell her that they'd decided to accept her offer.

"Hello, Darby!" Jeffrey called out, breaking into her thoughts.

Darby looked up to see him picking his way across the yard through a dozen or so chickens that pecked eagerly over the fresh feed that Aunt Birdie had just thrown them.

She led Blue up to the fence. "Hello, Jeffrey."

"Gee, Darby, I'm sorry to hear about the fire. Your friend sure took a beating."

"Yes, he did." Darby's ache for Luke had not lessened.

Jeffrey nodded at the big black colt. "This is your horse?"

"Yes," Darby said, and smiled.

"Wow, he's beautiful!" There was genuine admiration in his tone.

"I think so."

His gaze came back to hers. "I hope I'm not interrupting you."

Darby shook her head. "We're ready for a rest."

Jeffrey shifted his weight, pocketed his hands, and his steady blue-gray gaze caught and held her hazel one. "I hope you won't think I'm too bold, but I have to tell you I haven't been able to quit thinking about you, Darby."

She blushed, and Jeffrey rushed on. "I would like to spend some time with you now that I'm home."

He fell silent, and Darby lowered her gaze as she searched for the right words to put him off. "Oh, Jeffrey," she said, "I'm so flattered, but—"

"You already care for someone else." It was a statement, not a question.

Darby's eyes flicked back up to his. He was a very astute young man. "I guess you could say that."

He smiled. His smile was warm and understanding. "Do you want to tell me who he is?"

"Not really."

"But he's not a real beau?" Jeffrey said, cocking his head, remembering what she'd told him the day of Emma's wedding.

"Well, no," Darby hedged, "not in the true sense of the word."

"Then I have a chance." He held his hands out at his sides. Darby laughed, amused by his persistence. "Oh, Jeffrey . . ."

"C'mon," he said, his smile bright, "we'll have fun together, and if after a while you still feel the same for this fellow, you can tell me, and we'll remain the best of friends."

Darby searched her mind for an argument. "It doesn't seem very fair to you."

"Let me worry about what's fair for me. I'm a big boy now." His eyes were gentle on her face. "You don't have to protect me any longer, Darby."

Darby shook her head and lowered her gaze, warmth blooming within for the handsome young man who stood before her, so earnestly offering his attentions. "I don't know what to say."

"Say, 'Yes, Jeffrey, I would love you to escort me to church tomorrow morning!' "

She was quiet a long time, searching her mind for a valid reason not to accept the offer of his company. The sun shone down on them, and Blue nudged her with his nose. Then she lifted her eyes to his and smiled. "Yes, Jeffrey, I would like that very much."

"You sure you won't come to church with us, Aunt Birdie?" Darby asked, standing out on the porch the next morning while Jeffrey waited for her in his fancy new rig.

Birdie shook her head and smiled, her big brown eyes echoing an unspoken anguish. "Not this Sunday, honey. I'm not feeling myself."

Her eyes sympathetic, Darby sighed, knowing it was useless to argue with her. "I'll be home right after services."

"That's fine, Darby Lynn."

Darby turned, and Birdie watched her go. Her niece looked lovely dressed in a lavender silk blouse and a long flared skirt. Jeffrey leapt down from his seat and came around to greet her, handing her up into the buggy. Darby smiled at him, but Birdie knew there was something lacking in her smile. Jeffrey Morgan was a very nice young man, and it was obvious he had every intention of pursuing Darby, but Birdie also knew that Darby's heart belonged to another, and she understood the quiet reservation in her niece's eyes only too well.

She turned and walked back into the kitchen, her heart a heavy stone in her chest. Word traveled fast, and though Henry and Luke still refused to give credence to the rumor, it was common knowledge that Yancey was suspected of having set the fire at Rhinehart Stables. Folks said he'd probably lit out once he'd been paid for the deed.

Birdie could not accept the thought, so she simply tried not to think about it at all.

But at night, when she lay alone in her virginal bed, she stared into the darkness and thought of Yancey. She thought about the way he'd kissed her, the way he'd held her, the way he'd gazed down into her eyes, and her lonely heart ached for an explanation.

Jeffrey was pulling away from the house when Luke galloped into the yard on Toby.

He sat his horse with his usual easy confidence. He was dressed in black boots, brown britches, and a red plaid shirt, dented by wide black suspenders. He looked ready for work. His black hair fell across his forehead and gleamed in the bright morning sunshine; his blue eyes were clear and sharp and decisive. "Morning, Darby," he said quietly, then looked over at Jeffrey and nodded a greeting.

"Good morning, Luke," Jeffrey returned with an easy smile. "How are your hands?"

A slight smile touched one side of Luke's mouth. He held

one bandaged hand up. "Better, but these bandages are awkward as hell."

"I imagine so. I heard Doc Adams is taking care of you, but feel welcome to stop by my new office anytime if you have any problems with the healing. My office is located on Green Street, not far from Baxter Square."

Luke nodded. "Thank you. I'll keep that in mind." He turned to Darby. "You know the stables are back up, thanks to your father and many other good men."

"Yes." Darby smiled. "That's wonderful."

"I've come to get Blue and Effie," he said resolutely.

Darby's eyes brightened. "Oh, Luke," she said, her smile growing. He hadn't given up, and she was so proud of him. "I'm so glad." She wanted to get down out of the buggy to go with him, to help him collect the horses, but she didn't. Instead, she thought of Jeffrey, who sat so patiently beside her, and she said, "Eugene and Pa are out in the barn. I'm sure they'll help you."

Luke nodded and turned, then over his shoulder said, "Just so you know, training resumes tomorrow morning at dawn."

✦ 10 ✦

EARLY THE NEXT morning Luke called Darby into his new office. It was a small room, empty of furnishings as yet, located in the back of the stables as his previous office had been.

Once inside, he turned to her and said, "For the time being the outfit has been narrowed down to myself, Eddie, Tom, Ian, Bo, and you. Ian won't be able to ride for a while, and I need an exercise rider to cover for Bo. There's only one of us light enough for the job."

She waited for him to continue.

"I'd like you to be here an hour earlier every morning. I'll teach you how to put Blue through his paces."

Surprised, she studied him in silence. She'd always wanted to ride Blue, but both Luke and Bo had always discouraged it. Blue was a racehorse, they said, not a pet. She'd come to understand why they said that, even to see the wisdom in that protestation, but now the thought of actually riding him brought a rush of secret pleasure and anticipation.

"Well?" he said, cocking a dark eyebrow. "Do you want the job or not?"

"Of course," she said quietly. "You know I do."

He put his hands on his hips and went on. "I'd like you to trot Effie around the track every day too. She knows the track by heart and, despite her injury, she needs her exercise. If all goes well, I'll breed her next spring."

Darby nodded her acquiescence.

He fell silent, and she turned to go.

"Darby," he said, halting her.

She turned, and their troubled gazes locked.

"I'd like you to come in on Sunday mornings too." He paused, then said, "Early." He felt a twinge of guilt at the selfish request, and he wondered if she would refuse. He knew the request was for himself, not for Blue. Blue's exercise could wait until after Darby had gotten home from church, until after Jeffrey Morgan had left her at her door.

Bemused by his request, she was silent another moment. She knew he was short-handed now that Yancey was gone and he'd let the other stable hands go, but she also knew that without the other horses, the workload had also been significantly reduced. She suspected his true motive and was puzzled by it, but she finally nodded and said, "All right." Then she turned and walked out the door.

The hot summer days passed in a whirl of sweat and dust as Luke and Bo taught Darby how to exercise a Thoroughbred. They taught her how to sit a racehorse correctly, how to ride high in the saddle and lean low over the horse's neck, how to slow him down and speed him up. They even taught her how to fall and roll away from the horse's hooves should that action ever be necessary.

Riding the big stallion was a heady experience for her. The power of his fluent stride amazed her. When he was not on the racetrack, Blue was like a big, happy puppy, but on the track something happened, and he became a wildfire stoked by the wind. It took all her strength to remain on his back.

Luke warned her against ever letting him open up entirely. That part of Blue's training was for Bo and Bo alone.

Darby respected Luke's warning. In truth, she was happy just to ride Blue, just to be able to have a part in his training.

As the days wore on, they all missed Yancey, but his name was rarely mentioned. Sheriff Roth didn't come up with any other suspects, and Luke was not surprised. Roth's investigation into Benjamin Rhinehart's shooting six years ago had yielded nothing as well.

So Luke took precautions of his own. He put a cot back in his office, and he, Ian, Tom, and Eddie took nightly turns at guard duty, while they tried to concentrate on the coming Fall Meets.

Darby worked hard to cover Yancey's work along with her own. She went home bone tired and exhausted, yet she felt an exhilarating sense of accomplishment as she watched Blue's development and progress.

He was doing wonderfully, but he'd grown a bit stubborn about some things. He seemed to know Effie had been hurt and he refused to leave his stall in the mornings or run the training track unless Darby led the filly out with him.

One day while they were out at the track, Darby turned to Luke and asked, "What are you going to do when we have to take him over to the track for the Fall Meet? He won't want to go without Effie."

Luke shrugged, then simply said, "Then we'll take her too."

Conversation between Darby and Luke had become stilted once again, confined strictly to work matters. But there were times when the rigors of the day had taken their toll, and their guards were down, their gazes locked and a host of unspoken words passed between them.

Darby knew it was better that the words remain unspoken. Though her heart still ached to hear words of affection from Luke, and her body still ached for Luke's touch, Jeffrey was fast becoming a part of her life. He came courting regularly, even though he had to wait till the evening hours to see her. He didn't seem to mind, though. His new practice and patients were taking up a great deal of his time as well.

June swept by, and July sizzled in. Ian's leg began to heal, and Luke was finally able to work without the bandages on his hands.

On the second Wednesday morning of July, the Reverend Johnson rode out to the stables to find Bo.

His expression solemn, he climbed down out of his buggy and walked over to where Darby and Luke stood, watching Bo race Blue down the backstretch.

"Hello, Reverend," Darby said with a smile.

"Hello, Darby," the reverend returned soberly. His kindly face was bereft of anything even resembling a smile. He turned to Luke. "I need to talk to Bo, if I could."

Hearing the seriousness in his tone, Luke waited till Bo rounded the turn, then lifted his arm and waved him in.

Concerned, Darby wanted to ask what was wrong, but she didn't want to pry.

Sensing her hesitancy, the reverend answered the question for her. "It's Millie," he said quietly, his eyes clouded with sorrow. "She's losing the baby."

"Oh," Darby said, taking his hand. "I'm so sorry . . ."

Bo pulled Blue up. He swung down from the horse and handed the reins to Luke. "Hello, Reverend," Bo said pleasantly. "What brings you out?"

"It's Millie, Bo," he said without preamble. "You should come home, son. She's losing the baby."

Bo's face paled instantly.

"She came over to the house this morning after you left. She said she wasn't feeling well, so we sent for Jeffrey Morgan. By the time he got there, it was too late. There isn't anything he can do."

"Jesus," Bo swore softly without diffidence to his father-in-law's vocation.

Luke put a hand on Bo's shoulder. "Go home, Bo."

Bo nodded and ran for the stables. Within seconds he was on his horse and galloping through the wide-open doors, racing for town.

Darby and Luke walked the reverend back to his buggy. The reverend climbed up into his seat, then looked down at Darby. "Stop and see Millie after a few days, won't you?"

Darby nodded and patted his arm. "Of course I will."

When Bo reached the Reverend Johnson's house, he didn't bother to tether his horse's reins, but jumped down and ran into the house, then took the stairs up to the second level by twos.

He ran down the hall, searching frantically for Millie's old bedroom, and was met at the door by Rose Johnson, looking weary and sad. "Come in, Bo," she said kindly, stepping sideways so he could enter the pretty, feminine room.

Bo stood silent and uncertain as Jeffrey Morgan rose from the chair beside Millie's bed and took her hand. "You'll have more babies, Millie. You're young and healthy," he said quietly, giving her hand a gentle squeeze.

She nodded while tears leaked out of her eyes and slid down the sides of her temples into her thick red hair. Her hair seemed unusually bright against the white pillow.

Bo approached the bed, his heart thumping, his throat aching. Millie turned her head to look at him, her blue eyes filling with a fresh rush of tears. "Oh, Bo," she said, aggrieved, "I lost our baby."

Their gazes held, and they both realized at that moment how very much they had come to want the baby despite the fact that its conception had been untimely, even had seemed a bane to them both. The child had still been a part of each of them.

Now it was gone, and the void it left behind was a gaping, empty wound and a poignant feeling of loss.

Jeffrey walked away from the bed and with a silent nod to Bo he and Mrs. Johnson quietly left the room, closing the door behind them.

Bo reached out and took Millie's hand, sinking down onto the bed beside her. "Shhh," he whispered. "Don't cry, Millie." With his other hand he wiped the tears that seeped out of the corners of her eyes and pushed her hair back from her pale face. But her tears came fast and furious, and he couldn't keep up with them. "I'm so sorry, honey . . ." The words caught in his throat, and he leaned over and hugged her gently, laying his golden head upon her breast. Millie reached up and cupped his head to her chest.

Then, quite suddenly, a sob tore loose from his throat, and Bo let go and wept out loud—for Millie, for himself, and for the little baby girl they would never know.

After that day Bo was different. He began to spend more time at home.

Luke wondered if he did so out of guilt, but Darby believed that Bo had changed somehow. He still smiled and teased a lot, but he seemed more responsible as time went by, and he seemed eager to get home to Millie at the end of each day.

Bo and Darby were not the only ones to recognize a change in Bo.

Katrina was furious.

She had not seen him since the beginning of June. She'd heard that his wife had miscarried their baby, so she waited, certain that he would soon grow bored with his little Methodist wife.

But time drew on, and still he did not come to her. Her fury began to fester into a poisonous rage.

August rolled into September, and October rode in on a blaze of autumn color.

Blue's training grew more intense. He looked wonderful; his times on the track were excellent. Luke seemed pleased, though there was always a reserved quality to his praise. But Bo told Darby that he'd never seen anything like Blue and that next year's Derby was theirs for sure.

Early one morning, before Darby fed Blue, she sought out Luke. Jeffrey had begged her to take off time for a picnic. The weather had been especially pleasant and mild, and she'd finally given in to his request.

She knocked on Luke's office door.

"Come in!" he called out.

She turned the knob and entered the room, which now boasted a neatly made cot and a small, scarred, serviceable desk, cluttered with a lamp, a coffee cup, and countless news-papers. The walls were tacked with clippings about other horses and their statistics. Luke claimed it was good business to keep an eye on the competition.

He looked up from the newspaper he was reading. "The bookmakers have Blue's odds at three to ten," he said matter-of-factly.

"That's good, isn't it?" she asked.

A smile stretched across his face, reaching clear up to his eyes, and Darby felt a sweet tingle of pleasure at the sight. She had always loved his smile. "He's the favorite," Luke announced with quiet satisfaction.

"Oh, that's wonderful, Luke!" she said, almost forgetting the reason she had sought him out. Their gazes clung, and they shared a quiet moment of gratification. They had worked so hard; they had dared to dream, and tomorrow's race brought them one step closer to the fulfillment of that dream.

Awareness bloomed between them, and his gaze dropped to her mouth. She lowered her gaze to the neckline of his shirt, where dark, curly hair sprang out from the open V. She wished he would touch her. He wondered how much longer he could keep himself from doing just that.

The moment stretched on and grew awkward. He looked back down at his newspaper. She pushed her wispy bangs out of her eyes and said, "I wanted to let you know that I'll be gone for a while today. I'll be back this evening, though, to give Blue his bath."

Surprised, his gaze came back to hers, and he raised his brows. She'd never asked for time off. "Something wrong?" he asked, curious, his blue eyes penetrating.

She shook her head. "No."

He waited for her to explain, and when she didn't, he knew it was Jeffrey Morgan. He knew it as surely as he knew the sun would set that evening. She was going to spend the af-ternoon with him. Irritation lit within, and he fought the urge to tell her she couldn't go, that she had to stay, that he needed her there, but reason intruded and he remembered that in truth he worked for her. He had no right to make demands on her time, even though he had done so.

He had no right to try to keep her from the young doctor. Yet he was guilty of that too.

Regardless of his common sense, jealousy became a living, breathing thing within him, and he remembered the conversation Bo had instigated only yesterday.

"You know, Luke," Bo had said, his brown eyes uncharacteristically wise, "that young doctor sure has taken a likin' to our Darby." At Luke's silence he'd continued. "Seems to me there comes a time when a man has to look inside himself and decide what really matters the most to him." He'd given Luke a long, hard look. "How long you gonna wait before you tell Darby you love her?"

"What makes you think I love her?" Luke had barked.

"Hell, Luke," Bo had said on a short huff of laughter, "it's plain as the hair on your head every time you look at her. I knew it months ago." He'd paused a moment, then said, "I wouldn't wait too damn long if I was you. You just might lose this race."

"Luke?" Darby said, calling him back, a question in her voice and eyes.

With the memory of Bo's words haunting him, Luke forced the invisible curtain to fall down over his face. "All right, then." His tone revealed none of his turbulent emotions. He returned his attention to the newspaper spread out before him.

"All right, then," Darby repeated, wishing he'd said he couldn't spare her on this important day—the day before Blue's first Fall Meet.

But he hadn't. And she knew he wouldn't. So she turned and left his office to see to her morning chores.

Dressed in a simple blue gingham dress, Darby sat on one of Aunt Birdie's patchwork quilts. She leaned back on her hands and tipped her face up to the warm autumn sun.

"I'm so glad you came," Jeffrey said, stretching out on his side beside her.

"Me too," Darby said, smiling, her eyes closed.

He lifted himself up onto one elbow and propped his head in his hand. "You work too hard, Darby. You spend so much time out at the stables."

She opened her eyes. "It's worth it to me, though. Blue is a very special horse, and I'm so lucky to have him. My hopes and dreams are all tied up in him. I need him to win tomorrow's meet, and then the Derby next year, so I can build my own breeding farm one day."

"Is that what you really want?" he asked, searching her face intently.

"More than anything." Darby's voice was soft, wistful.

Jeffrey was silent a moment. "What about a family, Darby? What about children? Do you ever think about having a family of your own, about having a husband?"

She smiled and averted her gaze. "Oh, I suppose I do at times."

A thoughtful silence fell between them. The meadow was alive with the sounds and sights of autumn. A warm wind whispered through the brilliantly colored leaves, while a blue jay complained shrilly, swooped low, then sailed back up into the blue, cloudless sky.

Jeffrey reached out and covered her hand where it lay on the quilt. "I would take good care of you, Darby," he said quietly, earnestly, breaking the silence, willing her to look at him. "You would want for nothing. And if, after having our children, you still wanted to raise horses, well . . . I would not mind. In a couple of years I should be able to buy a sizable piece of land and build you a house and a fine stable. . . ." His voice trailed off, and she lowered her gaze and studied his chest while he studied her face.

Time ticked on while around them flies buzzed lazily, and somewhere off in the distance a dog barked. In time, she looked into his eyes again. He was so sincere, so undeniably handsome that she wondered why she could not feel anything more for him beyond a warm and abiding friendship. His gaze dropped to her lips, and she knew that he was going to kiss her. She did not draw away.

Maybe if he did, she thought, she would feel something more.

He leaned in close and pressed his lips to hers. His lips were warm and silky as they moved over hers. When his tongue slipped inside her mouth, she hesitantly answered, hoping for the slow tingle to begin, for that wonderful shattering response that Luke's kisses had ignited. He wrapped his arms around her and pressed her back onto the quilt, and she let herself melt beneath him. He threaded his fingers into her hair, and she stroked his shoulders, waiting, waiting, for that feeling to take her.

But it didn't.

When he lifted his head and stared down into her face, she found herself comparing the shade of his blue-gray eyes with Luke's much bluer ones.

She knew that she would never love him as she did Luke. No matter how much time passed, regardless of Jeffrey's kindness and success, regardless of the unconditional love he would give her, her heart would always belong to another.

That same night Raymond Miller came to see Bo at his home. Millie answered the door. She knew who he was and politely ushered him into the small entryway of their house.

"Mrs. Denton," Miller boomed, "how nice to see you up and about! I was so sorry to hear of your loss."

Millie attempted a smile. She'd heard about the race between Knightwind and Phantom and she knew Miller had quite a reputation for being relentless in his desire to win a race despite the cost to his horse or anyone else's. "Yes, well, thank you, Mr. Miller. I suppose you're here to see my husband, so if you'll excuse me, I'll go find him." She turned to see Bo coming out of the parlor. Relieved, she took her leave, then made her way back to the kitchen, where she was preparing dinner.

"Hello, Denton," Miller greeted Bo warmly, offering his hand.

"Miller," Bo said with reserve, though he shook the man's hand.

"I apologize for seeking you out here, but I didn't feel I should go to Rhinehart Stables to discuss this matter."

Bo looked skeptical, but he turned and led the way into the parlor. "I hope you're not going to ask me to jockey for you again," he said over his shoulder as he filled two glasses with a generous portion of bourbon.

"No, that's not what I'm going to do," Miller said, accepting the glass from Bo's hand. "At least not at first."

Bo sat down in a leather chair and gestured for Raymond to do the same in the one across from him. "Then why are you here?"

Miller lowered himself into the chair. "Because I intend to win the Derby next year."

Bo's expression was impassive. "I think I remember you telling me that same thing the day Knightwind died."

Miller shook his head sadly. "Nasty shame, wasn't it? He was such a beautiful horse."

"You played a part in his death," Bo said coolly, taking a sip from his glass, finding it hard to control his irritation with the other man.

Miller smiled amiably and lifted his glass. "I offered Rhinehart a challenge. He accepted. I can't help it if his horse wasn't up to the challenge. That's why I'm here. Kentucky Blue won't be up to the challenge either."

Bo's usually friendly gaze hardened. "What do you want, Miller?"

"I want you to throw tomorrow's race."

"Why?" Bo asked, his curiosity rife, his gaze sharp.

"I have my reasons."

Bo was silent a moment. He studied Miller behind heavy-lidded eyes. "You're jealous, aren't you?" he stated at length. "You haven't run Phantom against Kentucky Blue because you know damn well Blue would beat him and ruin his record of being undefeated.''

Miller's face reddened, but he shook his head in denial. ''Really, Denton, don't you think you're deduction is a bit adolescent?''

''Not for you it isn't.''

''Throw the race, Denton,'' Miller urged again.

Bo shook his head. ''Forget it.''

''Your loyalty to Richards and the Greene girl is admirable, but with the misfortune Richards suffered, I know he can't be paying you all that well. I also know the girl doesn't have any money. Every successful jockey should have enough good sense to contract himself to the person who can pay him the best. Throw the race tomorrow, and I'll make it worth your while, and you'll have a champion to run next year in the Derby.''

Bo stared at Miller in cold silence. There was an element of truth to what he said. His funds were getting low, and he could use the money. But he would never betray Luke or Darby. Not for any amount of money. If Blue placed well tomorrow, and Bo knew that he would, the outfit at Rhinehart Stables would have a payday. They'd all manage. He stood. ''I have a champion, Miller. The only one I need is Kentucky Blue.''

Miller rose, and the smile slipped from his face. ''You're a fool, Denton. That horse will break down on you just like his father did.''

''Maybe,'' Bo said quietly, ''but I wouldn't bet on it if I were you.''

In a seedy little saloon down on the riverfront, Bradley Rhinehart sat in a shadowy corner, drinking himself into a dull stupor. He was alone and lonely, tense and nervous. He'd placed the last of the money his uncle had paid him for the farm with a bookmaker that very afternoon, on tomorrow's race, on a horse named Bright Hope.

This time he was determined to collect his winnings. This

time he would do what he had to do to change the trend of his bad luck.

After her picnic with Jeffrey, Darby changed her clothes and rode out to the stables. The late-afternoon sun was already slipping down behind the Kentucky hills.

When she arrived at the stables, she immediately busied herself with Blue's bath, while the evening shadows crept across the stables.

Bo had gone home hours before, and Ian, Eddie, and Tom had retired to the bunkhouse.

Darby figured Luke must be in his office.

She thought it was just as well. She wanted to be alone with her thoughts. Tomorrow was an important day; the outcome of the race could make or break them. Darby knew they needed the purse money a first-place victory would bring them to get them through the long winter months ahead.

As she tended to Blue, twilight fell, and the gentle sound of cicadas sang out into the night.

She was so lost in her thoughts that his voice startled her. "Mrs. Brunsteader has dinner ready," Luke said matter-of-factly from the door of Blue's stall.

Darby glanced up at him.

"She said to ask you to join us." He found himself hoping she would accept.

"No, thanks," she answered quietly, returning her attention to Blue. "I'm not hungry." She busied herself with drizzling water down Blue's face. She felt Luke's gaze on her but she didn't look at him. She didn't trust herself. Just a few hours earlier she'd lain with Jeffrey and allowed him to kiss her, even kissed him back as she had never kissed anyone but Luke. She was sure that if she looked at Luke now, he would know, and though he had no claim on her and obviously didn't want one, she felt that she had betrayed him somehow.

"Well," he said, and shifted his weight onto the opposite foot, "I'll be up at the house if you need me. I won't be long. It's my turn for guard duty tonight."

"All right," Darby said, still refusing to look at him.

He turned to go, then hesitated, glancing back over his shoulder at her. "Darby," he said quietly, hating himself for what he was about to ask. But he had to know, even though the knowing would be torture.

"Yes?" She dropped her guard and lifted her eyes to his.

"Did you have a nice time today?"

Her lips parted, and she blushed. His chest tightened. He nodded and walked away. He'd received his answer.

Confused and frustrated, Darby wanted to call after him: *This is what you wanted, isn't it? You don't want me. You can't love me. What do you expect me to do?* But the words got caught in her throat, and so she said nothing.

"Oh, Blue," she whispered after he'd left. She laid her cheek against the colt's velvety muzzle. "What am I gonna do?" He snorted softly, and she hugged his damp neck.

A half hour passed.

As Darby rinsed Blue's legs off, she heard a sound behind her and turned, expecting to see Luke once again.

But it wasn't Luke who stood in the doorway of Blue's stall.

"So, this is the great Kentucky Blue," Bradley Rhinehart slurred thickly.

Darby recognized him at once. She instinctively put herself between Rhinehart and Blue. "What do you want, Mr. Rhinehart?" she asked, her voice polite and steady, though an alarm rang out in her brain.

"I want what belongs to me, but since I can't have it, I'll take care of things another way." There was an unmistakable threat to his words.

She was silent only a moment, then she quietly said, "I think you should leave."

Bradley laughed harshly. "Do you now?" He reached down into his crumpled suit coat and brought out a knife.

Fear ripped through her. The knife looked sharp and deadly.

"A little slice to a few tendons and that horse won't run tomorrow. He won't race ever again."

"Why would you do such a terrible thing?" Darby asked, trying to stall for time. She wanted to scream for Luke or the stable hands, but she was afraid if she did, she would force Bradley's hand. And she knew she was not strong enough to hold him off herself.

Bradley's eyes glazed over, and his expression grew morose. "I have no choice, you see?" he said with something akin to an apology in his tone. "I have nothing left."

Her mind churning, Darby's frantic gaze swept the stall, finally lighting on the pitchfork she'd left standing in the corner. There was not an ounce of hesitation or fear as she lurched for it. She lifted it, training it on Bradley's bulging stomach. "Get away," she warned, her voice low.

"Aw, c'mon now," Bradley slurred. "Just what do you think you're gonna do with that?"

"Run it through you if I have to," Darby said, her voice hard with purpose.

"I don't think you will."

"I think she will," Luke said from behind.

Darby turned her head toward where he stood in the shadows, and Bradley spun around to face him.

"Put the knife away, Bradley," Luke said tiredly.

Bradley lurched for him, but he was so drunk he lost his balance and fell to his knees. Luke wasted no time in kicking the knife out of his hand. Bradley grasped for Luke's trouser leg, but Luke agilely sidestepped him and shoved Bradley back down onto the floor. "Jesus, Bradley, what do you think you're doing here?" he asked in disgust, putting himself in front of Darby and Blue.

Darby clung to the pitchfork, refusing to relax her grip until she knew all threat of danger was past.

"Isn't that obvious?" Bradley flopped onto his back. "Making a fool of myself." He gave a harsh, bitter laugh. "Actually I'm trying to injure your horse," he said truthfully, "except I can't even do that right."

Luke felt a hot flare of anger, but surprisingly enough, he also felt a conflicting pang of pity for the man sprawled out on the dusty floor before him. Bradley's clothing was stained and crumpled, his face unshaven and dirty. He looked much older than his thirty-six years. To look at him, one would never know he had grown up with every opportunity. He was such a tortured soul who had brought nothing but hardship to his life at every turn.

"Why would you want to do that?" Luke asked, frowning, wondering if someone had paid him to hurt Blue, wondering if Bradley had been the man responsible for the fire that had killed his horses and ravaged his stables.

"Because I have nothing to lose," Bradley said, his voice full of self-pity. He struggled to sit up. "I've lost everything. You have what should have been mine."

Luke's patience snapped. "It's your own damn fault, Bradley! Everything your father ever built you all but destroyed with your addictions! Everything he ever did for you, you threw back in his face. Do you really think you can blame anyone else! For God's sake, man, take a good look at yourself and quit wallowing in self-pity!"

Bradley looked up at him through bleary, bloodshot eyes.

"Did you start the fire too?" Luke asked curtly, pushing his fingers through his dark hair in a gesture of frustration.

Bradley coughed out another short, bitter laugh. "I'd like to say I did. At least that was a success."

"I guess in your eyes it was," Luke said, forcing himself to rein in his temper. It was a difficult task, however. He thought of Effie and her injury, and the horses that had died in the fire that night, and he felt rage ignite and the need for justice burn hot in his breast. But somehow his instincts told him that that need would not be satisfied by striking out at Bradley.

He turned to Darby and took the pitchfork from her hands. "Are you all right, Darby?" he asked quietly, unable to mask the tenderness that crept into his gaze.

Darby managed a shaky smile. "I'm fine."

Luke turned back to Bradley, and his voice hardened. "Go on home, Bradley, and we'll forget this ever happened. I don't even want to waste my time on you, but the next time I catch you on my property, I'll put a bullet into your hide and ask questions later."

Bradley laughed again. The sound was harsh, humorless. "I'd really like to oblige you, but I'd rather you called out the sheriff. You see, I have no home to go to or any money to rent a room. At least in jail I'll have a place to sleep for the time being."

"What are you talking about?" Luke frowned.

"Oh," Bradley said, sobering somewhat. "You didn't know that Rhinehart Farms belongs to my uncle Nathaniel now?" At Luke's look of confusion, Bradley went on. "He was after it all along. It was only a matter of time."

Surprised by that revelation, Luke was silent a moment. There was much about Nathaniel Rhinehart that Luke did not understand, much he did not trust. But it seemed as though time was stripping away the mysteries surrounding the man, layer by layer.

Bradley coughed, and Luke's thoughts came back to the problem at hand. Bradley was such a pitiful sight.

He remembered Benjamin Rhinehart's kindness. He'd been a young trainer with a heart full of dreams, and Benjamin had given him a chance to make those dreams realities.

He returned his attention to Bradley. He and Bradley never liked each other, but Luke knew that Benjamin, though disappointed in his only son, had loved him dearly. Luke also knew what it was like to have no family and no place he could call home. His heart twisted with empathy and he tried to sort through a surge of conflicting emotions. "Are you telling me you don't have anywhere to go?" he asked at last.

"Exactly," Bradley said. He blinked, then burped loudly.

Luke sighed heavily, weighing the wisdom of his decision. It could be a very costly decision. But it was the only decision he could make.

With a quick glance at Darby, he leaned down and offered

Bradley his hand. "I have room for you here if you want to stay, but you'll have to pull your own weight if you want to get paid and you want to eat. You'll have to work right along with the rest of us."

Bradley eyed Luke's hand for the space of several moments. He'd never done a day's labor in his entire life. But he had no friends, no family, no money, no hope. He didn't even have a clean change of clothes.

He had nothing but the offer of Luke's outstretched hand. With a muffled sob, he reached out and took it.

❖ *11* ❖

THE NEXT MORNING dawned clear and bright.

The grandstand at Churchill Downs filled early with spectators from all over the state. The bright flags atop the spirals whipped wildly in the wind, while a rainbow of ladies' frilly parasols paled in splendor against the colorful backdrop of the surrounding trees.

Escorted by their elegantly clad gentlemen, the fashionably dressed ladies held their parasols high, shielding their faces from the warm autumn sun while they exchanged tidbits of gossip and speculated on the outcome of the day's race.

Darby wore brown britches and a bright red shirt and stood in the saddling area, holding Effie's halter and watching Bo trot Blue around the track. Blue held his head high. His coat shimmered with blue highlights in the brilliant autumn sun. Darby felt a swell of pride and love for the colt, and, yes, she felt fear for him too. Fear that he was just too perfect, too fast, that his pure, smooth, effortless speed would be his undoing, as it had been his father's.

She watched the other horses. Six strong contenders, the most threatening rumored to be Bright Hope, a big bay colt from Tennessee.

Horses came from all over the country to race at the Spring and Fall Meets at Churchill Downs, but nothing excited the crowd more than a horse born and bred in their home state, a horse like Knightwind, a horse like Kentucky Blue.

Luke took his place at Darby's side. "He looks good," he said after some time, glancing down at her. He wondered if she knew how pretty she looked, standing there with the sunshine glinting off her chestnut hair, her round cheeks flushed with excitement, her nose dusted with freckles.

"Yes, he does," Darby said, feeling the familiar rush of warmth Luke's presence always brought. She thought about last night, about Bradley and his pitiful attempt to hurt Blue. She thought about Luke and his compassionate response to Bradley's plight. After a few moments her thoughts found their way into words. "It was a kind thing you did for Bradley."

Luke shrugged and pocketed his hands. "I hope it wasn't a mistake." He looked out at the track, his gaze sharp as he studied Blue's movements. "Benjamin Rhinehart was good to me. Offering a bed to his son was the least I could do, although I have to admit it seems odd to offer a man a bed in what was once his own home."

Understanding his conflicting feelings about that odd development, Darby turned to him. "I suppose it would still be his home had he made better choices. You shouldn't blame yourself for his loss. From what I can see, Mr. Rhinehart left the stables to you because he knew you would do your best to continue in his footsteps. He trusted you."

"I suppose so," Luke agreed, silently acknowledging that she was right. Benjamin had taken a gamble on leaving Bradley the breeding farm, hoping he would take good care of the horses, hoping he could make a new start and a better life for himself. Luke was glad Benjamin did not know that Bradley had failed him again.

"Where is Bradley now?" Darby said, glancing around.

"He didn't want to come. He grumbled something about not wanting to see the last of his money float into the wind. So he stayed behind at the stables. He's supposed to be cleaning out Effie's and Blue's stalls." A small smile tugged at

Luke's mouth. "I wasn't kidding when I said he'd have to earn his keep like the rest of us."

"Do you think he'll stay?"

"I don't know. We'll see."

Darby fell silent. "How do you think his uncle got the farm from him?"

Luke's expression hardened. "I'd be willing to bet it had something to do with Bradley's gambling debts."

"But why would he take his own nephew's home away from him?"

Luke turned to her. He lifted one dark brow. "Maybe he believed that it should have been his all along."

They abandoned the topic of conversation as Ian, Eddie, and Tom joined them, and they all turned their attention to the track.

The riders circled once as they approached their starting positions. The track was dry and fast. Bo looked over at his outfit, then over at the nearly full grandstand and clubhouse. From their seats Jeffrey Morgan, Henry Greene, Birdie, and Millie caught his eye and waved to him. He returned their wave and felt the expected, familiar jolt of excitement shimmy down through his limbs. He loved being on the track. He loved having a horse like Blue beneath him.

Bright Hope approached on the left, and Bo gave him a curious glance. He was a fine-looking horse, but Bo was not intimidated any more than Blue was. They both loved a challenge.

The seven horses took their places, and the crowd hushed in anticipation.

The seconds ticked on, then suddenly the flag dropped and the horses bolted from their starting positions.

Kentucky Blue broke perfectly, but Bright Hope stumbled a bit, then recovered immediately.

The two inside horses edged slightly in front of Kentucky Blue, but Bo didn't panic. He knew he could pass them anytime he wanted to. He let the reins out slightly and allowed Blue to settle into his long stride. Within seconds he pulled ahead. He stayed well out from the rail, a full length in front, but Bo was aware that Bright Hope and a chestnut colt were coming out of the pack. Both horses were pressing close behind, not giving way.

Bo gave Blue a little nudge of encouragement, and he shot forward, but at the same time, out of the corner of his eye, Bo noticed that Bright Hope was gaining, pulling away from the chestnut colt, challenging Blue for the lead.

And then it happened.

For one split second Bright Hope was neck and neck with Blue, then suddenly he pushed his nose out into the lead.

The crowd gasped, rising from their seats.

Darby's hold on Effie's halter tightened, and Luke held his breath.

Bo knew what to do. He rose high in his stirrups, let Blue's reins out even more, and gave him a sharp nudge. Blue responded with such powerful and sudden acceleration that Bo was almost unseated.

In three great strides Kentucky Blue had sprinted away from Bright Hope.

The crowd breathed its relief.

Blue was out front again, pulling farther and farther ahead, and the cheering from the crowd grew jubilant.

When he crossed the finish line, the spectators continued their wild ovation, but Luke looked on in silence and felt an awful twisting in his gut. Something was wrong with Blue. He could feel it.

Bo turned Blue around and rode him back to the grandstand so the crowd could get another look at him. Blue stood before the cheering crowd, regal and poised, and gradually the crowd grew quiet. The beautiful black colt tossed his head and pranced sideways for them, sending the crowd into another roar of approval.

The crowd loved him. He was their favorite, their own Kentucky Blue.

But not everyone in the grandstand was so elated with

Blue's victory. From her seat beside her husband, Katrina Kirby looked on and felt a bitter resentment uncoil in her stomach. Bo had ended their affair without a word. He'd simply stopped coming to her, even though she still sent notes to him at the stables, letting him know when Frank was away.

Several seats above her, Nathaniel Rhinehart sat watching, his expression grim.

But down in the saddling area, joy was unbound. Ian, Eddie, and Tom hooted loudly and pounded each other's backs, and Darby turned to Luke, her face bright with a mixture of happiness and relief. "Oh, Luke," she said, smiling.

He almost reached for her, wanting desperately to crush her up against his chest and share her unfettered joy in the moment. But even as he weighed the thought, Jeffrey rushed to her side and picked her up, spinning her about in a circle.

"Congratulations, Darby!" he cried, then dipped his head and kissed her full on the mouth. When finally he released her, he turned to Luke and offered his hand. "Congratulations, Richards!"

His chest tight, Luke forced a smile. It was hard not to like the young man, but it was even harder to see him touch Darby. Yet he knew he had no one to blame but himself. That was the hardest realization of them all. "Thank you," he said, and felt Darby's gaze on him. He looked at her, and their gazes clung for the space of several seconds. He wanted to tell her so many things: that yes, Bo was right, he did love her. That he thought she was wonderful. That he believed she was the most selfless, sweet person he had ever known. That he wanted her for himself and himself only. But his own fears and Jeffrey stood between them like an impregnable wall. So instead he simply said, "Congratulations, Darby."

Her expectant gaze clouded, and her eyes lost some of their sparkle. "Congratulations, Luke," she returned, her smile fading.

Then he turned and made his way through the crowd toward the stables, where he would wait for Bo to bring Blue in.

That night Luke's suspicions about the colt were confirmed when Blue did not finish his oats for the first time. He sent Eddie into town for Josh Landers and voiced his concern to Darby.

After finishing their chores, the stable hands, Bo, and Bradley collected a portion of the winning purse, which had come to $1,000, and, since there was nothing more they could do for Blue, they left for the evening.

When Josh Landers arrived, Luke and Darby led him into Blue's stall. "Something's wrong," Luke said. "I felt it earlier at the track. Then tonight he didn't finish his oats."

"Well, let's take a look," Joshua said with a reassuring smile and busied himself with checking the colt's feet, one by one, then running his hands over each of his legs. After he'd checked all four legs, he returned his attention to the left hind leg. He straightened and turned to Darby and Luke. "There's some swelling in this ankle." He bent over and ran his big hands over the joint again, his brow puckering. "He has a slight fracture here." He looked up at Luke and nodded. "That's what it is, all right. It's a minor injury, and it should heal with no problem. But you'll have to scratch the rest of the meets for the fall season. He should spend the next ten weeks or so in his stall."

"Then he will," Luke said without preamble.

"Are you sure he'll be all right?" Darby asked.

Joshua Landers patted her on the shoulder. "Quite sure, Darby. This type of injury isn't a serious threat. As long as Blue is given time to heal, he should be fine."

For the next hour the doctor worked on Blue, wrapping his ankle in several layers of thick cloth strips to immobilize the joint as much as possible. At first Blue protested, kicking out, trying to shake off the offending bandage. But finally he quieted and accepted its presence.

Josh left extra cloth strips and told Darby and Luke to

change the wrapping every three to five days. They thanked him, then Luke walked him out to his horse.

As twilight fell, Darby went out to the water pump and filled a bucket with water for Blue's bath.

When Luke returned to Blue's stall, he hung his folded arms over the gate and watched Darby's ministrations for a few seconds in thoughtful silence. His eyes drifted over her. She still reminded him of a leggy colt. "It's late," he said at last, swinging open the gate and stepping into the stall, "and you're as tired as the rest of us. I'll help you finish."

Surprised, Darby glanced up at him. "You don't have to."

A slight smile touched his handsome mouth. "I know that, but I want to."

"All right," she said quietly, only too aware that they were alone in the barn, only too aware that something powerful and unavoidable had been building between them for a very long time and that it was ready to explode at any moment.

Minutes passed, and they worked on Blue together while they thought about him, while they thought about the day's race, while they thought about each other.

Then finally Darby broke the silence by asking, "Do you think it was Bradley who started the fire?" She stroked a brush over Blue's left hip, carefully keeping her gaze trained on her hands.

Luke dried off Blue's ears and forehead with a cloth. "I thought so at first, but I don't anymore. I wouldn't have left him out here alone today if I had thought it was him."

Darby waited through two beats of silence. "You don't think it was Yancey, do you?" There was a frightened urgency in her voice as she asked the question. She was afraid of his answer, but she needed to know what he thought.

"No," Luke said without hesitation. "I don't believe it was Yancey. I don't know why he left. Maybe he was afraid he would be blamed, who knows? But I don't believe for a minute he set the fire."

His words calmed her. "I'm glad," she said, a tiny smile

playing along her mouth. She loved Yancey, and she, like Aunt Birdie, could never accept the thought of Yancey doing such a terrible thing. "Who do you think did it?" she asked, her brow furrowing. She looked up at him. "And why?"

Luke shook his head. "I don't know." He paused a moment. "But I'll know in time."

They fell silent once more.

Their hands met over Blue's back, and their gazes locked and held. Luke's eyes darkened; Darby's breath caught in her throat. Time ticked on while their hearts beat as one, speaking the words that their mouths could not utter.

I want you.

I need you.

Panicked, she looked away and hastily picked up the bucket of water, sloshing part of the contents out onto the hay-covered floor. "I'll empty this," she said, and fled from the stall, head down, carrying the bucket out of the stables into the blessed cool night air and dumping the contents out onto the grass. When she returned, her movements were quick and agitated. She scurried around, hanging the bucket up and gathering her grooming tools, then putting them away in the little work room where the stable hands stored the equipment.

Luke stood outside Blue's stall, leaning up against the door, his arms crossed over his chest, watching her even as he warred with his conscience. The sight of Jeffrey kissing her had unleashed a host of irrevocable thoughts and emotions—feelings he'd tried hard to bury, thoughts he'd tried hard to suppress. But those thoughts and feelings had been present for a very long time regardless of his efforts to quell them.

Bo was right. He loved her.

Yet he still believed she deserved more than he could ever give her. She deserved stability, a man who could provide for her, a man who would love her completely, a man who knew who he was and where he'd come from. Someone other than himself. No one had ever loved him; no one had ever taught him how to love in the way that she deserved to be loved.

Without looking at him, she grabbed the coat and woolen cap she kept hanging on a nail over Blue's stall door and woodenly said, "I should be going now." She jammed her hat on her head and shrugged into her coat, then without looking at him said, "Good night, Luke."

He studied the dark bulk she made as she turned to go and, for all his reasoning, he knew he would not let her leave him this night. He reached out and caught her arm, staying her. Then he took her by the shoulders and turned her to face him.

She refused to meet his gaze. Her heart picked up its tempo. She knew she should think of Jeffrey, but all she could think of was Luke and how wonderful it would be to feel his arms around her again.

"I know I have no right," he said quietly, taking her hands, drawing her to him, knowing that what he was about to do was irreproachable. But a year and a half of furtive glances and suppressed feelings had built up within him like a roiling volcano, and it was too difficult to douse the fire any longer. "I don't want you to go, Darby . . ." He reached out and undid her coat buttons one by one, then pushed the garment from her shoulders, letting it fall to the hay covered floor in a dark heap. He pulled the cap from her head, letting it follow in her coat's wake. Her dark curls stood up from her head in wispy, static-teased tendrils. "Darby, look at me," he ordered in a deep, quiet voice, and she obeyed, lifting distressed eyes to his. "Do you want me to stop?"

She stared up into his eyes for several long heartbeats and, for all her resolution not to fall victim to his touch again, she honestly said, "No . . . but—"

With a strangled groan he ignored her halfhearted protest and pulled her up against his chest and kissed her with demand, his mouth open, his tongue seeking. She kissed him back, her breath breaking on an impassioned murmur. His hands roamed over her body, burning through her clothing from her waist to her ribs, to her neck, where they stopped to cradle her head. He kissed her cheeks, her eyes, her hair, and desire grew heady for them both. His hands found her ribs once again, then bracketed her breasts, touching her tenderly, carefully, reverently.

She followed his lead, touching him all over, his back, shoulders, neck, and face, marveling once again in the feelings his touch evoked. It was not like this with Jeffrey. It had not been like this with Bo. She knew it would never be like this with anyone else. It was Luke, only Luke, who could make her heart beat wildly, who could make her knees melt. His touch felt good and right and wonderful.

His arms slipped underneath her knees and around her back, lifting her, carrying her through the dimly lit, shadowy stables to his office.

He shouldered the door open, then lowered her onto the cot. It creaked a complaint as he followed, dropping his length onto hers.

"Darby," he whispered, pulling away slightly, giving one last thought to propriety.

But she whispered, "Don't stop," and propriety fled as she locked her arms around his neck, pulling him back down.

Their kisses grew hot and wild. They pressed close, rolling toward each other slightly, fitting their bodies together as one. He eased down her suspenders, then worked the buttons on her red shirt, pushing it off her shoulders, pulling it out from under her, tossing it to the floor. She did the same for him, pushing his shirt away, touching his heated bare skin for the very first time.

"Oh, my . . ." she said on a soft sigh as she ran her hands over his chest, his back, his shoulders. His skin was warm and male, hard and smooth.

His hands cupped her naked breasts, learning their shape, their weight, stroking his thumbs over the tender buds of her taut nipples. She gasped, and he lowered his head, taking her nipples into his mouth one by one, taunting them with his tongue till she arched against him. He buried his face between her breasts, breathing against her, heating her skin while she

cradled his head and allowed him to lead the way into a valley
of sensuality.

Growing impatient, he dragged her britches down over her
hips and tossed them aside, then his thumbs caught at her
brief undergarments and peeled them away also, leaving her
naked and vulnerable beneath him. She blushed and closed
her eyes, and he stroked her cheek tenderly. She was so
lovely, her skin a satiny alabaster glow in the flickering lamplight. He rose from her and shrugged off the rest of his clothing, then lay back down with her, taking her flush against his
naked body.

"I think I've wanted this since the first time I saw you,"
he said honestly.

"Did you?" she asked, opening her eyes, surprised.

"Yes."

"I didn't know."

"I couldn't tell you . . ."

"Why?"

He answered her with a series of wet kisses to her face,
her throat, her breasts, belly, and thighs. His mouth came back
to hers, and he kissed her deeply, his tongue entwining with
hers, teaching her, guiding her while his hand rode down over
her slender hip, over her smooth belly, and lower, touching
her within her warm secret place for the very first time.

Surprised by the sweet rush of pleasure his touch brought,
her breath caught and held while he stroked her intimately
and tutored her long limbs to part for him, her flesh to respond
to his exploration. Then he took her hand and guided it to his
own aching flesh. She touched him lightly, tentatively, thinking him beautifully made, her eyes lifting to his in wonder.
He groaned softly, and his eyes slowly closed as his breathing
grew ragged.

Then he could wait no longer. He hovered above her, pressing his distended flesh against her wet warmth, and she
waited, eager and unafraid. He watched her face as he entered
her, afraid he would hurt her. But his entrance was slow and

grand, a lovely thing, all she had imagined it would be, all she had hoped it would be. She looked up at him with trust, her eyes shining with all she felt for him, and he thrust into her fully.

She gasped, and her eyes sank shut.

Alarmed, he went still and whispered, "I'm sorry."

"Don't be . . ." She touched light fingers to his face.

"I thought I hurt you—"

"You didn't," she said, and lifted her hips to meet him, drawing him deep. "It's just so wonderful . . ."

"There's more . . ."

"Show me . . ."

And so he did, moving within her, rocking against her, his thrusts fluid, yet swift and strong.

He felt her arch, heard her gasp and, in time, felt her shudder as she discovered what lay at the end of this rainbow of passion.

She clung to him, still dazed, and felt him press deep, once, twice, then one last time as he found his own shuddering release and collapsed upon her.

Then came the quiet, still moments, as breathless, trembling, he held her tight, feeling a river of love pour out of his soul for her. He looked down into her face and wished the world away. She smiled. The smile was gentle and sweet, so like her, and the guilt came back to haunt him with force.

I love you . . . He saw the words reflected in her eyes.

I love you . . . She knew the words had to be in his heart.

But he did not say them. He could not say them.

For his old doubts had crept back and locked the words tightly within his chest.

The next morning Darby rose anxiously from her bed. Though her body ached from fatigue, her heart was singing. She was in love, and she knew Luke loved her too. He had not spoken the words out loud, but they were there in his eyes and in his touch. She took her time bathing, then brushed out her hair and tugged on a fresh shirt and a pair of britches, then went downstairs for breakfast.

While she ate, she explained Blue's injury to Aunt Birdie, a sleepy Eugene, and Henry, then hurriedly shrugged into her coat and left for the stables.

Luke was waiting for her outside when she arrived. Bo was not there yet, and the other stable hands were busy with the morning chores. She swung down from her horse and smiled at him, her eyes full of love and expectation. She started across the grass toward him, but something in his expression slowed her steps. The familiar shuttered look was back in his eyes.

"What's wrong?" she asked, the smile fading from her face.

The disappearance of her smile cut him deeply, but he said the words he'd rehearsed to himself all night long, just the same. "There won't be very much to do around here over the next few months with Blue's leg needing rest." He paused, then went on. "You don't need to come out for a while."

He watched her digest his words, work them over in her brain, try to make sense out of them. He understood her confusion. But he'd lain awake long into the night, thinking things over, trying to find a way to justify making love to her. What if he'd made her pregnant last night? Her father would shoot him, and he would deserve no less. If she wasn't pregnant already, she surely would be if they kept on doing what they had done last night.

He was twenty-nine years old and had nothing solid to offer her. No matter how successful he may or may not become, he knew she was better off with Jeffrey Morgan, a man with a real name, a man who knew who he was.

"But I want to come out," she said in answer to his last statement.

He dropped his gaze, and she watched him swallow. "It would be better if you didn't, Darby," he said quietly.

She was silent a moment. She suddenly felt very cold. He

didn't want her around. He didn't want to see her. But didn't he know? It was far too late. She could no sooner salvage her heart than she could restore her virginity. They were both gone, lost to him forever. She felt bruised, battered, wounded beyond healing. She ached to understand. "Better for who, Luke? For you?" Her voice was full of hurt and confusion.

He lifted his haunted gaze to hers. "Come March, when we start working Blue hard for the Derby, we'll both be thinking clearer about last night."

"There's nothing wrong with my thinking," she said softly. Her face was chalk white. "I know exactly what we did last night."

"It was a mistake."

"How can you say that?" Her brow was drawn tight, her hazel eyes vulnerable as they stared back at him. "I don't understand. . . ."

"We shouldn't have done it," he went on as if he hadn't heard her, and lowered his gaze to the ground once more. He shook his head. "I shouldn't have—"

She thought about that a moment. Tears stung the backs of her eyes. She whirled away, hooked her foot in her horse's stirrup, and swung back up into the saddle. She was determined he would never know how much he had hurt her. "You're right," she said quietly, not even bothering to look at him. "You shouldn't have." With that she turned her horse and galloped away.

Fall passed and winter set in, and the frosty days passed in a dull gray haze for both Birdie and Darby. The Greene farm was tranquil, settling into a slower routine than that of the other seasons.

Darby did not go back to the stables, though she missed Blue and Effie desperately. But pride held her back. Luke did not want her there, and that fact was enough to strengthen her resolve.

She avoided Jeffrey at every turn, seeing him only when she could not think of an excuse to put him off. She found it hard to look into his earnest face after what had passed between herself and Luke. She felt small and underhanded for not making a clean break with him, but the opportunity had not arisen. For the most part, they were always in the presence of others. When they were alone, the words just wouldn't come.

Then Christmas came, complete with a dusting of snow and a surprise visit from Jeffrey.

She served him a piece of Aunt Birdie's apple pie and sat on the settee with him while he visited with her family.

Ardis, Linette, and Emma were present with their families. Emma and Linette had special news to share. They were both expecting their first child the very same month.

After his second cup of coffee, Jeffrey leaned over to Darby and whispered, "Let's go outside for a while, shall we?"

She nodded, and they excused themselves. They grabbed their coats on their way out the back door and shrugged into them as they stepped out onto the porch. They stood shoulder to shoulder in the crystalline cold, their breath escaping into frothy clouds, listening to the bare tree limbs clacking in the wind.

Both lost in their own thoughts, they looked up into a clear, moonlit sky. It was sprinkled with countless shining stars.

After several moments Jeffrey broke the silence. "I've missed you, Darby."

Plagued by guilt, she looked at her hands where they gripped the porch railing. What could she say in return? "I've missed you too, Jeffrey," she returned softly. "But the days have all run together for me lately."

"Are you still going out to the stables?"

She shook her head. "No. With Blue's injury there's really very little for me to do out there. I won't be going back till March."

"Good," he said quietly, and gave a soft chuckle, then took her by the shoulders and turned her to face him. "That means more time for me. Selfish of me, I know."

"Oh, Jeffrey . . ." she began, pressing a palm to his chest, knowing she must tell him the truth—that her heart belonged to another, that his devotion was wasted on her, would always be wasted on her.

But he did not give her the chance. "Marry me, Darby," he whispered urgently, staring down into her face. "I love you so."

Those words, the very ones she'd ached to hear from Luke, caused a flutter of panic in her heart when spoken by Jeffrey.

She opened her mouth to still any further declaration of his feelings, but he hurried on. "I want to marry you. I want to have children with you. I want to build you a house. I want to give you my name."

She shook her head and gazed up into his ardent eyes. "Jeffrey, please . . ."

"Please what?" He shook his head in question, and a lock of soft brown hair fell onto his brow.

He looked so much like the vulnerable little boy she'd once fought battles for that she reached up and brushed the lock back into place. He captured her wrist and pressed a kiss into her palm.

The tender gesture touched her. "I don't know what to say—"

"Say yes."

She could not imagine it—married to Jeffrey, keeping his house, bearing his children. For all his charm, for all his goodness, for all his dearness, the thought depressed her beyond words.

"Say you will, Darby."

Her eyes were dark with regret. "I wish I could, but I can't. I'm sorry."

"Then say you'll think about it."

"I really can't—"

"Please?" His expression was so beseeching, it tore at her heart. "At least say you'll think about it?"

Because she could not bear to hurt him and because she could not find the words to explain what had happened between herself and Luke, she silently nodded her compliance.

He pulled her into his arms and hugged her fiercely. "Oh, Darby," he said, his voice ecstatic, rocking her back and forth. "Darby. You've made me so happy!"

She squeezed her eyes shut and willed away her trepidation, hoping she would never have to hurt him. . . .

❖ *12* ❖

THE MONTH OF January passed slowly.

The air was cold, but the sky was often a chilly, brilliant blue, a striking contrast to the deep green of the forest pines that lay beyond the rolling hills.

Darby kept busy most days, helping her father and Eugene around the barn and helping Aunt Birdie around the house.

But she also took some time for herself. She rode out to see each of her sisters, taking an entire day to spend with each one. The visits were good for her. She had matured over the past year and a half, and in spending time with her sisters, she came to know them in a new and different way that fostered friendship and respect.

She watched them move about their own homes, happy in caring for themselves and their husbands, happy with life, and she realized she had been foolish to judge them so harshly in the past.

Jeffrey came courting regularly, but she was able to limit his visits to twice a week. As he grew more persistent with his avowals of love, she became more uncomfortable and guilt-ridden. How could she accept his proposal when she had given herself to another? She had called Luke a coward, but she was every bit as cowardly herself. She knew she had to tell Jeffrey the truth. But she had the oddest feeling that if she told him of her night of weakness in Luke's arms, he would still proclaim his love for her and would still want her for his wife.

She was torn by her emotions—for Jeffrey and about Luke.

She tried her best not to think about Luke at all, but she was rarely successful. If thoughts of him did not plague her during the day, they surely did at night.

Her dreams were riddled with images of him. His eyes haunted her, his hands teased and taunted her. The words he'd said when he sent her away reverberated in her mind over and over again, and when at last she awoke, she was often sweat-soaked, her heart aching, her pillow wet from tears.

She did not understand how he could be so kind and compassionate, so strong and wise, could touch her with such tenderness and love, yet send her away.

She would never understand, and she feared that she would never let go of the hope that she someday would.

One chill February day, tired of her melancholy, she dressed in a long gray skirt and crisp white shirtwaist, climbed up into her father's buggy, and set out for Louisville to visit Millie. When she arrived she urged her friend to dress for lunch so they could eat at a quaint little restaurant on Main Street.

Surprised and happy for the diversion from her daily routine, Millie complied, dressing in a simple skirt and blouse. Then they rode through the busy streets to the restaurant.

The tables in the restaurant were covered with white damask and flanked by lit candles set in pretty silver candlesticks. Darby and Millie sat at a little table by the window, where they could watch the activity on the street.

Millie eyed Darby carefully from across the table. She lifted her goblet of water and took a sip. "What is it, Darby?" she asked at length. "What's wrong?"

"What do you mean?" Darby asked, smoothing her linen napkin onto her lap and lowering her gaze.

"You haven't been yourself for weeks. I've noticed the difference in you even though I've seen you only at church on Sundays."

Darby's gaze lifted. "I'm fine, Millie. Really."

"Oh, I can see that you are. On the outside, that is. You look absolutely lovely." Her gaze softened. "You always were lovely, Darby. Inside and out. And so much smarter than I. You were always a good friend. My very best." She reached across the table and took Darby's hand. "Please forgive me for ever hurting you."

Darby shook her head. "Don't be silly, Millie, you didn't—"

"Oh, yes, I did," Millie interrupted. "I was often a thoughtless ninny, saying insensitive things that hurt you and really only reflected my own insecurities. But since I married Bo, since I lost the baby . . . I've learned so much about myself, about life, about what really matters."

"What really matters, Millie?" Darby asked quietly.

Millie was silent a moment. "Friendship. Family. Being happy with yourself. Being quiet long enough to find out who you really are and what you really want."

Darby took a thick piece of warm bread from the basket on the center of the table and spread a thin layer of butter over the surface. "What do you really want?"

Millie smiled, but her expression was tinged with sadness. "I want to read more, learn more. I want to spend more time with the people I love. But most of all I want a child, Darby. Bo's child." She grew silent, her expression one of awed amazement. "The funniest thing happened after we lost the baby, Darby. We started talking and we got to know each other. We found out that we liked each other and we became friends." Her gaze softened, and her smile brightened. "We fell in love, Darby." She lifted her hands. "Can you believe it?"

Darby reached across the table and squeezed Millie's hand. "Oh, Millie, I'm so glad."

"We've been trying for another baby over the last couple of months, but nothing has happened yet."

"It will!" Darby said emphatically. "I just know it will."

They fell silent as the waiter brought their entrees. Darby

had ordered roast chicken and dressing. Millie had ordered roast beef and roasted potatoes. They turned their attention to their food for a few minutes, then Millie looked up sharply, her eyes widening. Her mouth dropped open slightly. "You've fallen in love too, haven't you?" she exclaimed loud enough that nearly everyone in the restaurant could hear her.

Darby blushed, realizing that some things about Millie would never change. "Oh, shhh, Millie!"

"But it isn't Jeffrey Morgan, is it?" she whispered, narrowing her eyes, leaning across the table, wagging her ornately designed silver fork at Darby. "I know you've been seeing him since Emma's wedding, but it isn't him, is it?"

Darby sighed heavily and remained silent.

Millie studied her face. "It's Luke Richards!" she whispered. "I should have known all along."

At Darby's pained expression, Millie's eyes grew compassionate. Then she smiled and leaned back in her chair. "Why, Darby Lynn, I never took you for a quitter!"

Two weeks later, on the first day of March, Darby rose early, dressed in britches and a blue work shirt, and set out for Rhinehart Stables. The weather had been unusually mild, and the forest and woods were particularly beautiful with the budding pink-and-white blossoms of the dogwoods. The air whispered of an early spring, and the sun shone down with golden promise. Gray squirrels skittered about, searching for nuts they had misplaced the previous fall, while birds sat in the trees and sang out a merry song of emancipation, happy to be delivered from winter's chill breath.

When she reached the stables, she swung down from her horse. Her jaw was set with stubborn resolve. On May 11, less than six weeks away, Kentucky Blue would run in the Kentucky Derby. She wasn't about to miss out on any part of the preparations, regardless of Luke Richards's feelings about her, regardless of her feelings for him. She would put all problems aside and once again set her eyes upon her goal.

Ian met her inside the barn. Though he walked with a noticeable limp, he no longer needed crutches. "Hello, Miss Darby! he called out, his face wrinkling into a wreath of smiles. He took her horse's reins from her hands. "It's about time you came back to work!"

"It's good to be back, Ian." She returned his smile with a bright one of her own. "How's your leg?"

Ian shook his leg and winked. "Not bad. Gettin' stronger every day. But the doctor says I still can't exercise that big colt of yours, so it's a good thing you showed up. Mr. Luke and Mr. Bo'll be glad to see you."

"Where are they?"

"Gettin' Blue ready for the track."

As she walked through the barn, she passed Eddie and Tom, who were cleaning out a corner of the barn, though it was almost as clean as a ship. They called out greetings, which she returned, then she walked over to Lady Effie's stall and leaned over the gate. "Hey, sweetie," she said, holding out her hand. Effie's ears pricked forward, and she gave an excited whinny. "C'mon," Darby urged, and the little filly hurried to Darby, pressing her nose into her hand. Darby leaned over the gate and hugged her neck. "Oh, I'm missed you so," she said softly, then glanced over at Blue's stall.

Bo and Luke were inside, saddling Blue.

Seeing her, Blue whinnied. Both men looked up at the same time. But it was Bo who smiled first and said, "Darby! Hello!"

"Hey, Bo," she returned, genuinely happy to see him again.

"Millie said you'd be out soon."

"Millie was right."

She entered the stall, and Blue nudged her. She hugged his neck tight. "Oh, Blue, you've grown. You're not my baby any longer."

He neighed softly, searching her pocket for a treat. She took out the carrot, broke it in half, and gave him a piece, then called Effie over and gave her the other half.

Then she turned to face the inevitable.

Their eyes locked on each other. "Hello, Luke," she said quietly, wishing he did not look so wonderful. He was dressed in dark britches and a green shirt, the neck open, the sleeves rolled up over his forearms. A lock of his dark hair fell onto his brow. His face was tan, his eyes bluer than ever. But the lines around those beautiful eyes, those lines she still found so attractive, seemed deeper, more pronounced.

"Hello, Darby," he said with a slow smile. His gaze swept her with a hungry tenderness. She looked as bright and lovely as spring sunshine. He'd missed her, and he was so glad to see her, so glad she'd come. He was afraid she wouldn't. But he should have known better. Darby had spunk. Time would have healed her wounds, and she would never give up on her dream, not for him, not for any man. That was one of the reasons he loved her. In banishing her from the barn, he had sentenced himself to four months of torture, for he had not been able to banish her from his heart and mind.

Now that she had returned, the light was back in his life, even if all he could do was look at her.

"Hello, Miss Greene," someone said over Darby's shoulder, pulling her attention away from Luke's hypnotic gaze.

She spun and was shocked silent. She almost didn't recognize him. He looked like a different man. He was trim and fit, dressed in clean britches and a shirt. His brown hair, though graying prematurely, was washed and combed, his eyes were clear and sharp, his face lean and handsome and sober, no longer bloated from whiskey. She imagined he looked very much like his father had at his age. "Hello, Mr. Rhine—" she began.

"Bradley," he interrupted with an easy smile. "Please call me Bradley." He was silent a moment while he shifted his weight self-consciously. "It's good to see you. I've been waiting for the chance to apologize."

She shook her head, but he continued with "I'm sorry about what I did, about Blue. I'm also very sorry that you had to see the tragedy I caused with Knightwind."

Feeling uncomfortable with his apology, she didn't know what to say, so she simply said, "You look so different. So good . . ."

He laughed good-naturedly and glanced over at Luke. "Luke's a hard taskmaster, but there's something to be said for hard work and a good meal every day."

She smiled, relaxing, her cheeks dimpling. "I'm glad."

He was silent a moment. "Luke tells me we're going to win the Derby." There was both pride and excitement in his eyes, and something else too—hope for the future.

Her eyes found Luke's, and she felt a jolt of pride as well. They were a team, all of them, Luke and herself, Bo, Ian, Tom, Eddie and, yes, Bradley too. Even Mrs. Brunsteader, who worked so hard to keep them fed, was an important member of their outfit. No matter what had happened between them, despite the devastation of the fire they'd all worked together toward the day they would win the greatest race of all. "He's right," Darby said, turning back to Bradley. "We most certainly are."

"Well, hell, then. Let's get to work," Bo said, leading Blue out of his stall. "Darby, if you'll get Effie, we'll see what this boy can do."

That same morning Nathaniel Rhinehart stood on Frank Kirby's doorstep and knocked at the expensive, hand-carved door.

The housekeeper answered his knock and ushered him into an elegant drawing room to wait for Mrs. Kirby.

Katrina took her time joining him, but when she did she swept into the room in a pink satin dressing gown.

"I'm afraid Frank isn't here, Nathaniel," she said, turning her back to him so she could face the fire that flickered eagerly in the hearth.

"I'm quite aware of that, my dear," Nathaniel said, coming up behind her. "I think you know I did not come to see Frank."

She turned to face him, her green eyes icing over.

"You know why I'm here, don't you?"

She held his gaze for two ticks of the mantel clock, then nodded. "Yes, I suppose I do."

"It's time to call in your debt, my dear Katrina."

"And just how are you going to do that?" she asked, lifting her chin, trying to mask her trepidation.

"By using your connections." He smiled, and it was a terrible thing to behold. "I do believe you have a bit of unfinished business with a certain handsome young jockey, don't you?"

For the first time since he'd arrived, Katrina smiled. "As a matter of fact, I do. . . ."

April brought an explosion of color. Rhododendrons and azaleas covered the hills with wild abandon, and trillium, bloodroot, bluebell, wild ginger, and lady's slipper colored the meadows. The tiny buds of bluegrass cast the fields in shades of blue, and the green pastures grew lush and dark.

Eleven months and three days had passed since the awful fire out at Rhinehart Stables. But not one day had passed that Birdie did not think of Yancey.

She thought of him that morning as she stood out on the porch admiring nature's beauty. Henry had gone into town for supplies, and Darby had left at dawn for the stables.

Birdie crossed the back porch to where Remus lay limp and asleep on the porch. As she stood over him, he raised his head from his crossed paws and blinked at her dispassionately. She reached down and patted his head. Yancey had loved the lazy old hound.

Out in the yard she scattered feed to the chickens, then stood in the sunshine, letting it warm her face, hoping that warmth would seep into her heart and warm the cold corners. She pushed a wayward strand of hair from her face and tucked it back into the loose knot at the base of her neck.

The wind kissed her cheek, and she fought against the ache of loneliness that threatened to overtake her.

She missed Yancey desperately.

She missed his grizzled face, his teasing blue eyes, she even missed his filthy, floppy old hat.

From out of the past came his words: "You look prettier than morning dew does on a rose. I mean it, Birdie."

Did you, Yancey? Did you really mean it?

It was a bittersweet revelation to her that she had known love at last, then lost it before she'd ever been able to consummate that love physically. At forty-three, her virgin heart and body ached for what she had never known.

She sighed heavily. *Where are you, Yancey? Where did you go?*

"Hello, pretty bird." His deep voice came to her on the wind.

She spun. As though her thoughts had conjured him out of thin air, he stood before her in a golden ray of sunshine. He was tall and lean, his gray eyes every bit as clear and lovely as she remembered them. His clothes were clean, his thinning hair neatly cut and combed, but he held his floppy hat—that beautiful, battered old hat—in one hand.

"Yancey," she whispered, wondering if she was asleep. She dreamed of his return so often, only to awake sad and disheartened.

He took two tentative steps toward her. "It's me, Birdie."

She shook her head, her big brown eyes disbelieving.

He nodded. "I know. You have so many questions." He closed the space between them and took her by the shoulders. "But I have one of my own first."

She stared into his face, speechless, still trying to believe he was real.

"Do you love me, Birdie Greene?"

She swallowed. "I should be the one asking the questions," she said, her voice husky with pain and accusation. "You left us. You left all of us without so much as a word of good-bye."

"I had to," he told her quietly. "But if you'll give me a chance, I'll tell you why. It's a long story, and I'll tell you all of it. I promise." He paused, and his eyes clouded. "I've made a lot of mistakes. I've done some things I'm not proud of. And I had to go back and try to right those wrongs. But one thing is as sure and true as that sun overhead. I love you, Birdie Greene, with all my heart and soul. So before I say anything else, answer me, Birdie. Do you love me?''

Seconds ticked by while he waited anxiously for her response. ''Yes,'' she whispered at last, her eyes sinking shut. ''Yes, Yancey, I do love you.''

''Then that's all I need to know.'' He pulled her into his arms and kissed her with a tenderness fraught with love and renewed hope.

They had both been given another chance and, though they had all the time in the world, they weren't about to waste a minute of it. They walked through the sunshine to the house, hand in hand, and she led him to her room. She closed the door and turned the key in the lock, then faced him once again.

Their gazes locked, and she took his hand and led him to her bed.

They stood motionless for several seconds, their hearts beating out their love for each other. ''Birdie,'' he whispered. The name was spoken like a prayer, an intonation. ''Are you sure?''

''Oh, yes, quite.''

They undressed each other, peeling away the garments with an unhurried reverence, wholly unencumbered by any modesty. When at last they were naked, she smiled and offered him her hand once again, pulling him down onto the bed with her.

They stretched out, thigh to thigh, face-to-face, touching, kissing, stroking, learning each other's shapes and textures, reveling in the fact that life had granted them this gift. It was a splendid, timeless moment, a moment of joy and discovery for Birdie, a moment of atonement and redemption for Yancey.

He thought her lovely, her body slender and youthful, her skin soft and silky beneath his work-roughened hands. She thought him beautiful, hard and lean, wonderfully male, as the mysteries she'd always wondered about came to light beneath his tender tutorage.

As morning fled and the noon sun arched a shimmering path through her window, Birdie Greene was no longer a dull little wren, but an ornately beautiful bird who had learned how to fly.

Kentucky Blue flew down the backstretch of the training track with Bo riding high on his back. Luke, Darby, Ian, Eddie, and someone Yancey did not recognize stood at the fence, watching.

The black colt was a sight to behold, and Yancey slipped down off his horse and watched, crossing his arms over his chest, a smile of pride and satisfaction creasing his weathered face.

Now a three-year-old, the horse had filled out significantly, his powerful rippling muscles evident beneath his glossy black coat. When Blue sailed across the finish line, Luke looked down at the clock, then said something to his outfit. A roar of approval went up while they hugged and clapped each other on the back.

Yancey's smile grew wide. How he had missed them all!

Luke looked over at Darby. "He's a winner, Darby."

She smiled. "Yes, I know." She no longer felt awkward with him. She was no longer threatened by his presence or hurt by what had been or not been between them. She had put those things aside to focus on the journey at hand. They were friends and colleagues again, at long last.

"That's some horse you got there."

Everyone turned at once. Darby's eyes widened. "Yancey!" she squealed, and was in his arms in a flash, hugging him, fighting back tears of joy. "Where have you been? Why did you leave?" she asked in an excited rush.

"Whoa now, slow down a bit," he said, patting her on the back. His eyes lifted to Luke's. "I need to talk to Luke first, then I'll explain everything to you and your pa over supper tonight.''

He released her, and she smiled up at him. "I knew you'd come back, Yancey. I just knew it.''

"I figured you did, Darby Lynn. 'Cause you got good instincts and spunk to boot, if ever anyone ever did.'' He looked at Luke once again. "Can we talk?''

Luke smiled. "It's good to see you, Yancey. Of course we can. Let's go on up to the house.'' He offered his hand, and Yancey shook it, hoping that Luke would still want to shake hands with him after he was finished telling him his story.

The two men left the others and walked up to the house.

"The colt looks great, Luke. You've done a fine job with him.'' Pride echoed in his voice. "But I always knew you would.''

"He's in top form,'' Luke answered. "I've never had a horse look better. But then, Kentucky Blue is a very special horse.''

"Yes,'' Yancey agreed quietly. "He is.'' He hooked a thumb over his shoulder. "Who is the new fella?''

Luke shook his head and chuckled at the irony of it all. "Bradley Rhinehart.''

Yancey turned his head sharply to stare at him, and Luke went on to explain what had transpired in his absence.

Yancey sighed. "Damn, but it's been a long winter.''

Luke looked over at him. "The longest one of my life.''

They reached the house, and Luke led the way through the entrance to the study. "Sit down,'' Luke said, gesturing to a leather chair. Instead of taking a seat at the desk, he chose the chair beside Yancey, turning the chair so he could face the other man.

Yancey's steady gaze held Luke's. "I'm sorry about leavin' like I did, Luke. But after the fire, I realized it was time to stop running from the past.''

Luke leaned back in his chair and crossed his booted foot over his knee, patiently waiting for Yancey to continue.

Yancey pressed forward in his chair, his expression somber. He took his hat from his head. "I don't know how you're going to feel about what I have to tell you, but I may as well start at the beginning. My real name is Yancey Larson, and I'm from New York." He paused, took a deep breath, then said, "I'm your father, Luke."

Nathaniel Rhinehart leaned back in his chair and steepled his fingers, fixing the young man before him with his icy gaze. The afternoon sun slanted through the window, but did little to relieve the chill in the office. "We have three weeks, Thomas."

Tom Haines looked down at his hands and picked at his fingernail. "I know."

"You must not fail this time."

Tom's gaze lifted. He ran a shaky hand through his red hair. "I don't want to do this, Mr. Rhinehart. Startin' that fire was bad enough. Killin' all those other fine horses. Horses I was mighty fond of. They were my friends. . . ." His young face spoke his distress.

"Now, Thomas . . . don't make me have a talk with the sheriff." There was a silky threat in Nathaniel's voice. "I would hate to see you go to jail for something that happened so long ago."

Tom pressed forward in his chair. "You know I never meant to shoot Mr. Rhinehart!" he cried, his eyes panicked. "I was only target-practicin'! I didn't know he'd be out ridin' so close to the edge of his property that day. I liked Mr. Rhinehart! I would never have hurt him on purpose!"

"*Tsk, tsk,* my boy. Do you really think the sheriff will believe you now? Especially after all this time? Especially when you left him lying out there to die?"

"I didn't, though. You know how it happened! You know I was coming to get help! You know I was on foot, and by the time I got back to the stables, Darby had already found Mr. Rhinehart and come and got Mr. Luke! I never had time to explain to anybody but you, and you said you'd take care of everything!"

"And I did. To this day no one knows who shot Benjamin."

"It was an accident!"

"That's not how the courts will see it."

Tom's eyes filled with tears. "It's the truth, and you know it."

Nathaniel shrugged. "Is it? It's not me you'll have to convince, my boy."

Nathaniel smiled inwardly. It had been a piece of luck for him that he had been out at the stables that day and caught Tom as he rushed by looking for Luke. The boy had been young, only fourteen, and scared out of his mind. It had been easy to convince him that he should remain silent for the time being, that he could go to jail if the truth ever came out. Then, as time passed, Tom's silence had strengthened Nathaniel's hold over him. Nathaniel knew that that hold would prove its worth in time.

And, of course, it had. . . .

· 13 ·

Stunned, Luke sat still and silent, waiting for Yancey to continue.

"I know what I just said might not make any sense to you," Yancey hurried on, "but please . . . just hear me out."

Amid a host of conflicting emotions, Luke managed to gather himself. "Go on," he said in a tight voice.

Yancey relaxed some. He crumpled the brim of his hat with his fingers and began to tell his story. "I was a trainer myself once." A small self-deprecating smile tipped up one side of his mouth. "But then, you already knew that, didn't you?"

"Yes," Luke answered quietly.

"When did you figure it out?"

"The day Bo and I came to tell Darby I'd train Blue. You had him out in the corral, showing Darby how to lead him in figure eights. You knew exactly what you were doing."

Yancey's eyes mirrored his respect. His son was a very astute man. "Why didn't you say something then?"

Luke shrugged. "I figured you had your reasons for remaining silent."

Yancey nodded. "You were right. I did." His eyes took on a faraway look. "It was thirty years ago in Upstate New York. I'd worked for several different Thoroughbred farms across the state over the past several years, starting out like most young trainers do, working as a stable hand. But I had finally been hired on as a full-fledged trainer by Clement Barclay of Barclay Farms. Mr. Barclay was a fair man with a stable of fine horses. It wasn't long before I was doing real well with his horses, placing in meets all over the state.'' Yancey smiled. ''I'd begun to make a name for myself even though I was only twenty-three.'' His smile grew soft, his eyes nostalgic. ''Then one warm summer day a young girl wandered into the stables. Her name was Abigail Spencer. She was eighteen years old and she had long, wavy black hair and the prettiest blue eyes I had ever seen. I even remember what she was wearing that day. She had on a blue dress that matched her eyes.''

He shook his head. ''She was the most beautiful girl I had ever seen. She was like an angel. . . .'' He fell silent, letting the memory take him. After several moments he collected himself and went on. ''She said she loved horses and just wanted to look at them. She lived on a big cattle ranch two miles north of Barclay Farms, and her family was visiting the Barclays.

''Well, the next thing I knew we were talking and laughing . . .'' He shook his head slowly, as though he still couldn't believe she had ever been real. ''She was the sweetest thing.''

His smiled slipped, and he looked down at his hands, which continued to mash the limp brim of his hat. ''As the days passed, she managed to slip back over to see me. Often it was late at night, after all the stable hands and grooms had gone to sleep. We were both young, and one thing led to another.'' Yancey lifted his gaze. His eyes were sad. ''I never knew she was promised to someone else until her brother told me. And I never knew about you until the day I saw you almost two years ago, and even then I wasn't sure.''

''Why did you leave her in the first place?'' Luke asked quietly.

''Because of the fire.''

''At Barclay Farms?''

''Yes.''

Disheartened, Luke's eyes slipped shut.

''No,'' Yancey hurried to say, holding out one of his hands.

"It's not what you think. I didn't do it. But I knew I'd get blamed for it. Abigail's oldest brother, Quinn, had come to see me one night after she'd left. He'd followed her. He was furious. She was promised to a young man she had known since childhood, a young man whom the family liked and approved of. Her brother made it very clear that they would never approve of me, a horse trainer with nothing of his own to offer her.

"I told him I loved her and that someday I would be able to give her everything she could ever want. But he told me to stay away from her. He threatened me. He told me that if I didn't forget about her, he'd make sure I had no choice about the matter."

Yancey gave a short, bitter huff of laughter. "I was young and headstrong and determined nothing would keep Abigail and me apart.

"One autumn night, about two weeks later, while Abigail and I were lying together out in a field, staring up at the stars, the fire was set. By the time we dressed and she left for home, and I got back to the stables, the horses and the barn were lost.

"I'll never forget the look of disappointment in Mr. Barclay's eyes when he asked me where I'd been and I didn't answer him. It was my night to watch the barn. All the other stable hands were in town that night." Yancey's anguish showed plainly in his eyes. "I couldn't tell him, you see. I couldn't tell him I'd been with Abigail. It would have ruined her good name for sure."

Yancey looked down at his boots. "Mr. Barclay said we'd talk about it in the morning. But morning never came for me. I knew what I had to do. I knew Abigail's brother had set the fire to frame me, to drive me away. So I left Barclay Farms before dawn.

"I headed south, working horse farms as a groom and stable hand until I couldn't stand it any longer. I was a trainer"—Yancey's voice echoed his frustration—"and it was hard for me not to voice my opinions, not to get involved in the training of the horses. So I quit the horse farms and found work wherever I could. The years passed all too swiftly, but I never stopped thinking about Abigail. I figured that she was better off without me, though. I imagined that she had married her young man and probably had a big house and a passel of children.''

His gaze rose and rested affectionately on Luke. ''Then you brought Darby the colt. I didn't get a good look at you that day, but I saw Kentucky Blue, and I knew I had a second chance in him. I knew he was a winner. When you came back with Bo to accept Darby's offer, I couldn't believe how much you looked like Abigail. It was uncanny. I started thinking and wondering, watching you.

''One day Darby mentioned that you had grown up in an orphanage in New York. Still, I didn't think it could be possible.

''But after the fire at the stables here, I knew it was time to face the past. My instincts told me the fire was set deliberately. And I also had a feeling that I was going to be questioned abut it. It was too familiar to be a coincidence. Someone knew about my past and was using it against me. I still don't know why. Maybe to chase me away, to cause a division here between us because of Blue and the Derby.'' He shrugged. ''I really don't know.

''But regardless of all that, I had to know the truth about Abigail. About you. I had to go back to Barclay Farms and tell Mr. Barclay the truth. I owed him that much. So I left for New York before anyone could stop me.''

His gaze steady, Luke shifted in his chair. He was almost afraid to ask, but he had to. ''What did you find out?''

Yancey sighed heavily, his pain evident in his gaze. ''I almost had to beat the truth out of her brother, but he finally told me that Abigail was pregnant with you when I left. I didn't know. I don't think she knew either, for that matter. When her pregnancy could no longer be hidden, her parents hid her away, claiming she had an illness that demanded complete bed rest and total isolation. When you were born, they forced her to give you up to an orphanage in New York City. She didn't want to do it, and she held on to you right up until the end, traveling to the city with you herself.

"When she returned home she married her young man like her family wanted." Yancey lowered his gaze, and his voice grew husky with emotion. "Her parents' ruse of an illness became an ironic reality when she fell ill two years later and died."

He shook his head sadly. "She never knew how much I loved her." He took a deep, shaky breath and lifted his tortured gaze to Luke's once more. "I went to the orphanage in New York City, afraid I would never know for sure if you were my son. But an elderly nun named Sister Frances—"

At the mention of the nun's name, a light came on in Luke's eyes.

"She remembered Abigail and the baby boy she had left with them so many years before. She said the boy had grown into a fine, intelligent young man." Yancey paused a long, silent while. "She said the name they'd given him was Luke Richards. . . ."

Luke swallowed hard, his Adam's apple riding up the thick column of his throat.

Yancey leaned forward in his chair and laid his hand over Luke's where it rested on his knee. "I am very glad to have found you. I know I don't have much to offer you as a father. But I want you to know this. I loved your mother deeply. Had I known of your existence, I would have tried to find you sooner. I've made a lot of mistakes. I've done some things I'm not proud of. But sometimes life gives us a second chance at happiness. I want that chance." His voice was husky with feeling. "I'm proud of the man you've become, Luke. And I want a chance to be a father to you. Please . . ."

Luke was silent. He looked into Yancey's eyes and finally understood the immediate bond he'd felt for the man. He also knew the affection he felt for him was real and true and would continue to grow as the years passed. Yancey had been a good friend to him before he'd been a father. And today Yancey had given him a gift. The gift of the truth. The gift of his parentage. "Yes," Luke said quietly, his heart swelling with emotion. He turned his hand over and clasped Yancey's firmly. "Of course I will."

Luke lay awake long into the night, thinking about Yancey and what he'd told him. A gentle serenity had overcome him, a quiet peace he had never known. His questions about his past had finally been answered. He was no longer a floating bit of dust without anyplace to land, without anything to cling to. He knew who he was. He knew who he had been and looked forward to who he would become. He had a name. A good name: Larson.

He thought about what Yancey had said: that someone had wanted to frame him for the fire. He thought about the newspaper article that Nathaniel had shown him, and he knew that Nathaniel was responsible for the fire—even if he hadn't set the fire himself.

But why? he asked himself, then quickly answered his own question. To break him, of course. To force him to sell out, as he'd done to Bradley, so he could claim his late brother's properties.

During the past several months Luke had talked with Bradley and come to know him. Bradley had told him how Nathaniel had used his weakness to bilk him out of the breeding farm.

Luke remembered Benjamin Rhinehart's belief that danger often came from within one's own camp. Luke wondered if Benjamin had ever guessed that his quiet, unassuming brother had been the source of danger he feared.

Luke decided at that moment that he would do everything he could to get the breeding farm back for Bradley.

He'd do it not only for Benjamin, but also for Bradley, who had become his friend.

In truth, Luke had always felt guilty about Benjamin leaving him the stables. He'd never felt that he deserved them.

But now he realized that he'd been wrong. Benjamin Rhinehart had loved him. Because of that love, he'd given him the gift of a home, a heritage he could build and pass on to his own children, just as Yancey had given him a past and a name. Rhinehart Stables was his home and, in acknowledging that truth, Luke felt a surge of determination: He would not lose the stables. He would not let Benjamin down.

Invariably his thoughts turned to Darby. He loved her. He wanted her. But would she have him now? Now that he had something to offer her—a home, a real name. How could he explain why he had sent her away? Would she listen? Would she understand? And what of Jeffrey Morgan? He loved Darby, also, and he was a decent fellow.

But the thought of her in Jeffrey's arms brought a piercing stab of pain to his heart. He rolled over onto his stomach, pressing his face into his pillow. Did she return Jeffrey's affection now?

Luke was sure she must, for she'd given no indication of any feelings for him beyond friendship since her return to the stables. She'd been her usual pleasant self, but the longing that had once been in her eyes when she looked at him was gone now.

He had been the one to chase it away.

With that thought in mind, he finally fell into a fitful sleep.

He awoke before dawn the next morning and went directly to Bradley's room, where they had a long talk about the future of Larson Stables and Rhinehart Farms.

When Darby arrived at dawn, she sought Luke out in his office. She stood for a moment, staring up at him, uncertain of what to say. "Yancey told us."

Luke smiled and shook his head, still having trouble believing it was true. "Beats all, doesn't it?"

Darby laughed softly. "It sure does."

He stared down into her sweet face, wanting so much to tell her of his feelings for her, but he was suddenly afraid— afraid she would reject him, afraid she was lost to him, afraid he could not have a second chance with her.

"Well," she said, and sighed, searching her mind for something to add. She sensed something different about him. The haunted look was gone from his eyes, which were as blue as a cloudless summer sky, and she was glad. "I'd best get Blue's gear ready. Yancey said he'd be a little late. He said he had something he wanted to ask Aunt Birdie. I have a feeling we're going to be attending another wedding before too long."

"Yeah?" Luke said, his smile riding up to his eyes. He was glad Yancey would have another chance at life and at love.

Darby nodded. "Yeah. They could hardly keep their eyes off each other all morning. I was afraid I was going to have to cook breakfast myself, and that's a scary thought."

Luke chuckled, and she did too. Then he said, "I was thinkin' . . . if Blue wins tomorrow, I should be able to afford a couple of yearlings. I was thinking about asking Yancey to help me train them."

"I'm sure Yancey would love that."

"I would like your help too. I can always use an exercise rider. I would pay you this time."

She was silent a moment. She felt a jolt of hope, of expectation, but she quickly quelled it. She could not afford to lose herself in false hopes again. "Oh, Luke . . ." she said softly, lowering her gaze and pocketing her hands. "I don't know . . ."

A fist squeezed his heart. He was afraid her hesitancy was due to her affection for Jeffrey. Because he could not bear the thought, he quickly changed the subject. "I talked to Bradley this morning, and if we can find a way to get his farm back, we thought we'd work together, sort of like independent partners. He has some fine horses out on the farm he could breed. Which would give me a group of yearlings to work with."

"Oh . . ." she said, truly pleased, her gaze lifting to his once again. "That's wonderful. His father would have been so happy."

The rising sun slanted a stream of golden light in through the window, causing dust motes to sparkle and float in the air. Outside the office, the stables began to awaken.

The silence grew awkward between them, and Darby turned to go.

"Darby?"

"Yes?" She looked at him over her shoulder.

"What do you think of the name Larson Stables?"

She smiled, and her eyes grew soft. "I think it's a fine name, Luke."

Later that morning, when Yancey arrived, Luke called the crew together. Everyone was there: Darby, Yancey, Bo, Bradley, Ian, Eddie, and Tom. Because they were his friends, he shared Yancey's glad news with them. Then he told them of his suspicions about Nathaniel. They would have to be especially vigilant with Blue and the stables, he said. With the Derby just weeks away, one lax moment could cost them everything.

That evening Darby asked Yancey to see to Blue's bath, and she went home to bathe and change into a skirt and blouse.

It was time to take care of her own business.

She could put it off no longer. The visit to Jeffrey was long overdue, and her conscience could bear the guilt no longer.

She found his office on Green Street easily. The front of the building was painted a rich dark brown and over the door hung a bright new sign that read: Jeffrey Morgan, Doctor of Medicine.

She left her horse and buggy at a livery down the street, then crossed the street and entered his office without knocking.

A middle-aged woman and an elderly gentleman sat in straight-backed wooden chairs in the waiting room. On the wall behind them hung the certificate that verified Jeffrey's medical license.

Darby smiled and nodded a greeting to both of them, then sat down in a chair to wait for Jeffrey.

After several minutes passed, the door to his examining room opened and she heard him say, "Take a spoonful of the tonic every evening for the next week, Mrs. O'Henry, and if you don't feel better, come back and see me."

"Oh, thank you, Dr. Morgan!" the little elderly lady said as he led her out into the waiting room.

Jeffrey smiled down at her, then lifted his gaze to see Darby. "Darby, hello!" he said, his surprise and pleasure evident in his tone. He returned his attention to his patient, walking her to the door and opening it for her. "Good-bye, Mrs. O'Henry. You take care of yourself now." He closed the door behind her and crossed the room to Darby, offering his hands, pulling her up and kissing her cheek. "What a pleasant surprise! I'll be just a little while longer, then we can go have some dinner if you like."

"We'll see," she said, forcing a smile. "Go ahead and take care of your patients. I'll wait."

"All right," he said, still smiling, though a shadow of concern clouded his gaze. He turned to the woman. "This way, Mrs. Collins."

Another forty minutes went by, with Darby dreading the passing of each and every second. She knew it was going to be hard for her to say the words she had to say. But she knew it was going to be even harder for Jeffrey to hear them.

When he finally showed his last patient out the door, he turned to her, rubbed his hands together, and cheerfully said, "Now, about dinner—"

Darby took his hand. "Could we just talk for a while, Jeffrey?"

He saw it in her eyes, and the smile slipped from his face. He nodded and sank down into a chair beside her. "I've been expecting this."

"You have?" she asked softly, surprised by his admission.

He touched her cheek in a gentle caress. "Oh, yes. Forever."

"Oh, Jeffrey," she said, her voice breaking on a note of misery. "I don't know how to say this." She lowered her gaze, unable to look into his dear face a moment longer.

"Then I'll say it for you," he said kindly, squeezing her hand. "I can't marry you, Jeffrey, because I love someone else."

Darby's gaze snapped up to his. She was quiet a moment. "Why do you always make it so easy for me?"

"Because I love you, my dear," he answered simply. He paused, his expression sobering. "It's Luke Richards, isn't it?"

She swallowed, and tears stung the back of her eyes. "How did you know?"

"Oh, my sweet Darby, I've known for a very long time." He smiled sadly and leaned back in his chair. "I guess if I were to be honest with myself, I'd have to say I knew the day of Emma's wedding, when I first saw you with him."

"Then, why—"

"Why did I pursue you?"

Darby nodded.

"Because I've always loved you, even when we were children. Having finally grown up, I saw a chance to court you at last. I didn't want to give it up. I thought I might be able to change your heart. I thought if I loved you enough, you would somehow love me back."

"I do love you," she said passionately, then added, "but not in the way you want me to."

He chuckled, but the sound was cheerless. "I know that, sweetheart." He rubbed a gentle circle into her palm with his thumb and put his arm around her, drawing her head to his shoulder. She went willingly, knowing there was no passion in the gesture, only quiet affection and the offer of comfort.

"Does he love you?" Jeffrey asked at length, rocking her slowly, as one would a weary child.

"I don't know," she answered truthfully.

"Well, he'd be a fool not to!" Jeffrey stated with such vehemence that she couldn't help but laugh.

They sat together in companionable silence for a very long time, her head pressed to his shoulder. Twilight fell, and the evening shadows seeped in through the windows, casting the unlit room in a milky semi-darkness.

"I don't suppose it would do any good for me to say that I love you anyway, that I'd give you some time to get this fellow out of your system. . . ."

Darby tipped her head back to look at him. "He's not a sickness you can treat with a tonic, Jeffrey."

"Damn," he swore softly, making a disgruntled face. "What a pity."

The days passed in a hurried blur as Blue's training intensified.

Louisville's newspapers announced that the judges for this year's Derby would be Meriwether Lewis Clark, R. A. Swigert, and Washington Hessing. The newspapers also published long accounts on each of the six horses expected to run in the big race.

Out in front fighting for top honors, the sportswriters wrote, were Kentucky Blue and Phantom, both Kentucky born and bred. Phantom was a strong, steady runner, they claimed, but Kentucky Blue's speed would astound the racing world.

The outfit at Rhinehart Stables read every word that was printed but didn't let the articles affect them one way or the other. They had more important things to worry about: keeping guard over their stables and keeping up with the pace of Blue's training.

May swept in on a whirlwind of warm days and balmy nights. Outdoors the air was filled with the scent of freshly turned earth and new plant life, while in the stables, nerves were taut.

Then it was May 10, Friday morning, the day before the eighteenth Kentucky Derby.

A newspaperman from the *Louisville Courier-Journal* came out to the stables, wanting to take a picture of Blue and get a jump on his story, but Luke sent him away, telling him he could get his picture and his story tomorrow. He wanted to keep Blue as calm as possible, and everyone in the stables was responsible for seeing that Luke's orders were carried out.

Which was why the young man who walked into the stables an hour later and asked for Bo was met with such hostile glances.

"You'll find him out at the training track," Eddie snapped impatiently. "And if you work for any of them newspapers, you might as well just turn around and git your tail back to town."

"I don't," the young man said, and hurried out the doors. He found Bo standing by the fence, talking to Luke. He handed him a folded note and said, "A lady said to give this to you, Mr. Denton."

Bo took the note, and the young man turned and left, glad to have completed his mission, eager to get away from the hostile crew.

Bo lifted a bewildered glance to Luke, then unfolded the note and read the words: *Come see me tonight. Frank will be gone. I know who started the fire last May. K.*

He handed the note to Luke, his expression as puzzled as ever. "What do you think?"

Luke arched one dark eyebrow. "I think you better be damn careful."

Bo arrived at Frank Kirby's house just after sunset. He had no intention of staying long. He wanted to get home to Millie. But he also wanted to know what Katrina had to tell him and how she had come by her information.

He, Luke, and Bradley had talked it over and decided that Katrina's information might lead to Nathaniel's arrest. If in fact they could prove his guilt, they might be able to find a way to get Bradley's farm back.

Bo knocked at the Kirby door, and the housekeeper answered at once. "Hello, Mr. Denton," she said, ushering him in. "Mrs. Kirby is waiting for you up in her room."

Bo frowned. "Please tell her I'll wait down here in the drawing room."

"I'm sorry, sir, but she insisted you were to come up to her room."

He was silent a moment, then he sighed heavily and strode across the fine Oriental carpeting to the stairs, which he took by twos. He wasn't going to waste time arguing. He knew how stubborn Katrina could be. He also knew the way to her room only too well.

The door was closed. He knocked once.

"Come in," Katrina called out.

He turned the doorknob and entered the room.

Katrina lay naked in the center of the huge, four-poster, her pose a practiced picture of seduction. She was as lovely as ever, her skin smooth and white, her beautiful blond hair spread out around her in a cloud of shining waves. "Hello, darling," she crooned in a sultry voice.

Bo left the door open, his hand still on the doorknob. "Hello, Katrina," he said dryly. "Seems like you never get out of that bed."

She chuckled and arched her back, trailing a perfectly manicured hand up her leg and over her smooth belly. "It's been a long time, Bo. Where have you been?"

"I think you know where I've been."

She lifted one eyebrow. "Tell me . . . I often try to picture it, but I can't. Does your little Methodist wife do for you what I used to do for you?"

Fighting to hold on to his patience, Bo shifted his weight. His expression hardened, and he got right to the point. "There's only one reason I'm here, Katrina. Who set the fire out at Rhinehart Stables? You said you knew."

She sat up slowly, her perfectly round breasts jiggling slightly with the movement. She turned to the wine decanter that sat on her bed table. She filled two goblets three-quarters full of the dark burgundy liquid. "*Tsk, tsk,* darling. Always in such a hurry. You know that always was your problem."

She held a goblet out to him. "Relax, we'll get to that soon enough."

"No, thanks," he said to her offer. "Let's get to it now, all right? I'm tired and I have a race to run tomorrow."

His offhanded tone put a match to her fury. Not only had he abandoned her bed, but also he had cut off her source of information. He used to tell her which horses were the safest to place her money on. Sometimes he had been wrong, but most of the time his tips had helped her avoid substantial losses. Without him she'd fallen further and further into debt with the bookmakers, and she knew her husband was sure to find out if Nathaniel did not bail her out again. So she would do this thing for Nathaniel. Because she needed his help. Because she owed him. Because Bo deserved it.

"Have a glass of wine with me, or I won't tell you anything." Her tone was clipped and unyielding, her eyes shards of green ice.

His impatience growing, Bo stalked across the room and took the goblet from her hand, quickly downing half of the bitter contents. "So talk," he snapped, his usually warm and friendly brown eyes now dark with disdain.

Katrina smiled. The smile chilled him to the bone. "It was one of your own men."

"Who, goddammit?" Bo demanded harshly, unable to hide his shock and surprise.

She lifted her glass and leaned back in the bed, resting her back against the cherrywood headboard. "A toast, Bo, to old times . . ."

He knew she toyed with him. He also knew he would never get his answer unless he humored her. He touched his glass to hers and quickly downed the remaining contents.

"All right, who was it?"

She smiled. "It was Tom Haines," she said quietly. "Stupid, slow-witted Tom Haines."

Bo's face registered his shock. "Tom?" he said in astonished disbelief. "Tom wouldn't hurt a fly. He would never do such a thing!"

She nodded. "Oh, yes, I'm afraid he would . . . under Nathaniel Rhinehart's orders, of course."

"But why?"

She lifted her eyebrows and shrugged one silky shoulder. "That I don't know, my dear."

As Katrina watched Bo's handsome face harden with anger, she gave a soft, satisfied huff of laughter. "I know what you're thinking, but it's too late. You won't tell anyone, Bo. And you won't be riding in any race tomorrow." Her voice grew soft with feigned sympathy. "You won't have time to do either, my love. You see, I'm afraid . . . you'll be dead. . . ."

It was then he glanced over at the glass she still held in her hand, and realization hit him with force even as the first slice of pain arced a wicked path through his extremities.

Her glass was full. She had never touched it. . . .

The first thing he did when he got outside was force himself to vomit. He vomited and vomited until his stomach was on fire, until nothing more would come up, until he was drenched with sweat. Then he swung up onto his horse and rode for home.

It was a slow journey, and he was wretchedly sick, his stomach cramping painfully, his face clammy and damp. He hung over the side of his horse, clamping a hand around his middle, feeling as though his guts had been sliced apart by a dozen knives.

Millie was watching out the parlor window for Bo when he finally rode his horse up into the yard. She'd been waiting for him. She was eager to tell him the happy news.

But when she saw him slide from his horse to the ground, her happiness quickly turned to alarm, and she rushed out the door to help him.

Through a haze of pain he told her what had happened, that he had to get to a doctor, that he had been poisoned. She didn't waste time with questions, but helped him back up onto his horse. It took her three attempts before she was able to mount behind him. It took all of her strength to keep him from falling off the horse's back.

But Millie Denton was stronger than she looked. She loved her husband fiercely and she was determined her baby would know his father.

Through streets lit only by the soft glow of gaslight, she headed straight for Jeffrey Morgan's office for the second time that day, hoping and praying that he had decided to spend the night in his office as he sometimes did.

❖ 14 ❖

As THE EVENING shadows fell, the cool night air wafted in through the open stable doors and windows, reaching Darby where she stood in Blue's stall, stroking his neck. Effie stuck her head over into Blue's stall, and Darby patted her too, and said, "I didn't forget you, girl. Don't worry."

The stables were quiet, the stable hands gone for the night. A couple of lanterns had been lit, sending shadows flickering into the far corners of the barn.

Darby knew this quiet moment would be the last she would have with Blue before the big race.

The day they had waited for was only hours away. The journey was almost at an end. Her heart swelled with a mix of feelings—eagerness, fear, uncertainty—all at once.

She thought about Knightwind, about the day he'd raced in the Derby, about the day he'd raced against Phantom, how his will to win had been so fierce, he had continued to run despite his injuries. He had been such a mighty contender.

Luke and Bo said Blue was faster than his father.

But was he stronger? Was he strong enough?

She wanted to believe he was. Most of the time, she did. "Oh, Blue," she whispered, afraid for him. The colt's ears pricked forward, and he stared at her with his huge brown eyes. He nudged her playfully, and she hugged his neck. "I love you, Blue," she whispered fiercely, leaning her forehead against his. "I love you so much."

"He's gonna be all right, Darby," Luke said quietly from behind.

Surprised, she turned to him and wiped the tears from her eyes. "Yes," she said, sniffling, and lifted her chin. "I know he is."

Her bravado touched him. "I promised you a long time ago that I would never race him unless I believed he was one hundred percent. Do you remember?"

She nodded. "Yes."

"He's one hundred percent. He's the best he can be."

There was a quiet confidence in his tone that calmed her spirit. She nodded, then took a deep, shaky breath. With one last pat to Blue's and Effie's necks, she turned and gathered her grooming tools. "I suppose I better try to get some rest," she said, swinging open the gate and stepping through, closing and latching it behind.

Luke crossed his arms over his chest and leaned his backside up against Effie's stall, watching her carefully. "Nobody sleeps much the night before a big race. Especially the night before the Kentucky Derby."

"No, I suppose they don't," she said with a small smile. She walked by him into the tool room and busied herself with putting away her brushes and curry comb, and hanging up the towels she'd used to dry Blue after his bath. When she came out of the room, Luke was still leaning against the wall, still watching her intently.

The moment was intensely familiar. She felt as though they'd stepped back in time, to another night that seemed a lifetime ago. She hesitated only a beat, then said, "I'll see you at dawn." She turned to go.

"Darby."

A warning pricked within.

"I have something I need to ask you."

She didn't want to turn around. "What is it?" she asked over her shoulder, trying to see Luke's face through the shifting shadows.

He hesitated a moment, then pushed himself away from the

wall and walked to where she stood near the open stable doors. From somewhere outside came the soft hoot of an owl, and much farther away the long, lonely cry of a train's whistle. "It's about Jeffrey Morgan."

She didn't look at him but waited for his question, anxious, afraid, her heart pumping painfully in her chest.

He gently took her arm and turned her to face him. He stared down at her and willed her eyes to lift to his. They did ever so slowly.

His handsome face was somber. "Do you love him?"

Silence. The owl hooted softly again. Then, "Yes," she said softly, honestly.

He swallowed. "I see."

"He is my dear and true friend. I will always love him."

Luke opened his eyes and took her by the shoulders. His brow puckered, and his ink-blue eyes bore into hers. "But are you in love with him, Darby?"

A heavy blanket of silence hung between them. She shook her head, lowered her gaze to his shirtfront, and whispered, "No."

He sighed, his eyes slipping shut in relief. "I was so afraid . . ."

"Of what?" she asked, her gaze snapping back up to his.

"That you had fallen in love with him, that—"

"And if I had?" she interrupted, feeling a flare of frustration and anger.

He shook his head and shrugged. "Then I would have to accept it, even though it would kill me."

She studied him for one pained moment, then took a step back from him, causing his hands to fall away from her shoulders. "What do you want from me, Luke?"

He reached for her hand and pressed a long, lingering kiss into her palm, his dark head bowed as if in prayer. "Everything."

"No," she whispered, aggrieved.

He lifted his head, and their eyes met.

"I don't believe you. I don't trust you anymore," she went

on, her voice soft but firm with resolution. "Not this time."

He saw the hurt in her eyes and damned himself for being the one to have put it there. "I never meant to hurt you, Darby."

Despite her vow never to let him know how much he had hurt her, she jerked her hand away from him, and the words stormed out in a terrible rush. "But you did! You did hurt me!"

"Listen to me, please . . ." He tried to reach for her again, but she spun away, shaking him off.

"I have to go." She stalked out into the moonlight, but he ran after her, catching her arm, spinning her around to face him once more.

"Darby, please! Don't you see? I had nothing to offer you! No name to give you! I still don't know what the future holds! I don't know whether I'll be able to make these stables a success, whether I'll even be able to hold on to them. But I know who I am now and I know what I want. I want you, Darby. I want to share my life with you. I want that more than anything in the world."

"You didn't trust me, Luke!" Her voice broke on an anguished sob. "It didn't matter to me what you had or didn't have! You didn't trust me to love you for who you are. *I* always knew who you were!"

"But I didn't," he whispered harshly. "Don't you see? I had to know . . ." Silence, then, "I love you, Darby." His eyes were ardent, his expression impassioned. "I want to marry you! I want to have children with you if you want them too." He smiled. "If you can find the time to have them." His smile grew tender. "I love you more than I can say. You're everything to me. You're the sunshine in my days, the light in my nights. While you were gone, I counted the days until you came back. I damned myself a thousand times for sending you away, for sending you into Jeffrey's arms." He took her hand and softly said, "We belong together, you and me . . ."

She stared up into his face, lit by silvery moonlight, so

darkly handsome, so earnest, so dear, and her heart began to open like a summer rose warmed by the sun.

He loved her. He'd said the words, and his eyes told her he meant those words with all his heart. It was impossible to argue in the face of such love.

Tears threatened to fall. She rested her palm against his chest, realizing she could no more turn him away than she could stop breathing. "Oh, Luke," she choked out, shaking her head. "What am I gonna do with you?"

He took her chin and tipped it up, his face descending, his breath stirring her hair. "Marry me."

She shook her head again, overcome by emotion.

"Say it, Darby. Say you love me . . ."

She sighed and let her doubt slip away on a whisper of cool night air, realizing that he was right, that she had known it all along: They belonged together, fate had brought them to each other, and so it would be. "Oh, all right," she said, a soft smile touching her lips. "I love you. I love you . . ."

His heart took flight. Those precious words. How he'd longed to hear them. He did not realize how healing they would be till that very moment.

He smiled down into her eyes and pulled her into his arms, hugging her close. He kissed her then, and his soft, open lips touched hers gently, awakening the latent passion within them both.

When he lifted his head, they joined hands and, with their hearts leading the way, they walked back into the stables, closing and latching the door behind them. They walked to his office and closed that door also.

They undressed slowly, helping each other, anticipating eagerly what was to come. He drew her down on the cot and kissed her with tender deliberation, wetting her mouth, face, and breasts while he whispered words of love and told her all he felt for her, all the special things he'd kept hidden in his heart.

"You're beautiful," he murmured against her neck.

"You are too."

"Not like you. You're like a colt, all long legs and silky-soft." He ran his hands over the sweet curve of her hips.

"I'm a girl, silly," she said on a chuckle.

"I know," he said, nipping playfully at her shoulder.

Their joining was different this time—magical and golden, an unhurried blending of their bodies and souls. They knew they would have many nights such as this, a lifetime to share their love.

He touched her gently, his caresses lingering and reverent. She touched him all over, no longer shy, exploring his body with eagerness, knowing she had every right, for this man would soon be her husband.

Their reunion was slow and supple and splendid. He took his time entering her; she guided him in lovingly, while their hearts billowed, and their breathing quickened.

When at last they'd each found completion, they lay side by side, smiling into each other's eyes, arms and legs entwined, pressed together like two dew-kissed flower petals.

"I love you," he whispered, stroking her dark hair back from her face and kissing the tip of her nose.

"Yeah?" she asked, smiling, her cheeks dimpling.

"Yeah."

"Remember the night of the benefit dance?"

"Of course."

"I bought all of your tickets," he confessed, then kissed her forehead.

"I know."

He pulled back and stared at her with surprise.

"How did you know?"

She shrugged one bare shoulder and winked at him. "Instinct."

The stables at Churchill Downs were shadowy and cool early the next morning. The smell of horses, hay, and leather hung in the air.

Nathaniel Rhinehart slipped unnoticed through the open stable doors. He walked quietly past a group of Pinkerton agents, but one of them saw him and called out, "Hey, there, fella! No one's supposed to be in the stables this early 'cept owners, trainers, and their outfits!"

Nathaniel Rhinehart turned to face him, and the agent, who had worked the race grounds for several years, recognized him as Benjamin Rhinehart's brother. "Oh, sorry, Mr. Rhinehart," he said, reddening with embarrassment. "I didn't know it was you."

"That's quite all right." Nathaniel tugged on his vest importantly. "It's good to know you men are doing your jobs." With a superior nod of dismissal, Nathaniel commenced with his walk past the many stalls, some already filled with the horses that would be this year's Derby contenders.

Though his demeanor gave nothing away, Nathaniel was tense. He was determined to make sure nothing went wrong with his plan this time. Katrina had taken care of Bo Denton. Tom would take care of Kentucky Blue.

Denton would never ride for Richards again. He would never ride for anyone, and Nathaniel would never again have to fear the young jockey's skill. He had nothing in particular against Bo Denton, except that he was the best jockey in the state, he could not be bought, and was far too loyal to Luke Richards. It was rumored that Raymond Miller had tried to buy him out, but the young fool wouldn't accept the offer.

Bo Denton was a detriment to Nathaniel's future. As long as he was alive, he had a semblance of control over the outcome of any race he rode in. Therefore, he affected Nathaniel's power over the local racing industry. There were other jockeys like him, Nathaniel knew, men who rode horses for the sheer pleasure of winning the race.

Nathaniel would see to them also, in time.

But it was that day's event that was imminent in his mind.

Richards and the girl could have hired another jockey to ride the stallion. Nathaniel was determined to see that Tom carried out his order.

He found Kentucky Blue's stall, the last one on the left in the back of the stables. A sign overhead sported the Thoroughbred's name and the names of his trainer and owner. A little bay filly stood in the stall next door.

"Hello, Tom," Nathaniel said, stopping before the stall door.

Tom was inside, brushing the big stallion's glossy coat with his usual gentle patience. The horse faced the window. Tom's rifle stood in the corner of the stall, just as Nathaniel had ordered it to be. Tom turned. "Hello, Mr. Rhinehart."

"Where is everyone?" Nathaniel asked, his eyes boring intently into the younger man's.

"They're comin'."

"Then it's time, isn't it?"

Tom nodded. "Yes, it's time, Mr. Rhinehart."

"Then do it," Nathaniel ordered curtly.

"I can't, Mr. Rhinehart," Tom said resolutely.

"Shoot the horse, damn you, then make a run for it. I told you I'd cover for you. They'll never know you did it."

"You're right," Tom said, drawing himself up to his full height. "Because I'm not gonna do it."

"You'll go to jail, Tom," Nathaniel's tone became soft and silky. "You'll go to prison. I've sent other men there. Do you know what they do to young men there?" Nathaniel shook his head slowly and smiled. The smile was so cold it froze on his face. "Unimaginable things, my boy. Things you haven't even begun to think about."

Tom lifted his chin, meeting the other man's gaze head-on. The fear was gone from his eyes, replaced by a quiet serenity. "An' I won't have to think about them anymore."

"What do you mean?" Nathaniel snapped, feeling a shiver of apprehension as he felt his hold on the young man dissipating.

"I went to see Mr. Luke early this morning. I told him everything. I told him about how I accidentally shot your brother. I told him I was responsible for setting the fire and killin' his horses too. And I told him what you wanted me to do to Kentucky Blue today." Overcome with emotion, Tom's bottom lip began to tremble. "An' you know what, Mr. Rhinehart? You were wrong. You were wrong all along. Mr. Luke believed me. An' he said I wasn't to worry or feel bad anymore 'cause he was gonna take care of everything."

At that moment the horse in the stall neighed softly and turned his head. The horse was not Kentucky Blue. Tom and Luke had moved the real Kentucky Blue to a safe place to await the race.

"It's over, Rhinehart," Luke said from behind.

Nathaniel spun around.

Luke and Darby came out of the shadows. Behind them followed Yancey, Bradley, Ian, Eddie, and Sheriff Harvey Roth.

Nathaniel felt his rage begin to boil up from within. He felt cheated, wronged, just like when his brother was alive and loving the woman that should have been his—living the life that should have been his.

Bo stepped out of the shadows. He was pale but very much alive. Shock widened Nathaniel's eyes. "You're supposed to be dead." The words escaped on an angry whisper.

Bo snorted and grinned. "Well, hell, I almost was. I still don't feel too damn good." He rubbed his stomach and winced. "But thanks to my wife and Doc Morgan, I'm gonna be around awhile longer." His smile grew. He was enjoying himself immensely. "Sorry to disappoint you."

Nathaniel's gaze found Darby. "This is all your fault, you know. Benjamin wanted to give you the colt, but he wasn't sure that he should. He felt Luke should have the chance to train him into a champion. But I encouraged Benjamin to give you the colt anyway. I told him Luke had so many others, and you had nothing."

"I don't understand," she said, her brow knitting in confusion.

His eyes glittered with madness, and the truth spewed out of him in a rush of self-condemning words. "I couldn't change his will without drawing suspicion from his friends. They all knew he intended to leave the horse stables to Luke and the breeding farm to Bradley, hoping one day they would join forces. But I knew I'd eventually get Bradley's farm.'' He looked at Bradley, his lip curling with disdain. ''It was so easy. He was so weak.'' His gaze found Luke. ''I knew I could get Richards's stables too. I knew if I divided his camp, if I burned him out, and if he didn't have the colt to depend on, he would eventually fail. I just never planned on the two of you joining forces.'' He gave a harsh, bitter laugh. ''Foolish of me, though. I should have figured that one.'' His obsession to have what he believed was rightfully his was like a volcanic poison within him. ''It should have been mine!'' he suddenly cried, his face turning purple, his fists clenching with impotent rage. ''Everything Benjamin ever had should have been mine!''

He reached into his coat and withdrew a small pistol. ''It's your fault!'' he screamed at Darby, and pointed the pistol at her.

Luke reacted quickly, shoving her out of the way, knocking her to the floor, covering her body with his own even as the shot rang out and the bullet sliced into the wall directly behind where she had been standing.

Tom's rifle was on his shoulder in a flash. The sound of the rifle shot ricocheted through the barn, causing the birds in the rafters to flee in a frenzied panic while the impact of the bullet flung Nathaniel onto his back.

A shocked silence followed, with Luke clutching Darby to his chest while a dozen Pinkertons, as well as other horse owners and trainers, came running from all corners of the stables.

''Are you all right?'' Luke asked Darby.

''Yes,'' she whispered, stunned. ''I think so.''

''Is everyone all right?'' he asked, getting to his feet and pulling Darby up with him.

''We all seem to be,'' Bo said, glancing around at the others and checking his own body for holes, wondering how much more he could take. He'd thought hard drinking and chasing after women had been dangerous.

''What the hell is goin' on here?'' Raymond Miller bel-

lowed, then, seeing Nathaniel, his mouth fell open in surprise.
"Jesus," he whispered.

Nathaniel's eyes were open but unseeing. The bullet had
pierced his heart dead-center.

Tom lowered his gun and opened the gate. He walked over
to where Nathaniel lay. "If I had meant to kill your brother
that day, Mr. Rhinehart, I would have," he said quietly, matter-of-factly. "I'm a real good shot."

Bradley stood over his uncle. He felt no grief, only a sense
of relief that the nightmare his uncle had created was over.
Nathaniel Rhinehart had been a cowardly, manipulative man
who fed off the weaknesses of others. But he would wield
his evil power no longer. He would never again hurt anyone
or anything.

The sheriff turned to Bradley. "He has no living relatives,
Bradley. You'll get your farm back."

Bradley nodded. "And this time I'll keep it." His eyes
lifted to his friends, and his clear gaze softened with affection.
"I know the value of my farm now, and the value of a hard
day's work. I don't intend to ever forget the lessons I've
learned this year. I just wish I had learned them sooner, for
myself and for my father."

Sheriff Roth placed a hand on the younger man's shoulder.
"If it's any consolation, Bradley, your father would have
been proud of the man you are now." He sighed wearily,
then said, "Well, I'd best go collect Mrs. Kirby. I can't help
but feel sorry for her husband. This whole thing is gonna
come as quite a shock to Frank. Who would have thought
she'd be in cahoots with Rhinehart?" He looked over at Bo.
"Who would have thought she'd be desperate enough to try
to kill Bo?" He sighed again and shook his head. "Thank
god she failed . . . Well, things have a way of comin' to light,
don't they? This'll be the last horse race Katrina Kirby will
attend for a very long time."

The air was charged with excitement.

The colorful flags on the towering steeples rose high into

the air and whipped gaily in the brisk May breeze. The sun shone down graciously, creating a golden splash of warmth over the sculpted grounds of Churchill Downs.

The grandstand and clubhouse were filled to capacity, and outside along the rails, hundreds of onlookers crowded around the paddock, hoping to catch a glimpse of the horses.

In his own official seat, Governor John Young Brown talked animatedly with his friends, while a beaming Millie, Henry, and Aunt Birdie sat with Darby's sisters and their husbands and waited eagerly for the race to begin.

Down in the saddling area, Ian, Eddie, Bradley, and Tom stood with Darby and Luke. Luke held Darby's hand while Darby held on to Lady Effie's halter. She fought down a ripple of trepidation, remembering Luke's words: Blue was one hundred percent. He would be fine.

She stole a glance up at Luke's face. A soft wind lifted his black hair from his forehead, and he squinted up into the sun, the lines around his eyes crinkling attractively. He had a fine face, strong and handsome, a face that would only grow dearer to her with the passing of time. She loved him so much. She felt it so keenly, so deeply that her throat swelled shut, and tears stung the backs of her eyes.

He felt her gaze and looked down at her, giving her hand a squeeze while a slow smile rode up to his eyes—those summer-blue eyes that she so loved. "This is it, sweetheart," he said. "Win or lose, we're still winners, and so is Blue. Don't you ever forget it."

"I won't," she said, smiling. "But he'll win. I know he will."

Kentucky Blue emerged from the stables first. He was calm, poised, majestic, his ears flicking back and forth, his head held high and proud.

The Rhinehart outfit whistled and cheered.

Sunshine glinted off his glossy black coat, casting blue spears of light to dance around him. As he trotted out onto the track, the crowd stood from their seats, and a great roar arose.

Katrina Kirby did not rise from her seat as her husband did, however. She could not. She was rooted to her seat by shock and fear. She knew the jockey who rode the black colt. She knew him by the way he sat the horse. She knew him by the golden fringe of hair showing beneath his helmet.

And she knew she was finished: Bo Denton was alive.

Behind Kentucky Blue came Phantom and his jockey, Thaddeus Martin, drawing their own share of cheers from the crowd as they paraded down the track. Phantom was a picture of regal beauty also, a shining white stallion that moved powerfully and effortlessly.

Then came the other great contenders. Aladdin, a bay colt ridden by Robert Clayton. Memphis, a chestnut gelding ridden by Roger Briggs. And Whiskey, a brown colt ridden by Howard Alexander. All of the contenders were worthy. All held impressive records of their own.

A hush fell over the crowd as the horses and their riders took their places on the track.

Time seemed to stop as the jockeys rose high above their mounts.

Then, at last, the flag dropped, and the Kentucky Derby was on.

Kentucky Blue and Phantom broke cleanly, with the other horses only seconds behind.

A roar rose up from the crowd, and Darby felt Luke tighten his grip on her hand.

As they approached the first turn, the pack began to separate. Kentucky Blue pulled ahead slightly, with Phantom sticking tight.

Bo shot a glance over at Phantom. He figured Martin would try to squeeze them over toward the inside of the track, and Bo did not want to get stuck there. He steered Blue out, slightly bumping against Phantom's shoulder.

In seconds, Blue stuck his nose out and pulled away smoothly. Everyone in the stands was on their feet, screaming.

As they entered the first turn, Bo felt Blue's power gather

beneath him. The stallion was a tornado of raw energy waiting to be unleashed.

But Bo was fighting a battle of his own as a wave of nausea rocked him. Jeffrey Morgan had warned him against racing today, saying he should rest, that he simply wasn't up to it. But Bo had to race this race. He simply had to.

He blinked hard against the dizziness that threatened to overtake him. He could not give in to it. He would not give in to it. This was their dream. To win the Derby. The dream he had not been able to realize with Knightwind. The dream he was determined to win with Blue. He had to hang on, to finish the race—for Millie and their baby, for Darby and Luke, and for Blue, whose courage and spirit would allow him to settle for nothing but first place.

Kentucky Blue thundered down the backstretch, his stride settling into a rolling gallop that quickly put him a full length in front of Phantom. The other horses were close behind, their jockeys pushing and pumping.

As they entered the far turn, Bo knew it was time to make the move. He loosened his hold on the reins and said, "All right, Blue. Let's show 'em what you can do." Blue exploded, stretching his lead out by two lengths, then three, riding into the wind, his long legs taking flight as he became the magical, mystical being his father had once been.

The noise in the stand was deafening. It blended with the pounding of hooves and the swift and steady intake of breathing as the horses pounded down the stretch, heading for home. Bo shut all the sounds out. There was nothing else but him and Blue, the rushing wind, and, ahead of them, victory.

He smiled, rose up in his stirrups, and welcomed it.

As Darby watched them thunder toward the finish line, tranquility overcame her. She knew Knightwind's gift to Blue had been an almost unearthly speed, but Merry Molly had graced her colt with the strength and the endurance to win the greatest race of all.

Kentucky Blue was going to win the Kentucky Derby.

Even as that thought jelled, it became a blinding reality,

and Blue sailed across the finish line, eight lengths ahead of
Phantom and the other horses.

Ian, Bradley, Eddie, and Tom went wild, jumping up and
down, lifting each other off the ground, banging one another
on the back so hard, they hacked and coughed.

The crowd in the stands was on its feet, screaming, stamp-
ing, and clapping.

Darby was in Luke's arms, her head thrown back to the
sun, laughing and crying at once.

Luke quieted her with a kiss, a long, deep, passionate kiss
that proclaimed his joy and love for her, and when at last he
released her, she hugged his neck tight and cried, "I knew
he'd do it! I knew *you* could do this! I always knew! He's
the best. Just like Knightwind was!"

"Yes, Darby, he is," Luke said, smiling, holding her body
close to his. He stared down into her hazel eyes, and the wind
caught her curly chestnut hair and teased it back from her
face. He touched her smooth, round cheek, tracing over one
of her darling dimples, and he knew he had found all he
would ever need in this bright young woman who would be
forever young in his eyes. He was home at last, here with
Darby, here in Louisville, Kentucky.

They stood together, side by side, arms looped around each
other's waists, watching Blue trot over to the area where the
officials would conduct the award ceremonies. Darby, as his
owner, would be presented the winning cup, an elegant silver
one that would grace the fireplace mantel in their study, over
which would appropriately hang Knightwind's picture.

Kentucky Blue lifted his head and danced sideways for the
crowd. They screamed their adoration, and Luke's and Darby's hearts filled with pride and love for him, for each other,
for their friends and crew, who had all played intricate parts
in seeing their dream to fruition.

Bo rose up in his seat and blew a kiss to Millie, then
whipped his helmet from his head and waved it high overhead. He turned and flashed his wide, white smile at Darby
and Luke, gesturing for them to join him.

''Shall we go?'' Luke asked her, holding out his hand.

''Yes,'' she said, taking his hand and turning Effie over to Ian.

''Just think,'' Luke said, smiling down into Darby's radiant face as they turned to go. ''In a few years we just might be watching Blue and Effie's baby out there.''

''Imagine that,'' Darby said, her eyes shining.

Behind them, Lady Effie whinnied softly. . . .

AUTHOR'S NOTE

THE HISTORY SURROUNDING Churchill Downs and the Kentucky Derby is rich and colorful and now spans over 120 years.

Every effort was taken to depict the city and the Thoroughbred racing track and grounds as accurately and authentically as possible. For the sake of fiction, however, I decided to alter history in a few areas.

In doing so, I added a fictional contender to the 1885 Kentucky Derby, although the true winner, Joe Cotton, remained the winning champion. And, in addition to this change, with all due respect to the true Derby contenders of 1892, all the horses and jockeys in my story during that year are fictional.

My reason for doing this was that I did not wish to take away any glory from the true champions and heroes of that year's Derby by altering their positions in the race.

It is also important to note that the clubhouse, grandstands, and grounds of Churchill Downs went through a series of changes and renovations from 1875 through 1895.

Since my story opens in 1885 and closes in 1892, I tried to portray the racing track and the surrounding buildings and grounds as they would have been during the early years before the final changes were completed.

All of this was done in the hope of giving you a wonderful, exciting story.

I hope you will forgive me my few liberties and, in return, I hope you enjoyed taking this ride with me back in time to Louisville and the magnificent Kentucky Derby. . . .

—Jessie Gray